THE WOLF

LORENZO CARCATERRA

BALLANTINE BOOKS · NEW YORK

THE WOLF

A NOVEL

The Wolf is a work of fiction. Names, characters, places, and incidents are the products of the author's imagination or are used fictitiously. Any resemblance to actual events, locales, or persons, living or dead, is entirely coincidental.

Copyright © 2014 by Lorenzo Carcaterra

Published in the United States by Ballantine Books, an imprint of Random House, a division of Random House LLC, a Penguin Random House Company, New York.

BALLANTINE and the HOUSE colophon are registered trademarks of Random House LLC.

LIBRARY OF CONGRESS CATALOGING-IN-PUBLICATION DATA
Carcaterra, Lorenzo.
The wolf : a novel / Lorenzo Carcaterra.
pages cm
ISBN 978-0-345-48394-2 (hardback)—ISBN 978-0-8041-7729-0 (eBook)
1. Organized crime—Fiction. I. Title.
PS3553.A653W65 2014
813'.54—dc23
2014017538

Printed in the United States of America on acid-free paper

www.ballantinebooks.com

9 8 7 6 5 4 3 2 1

First Edition

Book design by Liz Cosgrove

This one is for Susan Jill Toepfer.
March 9, 1948–December 24, 2013
A great wife. A great mom. A great friend.
I will miss her the rest of my days.

INTERNATIONAL ORGANIZED CRIME CONTROL BUREAU

MEMORANDUM

RE: Internal Investigation

            Marelli Crime Syndicate/Russian Mafiya Terrorist

            Connections

STATUS: Active File

FOR OFFICIAL USE ONLY

Marelli Crime Syndicate

PERSONAL WAR— CAN HE HOLD THE GROUP?

1. VINCENT "THE WOLF" MARELLI. Head of the Marelli Crime Syndicate, leader of the Organized Crime Council. 34 years old.

2. CARLO MARELLI. Retired head of the Marelli syndicate, passing the torch on to his nephew, Vincent. Still keeps tabs on day-to-day business and is a trusted and respected member of the International Crime Council.

RETIRED? OR MAKING SILENT MOVE?

3. JIMMY MARELLI. Disabled since birth but a power within the Marelli syndicate. Vincent's most trusted advisor and number two in the family command chain.

Russian Mafiya

FEEDING $$$ TO RAZA? WHY HIM? WHY NOW?

1. VLADIMIR "THE IMPALER" KOSTOLOV. The youngest (37) and most powerful member of the Russian Mafiya and a willing banker to international terrorists.

WOLF AND VLADIMIR MEET—WHY?

2. ALEXANDER ZAVERKO. Kostolov's cousin and feared right hand. Weakened by lung cancer, but still a threat. Operates Kostolov's sex trade and drug operations.

3. KLAUS MARNI. One of Vladimir's advisors, a trusted and dependable assassin.

PIT ONE AGAINST THE OTHER?

4. KLENSKO. Legendary leader of the Russian mob. Organized a loose network of young thugs into one dangerous and profitable outfit.

5. RUSLAN HOLT. Vladimir's muscleman and major earner for the Russian mob.

International Crime Council

1. VITTORIO "THE COBRA" JANNETTI. The leader of the Neapolitan end of the organized crime world—the Camorra.

TEAMS W/ WOLF. WHY NOW? EYES ON BIG TABLE.

LAYING LOW IN NAPLES. WHY? WHAT'S THE PLAY?

2. ANGELA "THE STREGA" JANNETTI. Vittorio's daughter and heir to the Camorra throne. She is the crime queen of Naples and one of the most feared criminals in Europe.

3. ALFREDO LAMBRETTO. Vittorio Jannetti's confidant and the muscle end of the Camorra. Has been a loyal capo for more than 30 years.

INSIDE MAN— MAKE A REACH?

4. LUIGI MANZO. Enforcer for the Camorra and one of the Strega's two most trusted hitters.

5. BARTOLO "BRUNELLO" VINOPIANNO. The Strega's lead enforcer and hitter. He has been by her side since she was a teenager.

6. ANTHONY ZAMBELLI. Head of the Sicilian branch of organized crime—the Mafia. Son of the legendary gangster FRANCISCO ZAMBELLI.

TOO DANGEROUS TO BE THIS QUIET.

7. KODOMA. The leader of the Japanese crime syndicate, the Yakuza.

POWER MOVER—WORKING BEHIND THE SCENES?

8. JOHN LOO. Yakuza leader Kodoma's nephew. Expert computer hacker and tracker. Being groomed for top spot.

NEXT YAKUZA BOSS!

9. QING. The Triad Dragon Head, ruler of all criminal enterprises in China.

10. WEINER. Former Mossad agent and now the titular head of the Israeli Assassin Squad.

11. CARBONE. The brutal and difficult-to-control head of the French crime syndicate.

12. ORTO. The last link to the dreaded Gypsy Kings and the head of the Albanian syndicate.

WEAK LINK IN OC CHAIN.

WORK AS A TEAM— W/ WOLF— STREGA.

13. BIG MIKE PALEOKRASSAS. Ally to Vincent Marelli and Angela Jannetti, he runs the Greek syndicate.

Loners

$$$—CI POTENTIAL. MIGHT FLIP. WORKS TWO SIDES OF EACH COIN.

1. SANTOS. High-level gunrunner and the liaison between Raza and the Mexican drug and ammo gangs.

2. CARLOS MENDOZA. Colombian gunrunner. Deceased. Rumored to have been a Raza target.

LINK TO RAZA.

Terrorists Funded by Russian Mafiya

1. ALI BEN BASHIR. Terrorist funded by Russian Crime Syndicate led by VLADIMIR "THE IMPALER" KOSTOLOV. Died in a 2012 terror attack in Florence, Italy.

2. RAZA. The rising star of the terror world. At 36, he is wanted in connection to half a dozen attacks and is a suspect in at least

FED BY VLADIMIR. WHY? CONNECTION? TARGETS?

half a dozen more. Considered dangerous, unstable and intelligent. Does not fit the profile of the average terrorist. Not to be trusted. Not to be denied.

3. ALSHAIR AL-MADEL. Chemical engineer by training and terrorist by choice. Leads a group of 200 rabid followers, eager to die at his command.

4. ANWAR AL-SABIR. The ranking number two in Raza's terror organization.

5. AVRIM. Loyal follower of Raza. Working closely with the terror leader as he plans his attacks.

6. KAZMIR. Terrorist recruiter for Raza's network.

7. DAL. Bomb courier working for Raza.

8. PANDI. Terrorist in Raza's network. A person of interest in the attempted bombing of the port area of Margellina, Italy.

SUICIDES. BOMBERS. CAN BE FLIPPED.

Law Enforcement

1. REMI FRANTONI. At 27, the youngest member of Italy's feared and respected Antiterror Unit.

2. FRANK TONELLI. Retired NYPD detective. Worked the OC Task Force. Both a friend and a foe to Carlo Marelli.

3. LUCA FRANTONI. Member of Rome's Antiterror Squad.

DIRTY? OR PLAYING THEM?

HEAVY LINKS TO STREGA. ROMANTIC LINK?

The Silent Six

1. DAVID LEE BURKE. Team leader. Decorated Green Beret. Reports only to Vincent Marelli.

2. JENNIFER MALASSON. Lethal weapon with either knife or rope.

THE WOLF'S ASSASSIN—MILITARY WON'T FLIP—WORKS UNDER RADAR.

3. ROBERT KINDER. Iraqi war veteran and proficient sniper.

4. FRANKLIN J. PIERCE. Martial arts expert.

5. CARL ANDERSON. Former US government chemist. Can poison an opponent in a dozen different ways.

6. BEVERLY WEAVER. One-time member of the North Carolina bomb unit. Munitions expert of the team.

POSSIBLE CONNECTION?
CI? WIRE???

THE WOLF

Prologue

Florence, Italy

SUMMER, 2012

It was not yet noon but already humid on this mid-August Sunday. Stalls and carts lined the Piazza Santa Croce as the statue of Dante glared down at hundreds of tourists and locals. Visitors wearing cameras like jewels around their necks ordered quarter kilos of prosciutto, salami, and fresh mozzarella, each slice laid evenly across the open face of bread just removed from small portable ovens. Others asked for pizzettas covered with toppings and wrapped in wax paper.

The locals lingered, scanning the goods, preparing to buy enough to get through the early part of the week. Many had been to mass and now anticipated the family meal. Street clowns and mimes provided levity to the congested and boisterous setting.

The young man was in his early twenties, clean-shaven, and dressed in casual Florentine attire: a tan jacket, cream-colored slacks, and white button-down shirt. One hand hid inside the left pocket of his jacket while the other held a chocolate gelato cone, the mound of cream melting in the heat. The man ate in the manner that he walked, slow and leisurely, and he wiped at thin veins of melting chocolate with a folded napkin. He studied the people around him and smiled. If many in the crowd were to die within the next several minutes, they had chosen a glorious day in a splendid setting.

The man's name was Ali Ben Bashir. He was the youngest son of an Iranian father and an Italian mother. His parents met when both were medical students at the university in Siena, then separated when Ali was six. After, his life was divided between two families, two cultures: summers in Italy with his mother, the rest of the year with Iranian relatives, none of whom had kind words for any Western nation, especially a Catholic one. He was encouraged to absorb the lessons of Islam and not fall prey to the easy temptations of a city like Florence, as his father's family mocked any mention the boy made of the Renaissance or his excursions to museums and churches designed and built centuries earlier.

Ali became a confused and angry young man, uncertain if the long looks he was given and questions he was asked each time he passed through Italian customs were routine or designed for him alone. His Italian relatives would poke fun at his concerns, dismissing them as paranoia planted by the ramblings of radicals. "They signal you out because you're from a place where today's terrorist comes from," his uncle Aldo told him over coffee one afternoon. "When I was your age, they asked those same questions of us, Northern Italians, because of the Red Brigade and before that of the Germans because of their terrorist problems. It doesn't mean you're special and it doesn't mean they hate you. It just means your time is now, until the next group of madmen come along."

Ali would listen, smile, nod as if in agreement, but remain unconvinced. He had caught too many looks of disdain, not only on the streets of Italy, but when he traveled to other cities as well—a student trip to New York, a vacation in Paris, a biking trip into northern Spain with friends—the same signal was delivered, the same message implied. He was not to be trusted and would never be welcomed. He was an outsider.

To the fundamentalists among his father's friends, Ali was a candidate ripe for radicalization. Over three years, they would visit Ali in small groups. During these meetings, hidden under the guise of dutiful prayer and worship, they would talk about all the ills Western society had placed upon Muslims. Ali grew agitated when told of the atrocities committed against women during the American invasions of Afghanistan and Iraq and of how their most religious book was held up to ridicule and in some cases burned, often by people who had never bothered to read even one word.

The journey of Ali from child of divorce to young student to proud Muslim willing to die for a cause culminated with the death of his father in the spring of 2010. Ali had spent three weeks by his father's bedside, leaving only to attend prayer services. He fed his father what little food he would eat and read to him in the back room of the small apartment. During that time, the two shared many moments and spoke as often as sickness allowed. Ali not only loved the man who had taught him how to read, lace his shoes, and say his prayers, he *respected* him. He knew his father in ways few sons took the time to know their own. But in that three-week period, when he watched the body of the man he most loved in this world surrender to the pain of a disease that could not be conquered, he came to understand why his father hated Western society and all it represented.

"I am sorry to see you this way," Ali said to his father during one of their final moments. "I hate to see you in such pain."

"The price one pays for living a long life," his father said.

Ali smiled and wiped his father's sweaty forehead with a damp cloth. "So, no regrets?" he asked.

"Just one," his father said.

"Does it have something to do with Mother?" Ali asked.

His father shook his head. "No," he said. "If I had not made your mother my wife, I would not have had you as my son. For me, our marriage remains a blessing."

"Then what is your regret?" Ali said.

His father stared at him, laying still, barely catching breath, in the warm confines of a room filled with only a bed, a prayer mat, a night-stand, a bureau. "I wish I had the courage to do what so many others braver than I have done," he finally said.

"What is that?"

"To give up my life," his father said. "To surrender flesh in the name of Allah."

Fourteen months after his father's death, Ali Ben Bashir stood facing a crowded piazza in one of the most beautiful and serene places in the world, across from a church where many of the giants of the Renaissance were buried. He unbuttoned the front of his starched white shirt, revealing an intricate series of wires, timers, and small explosives taped across his chest. He spread his arms out, a small black box with a red button in the center clutched in his right hand. "I do this for you, dear Father," Ali said. "I do this in your name."

Then, head lifted to a cloudless sky, Ali Ben Bashir pressed his thumb on the red button.

I.

"There is no crime of which I cannot conceive myself
guilty."

–JOHANN WOLFGANG VON GOETHE

Los Angeles, California

It should have been me.

Not Lisa.

And not my girls, that's for damn sure.

And not anyone else, not when you take a hard look at it. It was me they targeted. Me they wanted. It's me they've always wanted. But they couldn't touch me. So they reached for the ones they could get. And I let them walk right into it.

I wanted Lisa and the girls to fly on a private jet with bodyguards sitting in front and back and another team waiting on the ground. That was the way it was meant to happen. That's the way it would have happened if I had held firm. But I let myself be talked out of it.

Lisa didn't want our three kids raised in a bubble. She wanted them to grow up as normal kids leading normal lives—or as normal as they could be when you consider who I am and what I do. She had always wanted that—a normal life. We both knew going in that normal was never going to be easy, not with me around. You want safe and secure, move to a small town and marry the local grocer. But when you fall in love with a guy like me, the unthinkable comes with the vows.

I am a cautious man.

I don't trust strangers, am uneasy in large gatherings—from weddings to concerts to dinner parties of more than ten—and travel with a discreet security detail close enough to take action if the need arises. I have a carry permit and never venture out minus at least one loaded weapon. I don't adhere to a regular schedule, instead I vary everything—from workouts to the times I eat my meals to the routes I take to work sites and meetings. I am not troubled by any of these habits and, in truth, I derive comfort from knowing I'm in control of my surroundings. It allows me freedom and enables me to focus on the tasks I need to accomplish.

These habits help me excel at what I do. But they do not make me an ideal husband or father. I imposed these restrictions on my family, and while *I* see them as a necessary precaution, *they* chafed at their existence. My wife detested any security outside of a home alarm. The kids wanted to be able to have sleepovers minus background checks, go to parks and outdoor events without being in the company of armed men who made their presence known. The resentment was a cause for friction.

"Why can't we, just this one time, go on vacation like everyone else?" Lisa had asked me.

"We *are* going on a vacation like everyone else," I said. "Does it really matter how we get there?"

"The kids are not going to live your life when they grow up, Vincent," Lisa said. "They'll be out there on their own. The sooner they see what that's like, the better it will be for them. And as I recall, you went to Italy when you were a teenager and you went alone."

"Not exactly," I said. "But I get your point."

"We've never traveled as a family," Lisa said. "I don't think our kids have even seen the inside of an airport."

"They're not missing much," I said. "Long lines, bad food, lost luggage. Am I leaving anything out?"

"I'm serious, Vincent," Lisa said, reaching for my hand and holding it gently against her side. "Let them be kids, just this once. They're so excited about this trip. I am, too."

"If I get on that plane," I said, "it might as well be a private jet. First class will be me, you, the kids, and our bodyguards."

"Then don't get on the plane," Lisa said. "I'll go with the girls and you follow us later with Jack. You still have that real estate deal to close, right?"

I felt the argument sliding away. "That's right," I said.

"Get that off your plate and then you and Jack can meet us in New York," Lisa said. "Give the two of you some time together."

"It doesn't feel right to me, Lisa," I said. "At least not now. In a few years, maybe then might be a better time."

"You said you wanted a normal life for them," Lisa said. "Did you really mean that or were they just words?"

"I meant it," I said. "I don't want them to be like me in any way."

"Then normal needs to start right now," Lisa said. "With this trip."

I pulled Lisa close to me and held her in my arms. "I love you," I said. "And I'll do anything not to lose you or the kids."

"I love you even more," she whispered in my ear. "And always will."

So, going against my nature and judgment, I agreed to allow some air into my hermetically sealed world. For my kids and for Lisa. They wanted a taste of what passes for normal life, to move about freely, not be confined by my rules. And I went along with it, deluding myself into thinking that they would still be safe, they would still be there for me to hold them close.

That no harm would come to them.

That I was the only target of interest.

It was a move that should never have been made. I allowed my love for family to obscure my distrust of the world. I put them out there without the protection they needed, the safeguards required. I let them go. And I will never forgive myself for that.

My name is Vincent Marelli and I own your life.

I know you've never met me, and if you are lucky you never will. The chances are better than even you've never heard of me, but in more ways than you could think of, I own a piece of you. Of everything you do. I don't care where you live or what you do, a percentage of your money finds its way into the pockets of the men I lead. We are everywhere, touch everything and everyone, and always turn a profit. And once we've squeezed every nickel we can out of you, we toss you aside and never bother giving you a second thought.

You lay down a bet at a local casino or with the bookie in the next cubicle, we get a cut. You take the family on that long-planned vacation, a large chunk of the cash you spend—highway tolls, hotel meals, the rides you put your kids on—finds its way into our pockets. You smoke, we earn. You drink, we earn more. Buy a house, fly to Europe, lease a car, mail your mother a birthday present, we make money on it. Hell, the day you're born and the day you're buried are both days we cash out on you.

And you'll never know how we do it.

That's *our* secret.

We're never in the headlines. Oh, you'll read about some busts and see a bunch of overweight guys in torn sweatshirts with tabloids folded over their heads do a perp walk for the nightly news, but that's not us. Those rodeo clowns are the ones we want you to *think* we are. Those are the faces that get Page One attention, headline trials, and triple-decade prison sentences. We have thousands of guys like that and we toss them into the water any time federal or local badges need to make a splash, make the public think they're out there serving and protecting.

We remain untouched.

At least, we did. Until this happened.

We are the most powerful organization in the world.

In the last twenty years nearly every top-tier branch of organized crime has joined our union: from the three Italian factions to the

Yakuza in Japan, the Triads of China, the French working out of Marseilles, the Algerians, the Israelis, the Greeks, the Irish and the British. We are now one. A powerful and ruling body so strong, we are beyond the reach of any government, let alone an ambitious local district attorney out to make a name. We have become what the old-timers like Lucky Luciano, Frank Costello, and Meyer Lansky dreamed about.

We are a United Nations of crime.

We took the business of crime off the streets and brought it into the dark, wood-paneled rooms where the real money and power live. It didn't happen overnight and there were some bodies dropped along the way. In those early years, not every crew greeted the plan with applause. That's understandable. These were men and women used to doing business their own way. It wasn't easy to make them look at the bigger picture, have them see that the arrival of a new century brought with it an opportunity to take what we did in a more lucrative direction. But enough of them got it. They understood that the way we had accumulated wealth in the last century would take us only so far in this new one. That in order not only to compete but thrive and control the power levers, a modern gangster needed to be educated, as skillful with a spreadsheet as he was with a gun and a blade. The modern mob boss would need to be as comfortable inside a boardroom as his relatives had been inside a union hall. The muscle end would always be easy to find. The ones with the knowledge and expertise to dominate a corporate structure would take time to develop.

By the time the new century was welcomed, my group was in complete command. We had infiltrated the corridors of power from Wall Street to hedge funds to insurance companies and oil conglomerates. We were knee-deep in the political and medical worlds and cut a wide path in the hotel, art, jewelry, and airline businesses. You add to that gambling, drugs, sports, and sex and we owned it all. By the spring of 2011 thirty-one percent of the currency spent in the world found its way into our pockets.

It should have been a gangster's paradise, but in my world, hell is never far away. Terrorist organizations wanted no part of our methods and we wanted even less to do with their chaos. Besides, the way those groups traveled, the light of the law was never far behind. If they crossed into our turf for any reason, they were taken out, no questions asked, no arguments given. It worked pretty well for a few years.

Then along came the Russians, 1.5 million members strong, well-organized and even better financed. They laid low for close to a decade, letting the Cold War dust settle before tossing their muscle and cash to the terrorists. My group liked to get the bulk of their work done under the radar and preferred to conduct business in countries with stable governments. The Russians were the opposite. They thrived on worldwide unease—the more of it there was, the better they liked it. They had connections with forty-seven of the 191 terror organizations around the world and were the key financial suppliers for twenty-three others. Their money flow was endless and they were quick to supply them with any weapons and high-tech equipment they desired. The Russians also knew their way around what any terrorist outfit most craves—a dirty bomb. Thirty percent of the Russian crew came out of the Cold War with degrees in physics and chemistry. That combination alone, working with the wrong people looking to cause serious damage, would deal my business a lethal blow.

If all that wasn't bad enough, we also faced a growing problem south of the border. In 2008 the Mexican gangs got their hands on some terrorist money, working on the simple assumption that any enemy of the United States was sure to be a friend to them. The cartel bosses set up a drug pipeline, buying thousands of kilos of hash and heroin from the eighty-seven terrorist outfits around the world functioning as suppliers. In return, instead of paying in cash, they closed the deal with shipments of all calibers of guns, tossing in the clips for free. It wasn't lost on me that the guns traded by the Mexicans to the terrorists were American-made and stolen.

Any spot I could point to on a map was about to turn into a hot zone. There was too much trouble brewing for it not to bubble over, and by the summer of 2012, I had a major decision to make. One of those calls a guy like me gets to make once, maybe twice, in his life.

I could walk away from everything I built, turn my back and enjoy what was left of my time, proud of the criminal empire I helped create. I was thirty-three, with a wife I adored, two daughters, and a son who only had to smile in my direction to make me feel special. I had millions saved and millions more securely invested, every cent clean and legal. I had a thriving real estate and construction business that would keep my days busy and fuel a good and quiet life.

But something gnawed at me, held me back from taking the easy way out.

If I walked and let the terrorists and their criminal enablers have their way, they would bring everything I helped build down in one tumble. Besides, guys like me never walk away. We like to think we can, but the truth is I could never leave a problem—*any* problem—on the table and ask someone else to handle it.

There was never a doubt in my mind these terrorist groups needed to be taken out. And my organization was the only one with the money and the manpower to take them head-on. We would need to be as ruthless and determined as our enemies, use all our resources, skills, and connections to bring them to ruin. In the process we would sustain heavy losses—both financial and in blood—but there could be no other way. You don't talk peace with a guy looking for a fight and you can't cut a deal unless you trust the hand you're shaking. I looked at the situation from every possible angle and could figure no other way out. It was a war that needed to be fought. It would be a war foreign to us all: the power of modern organized crime against the Russian mob, the Mexican crews, and every terrorist outfit on the grid.

I had no way of knowing if it was a war we could win.

I only knew it was a war we couldn't lose.

I needed time to work up a plan.

I took a leave of absence from running day-to-day operations of the syndicate—the three months I would need to prepare.

I would have to make the first move, to dictate the course of the action. But before I could even make a move, I got blindsided, hit as hard as I've ever been hit in my life.

That was *my* mistake.

I had planned a two-week Paris vacation with my family, kicking it off with a long weekend in New York. My wife and kids were anxious to get going, thrilled I had set aside so much time for us to be together. I've never been big on vacations, so when I agreed to one it was greeted with shrieks of happiness.

I can't tell you how good those few minutes made me feel.

I let Lisa handle the details as she had requested. She and our daughters were scheduled to take an early flight out of Los Angeles and get into New York a few hours before me, giving them time to settle in and hit the city for a girls-only afternoon of shopping and more shopping while I put the finishing touches on a Nevada land deal I had been working on for two years. Our son Jack would stay behind and keep me company on the plane. I would even pretend to lose to him at chess while our flight headed east.

Lisa had talked me out of taking even the most basic safety precautions. Instead, I sent the three of them out there alone, defenseless. I tried to cover it a bit, putting one of the new bodyguards on the flight, sitting him two rows behind my wife. But that was hardly enough.

Less than one hour into their flight, six men—all armed with Swiss Army knives, one claiming to have an explosive device rigged to his groin—took control of the plane, taking the 187 passengers on board hostage. Among those 187 were two undercover air marshals, one in coach, one in first class, sitting across the aisle from Lisa. Both were armed with semiautomatic weapons. The six terrorists spread themselves out between coach and first, each holding a female passenger as cover. The two marshals waited until they had clear shots and then made their move. But a packed airplane is never a good place for a shoot-out, regardless of how much training a person received. There's never enough time or space and simply too much that could go wrong.

Delta Flight 33, LAX to JFK, was no exception.

I got my hands on the airline agency's report of the events as they happened after the marshals announced themselves and pulled their weapons. There was quite a bit of screaming, which grew louder as panic took hold and chaos replaced silent menace. Two of the terrorists managed to get the drop on one of the marshals, slicing a vein in his right arm and taking his weapon. The marshals were brave and tough and fought like wild dogs. The terrorists acted as they had been trained, fearless of death, caring little for the lives of those around them. The end result was as predictable as it was painful: sixteen dead, including the six terrorists and the young bodyguard I had placed on the plane, and eight others seriously wounded. Half the passengers who died were from gunshot wounds, including a Silicon Valley executive and his teenage son seated in the two seats that had been meant for me and Jack. Three had been strangled. Several others fell to multiple stab wounds. Two on board suffered massive heart attacks.

Three of the dead belonged to me.

My wife Lisa had her throat slashed and, according to the medical reports, bled out, unable to move, the pain of her dying moments made even worse by an inability to aid and comfort her daughters.

My youngest, seven-year-old Paula, had her skull crushed by the blunt end of a fire extinguisher, brutally murdered by a teenage terrorist with six young sisters of his own. Her head rested against the side of a small window, eyes open, staring at a clear blue sky.

My oldest, ten-year-old Sandra, was hit with two bullets, each one potentially the kill shot. One bullet lodged in her throat, the second entered below the right cheek. The bullets left her face brutalized, her young body lifeless.

In those horrendous final moments, when three people I loved were facing the dark hand of death, I was in the company of strangers, signing seven-figure contracts, bringing an end to a successful— and now meaningless—business transaction.

Once the attack had been brought under control, the plane was rerouted back to Los Angeles, under the supervision of the U.S. marshals on board, one of whom was in need of medical care. Within an hour of its safe landing, I received a call from a friend in law enforcement. I didn't need to hear anything beyond "There's been a situation" to feel the brunt of the awful truth.

I identified their bodies, buried my family, went through the empty ritual of a memorial service, and stayed inside my home for two months. My twelve-year-old, Jack, was my only companion. I worked out every day; endless hour after hour spent lifting weights, running hard on the treadmill, pounding the heavy bag, my anger an equal match to the tears I shed. I spent my nights sitting and talking to Jack, both of us refusing to take condolence calls or visits from friends or relatives.

The enemy had made the first move.

They had started the war.

It should have been me on that plane.

It should have been me they targeted.

It should have only been me.

That was *their* mistake.

And in my business, one mistake is all you get.

2.

Zurich, Switzerland

He was up early. The air was heavy with moisture, the sun not yet ready to shine. These were his favorite mornings, the ones that reminded him of the childhood in a town so small it could not be found on any Russian map. On those mornings, before the local steel factory opened its doors and shrouded the sky in dust and soot, he would stand in bare feet and stare out at the landscape surrounding the two-bedroom shack he shared with his parents and four older siblings. Two of his brothers had already stopped attending school and started on the only career path the town offered its young men—daily twelve-hour shifts stoking the fires.

But young Vladimir Kostolov knew he would rather die than do one day of work in that heat. The factory's owner lived in a large house miles away and never saw the toll the place took on the men who walked through its doors. Vladimir's father was one of those men, and Vladimir vowed he would never be his father. He would turn his back on the town and the factory and earn his living by other means.

By *any* other means.

His road out went through Moscow a month shy of his twelfth birthday. He'd been sent to live with his mother's cousin and was eager to breathe in the air of the big city. He hoped it would help ease the pain of a cough and congested chest that had plagued him since infancy. He had never met his cousin Alexander, who was only seventeen but had been living on his own since the death of his father two years earlier. Where Vladimir was thin and frail, Alexander was muscular and sturdy, running regularly through the empty streets of a working-class neighborhood, the shadows of Kremlin headquarters looming in the mist. Alexander had asked for the boy to come live with him, had convinced his aunt that when her son returned home he would be healthier. Maybe even useful.

In truth, curing Vladimir and helping him cope with life in a factory town were the least of Alexander Zaverko's concerns. He was a recruiter for the Red Mafiya, the Russian branch of organized crime. Alexander had already proved to be of value to senior members of the Milcheko crew who just in his cluttered neighborhood numbered two dozen. Alexander was a skilled car booster, taught by his mechanic father, able to start a car, move it to a hidden site, and lift the motor in under two hours. For this task he was paid the equivalent of four dollars per car. He often boosted four cars a day, doing his best work under the darkness of Moscow's winter nights.

Alexander earned a black dagger tattoo, the first of what he hoped would be many, on his sixteenth birthday when he shot and killed a retired KGB agent turned Red Mafiya enforcer who had pocketed more than his share of the neighborhood drug proceeds. He was allowed to keep the semiautomatic he had been given for the execution as well as any money found in the dead man's pockets. The Mafiya liked the way Alexander went about his business, calm and deliberate, and they gave their approval whenever he made a request to recruit younger members to the organization.

"Life is different here than in the village," Alexander said to Vladimir, tossing the younger boy's overnight bag on the center of a small bed in the rear of the barely furnished apartment.

"It cannot be worse," Vladimir said, taking a quick glance at his new surroundings.

"There's work to be had," Alexander said. "Money to be made. How much depends on what it is you're willing to do."

"Anything but work in a factory," Vladimir said. "I will kill before I step foot inside one."

Alexander nodded stiffly. "You will have to."

VLADIMIR RETURNED TO his town after two weeks with Alexander. His cough had not improved, but he had been introduced to Alexander's older associates and was given an indication of the type of work that would be expected of him were he to return and have his name placed on their ledgers. He was given two gifts by the Mafiya boss, a tall man whose upper body, back, and arms were covered in tattoos, in the tradition of the criminal underworld. The man's history could be read like chapters of a book written into the contours of his skin. The man had stared at Vladimir for several moments, charcoal eyes and black beard hardly disguising the cold indifference that fueled him. He had handed Vladimir a small caliber handgun and a folded roll of cash, waiting for the boy to accept them and nod his head in appreciation. "These are for you to do with as you choose," the man had said. "And if we never see each other again, we part as friends. But if you wish to return, come here to live, there is a place for you. You will be one of our own, a member of our group until the day one of us is found dead. Have I made myself understood?"

"How soon can I return?" Vladimir had asked.

The bearded man had shrugged.

Vladimir put the gun in his jacket pocket and held the cash in the palm of his left hand, fingers wrapped tight around it. "I won't be gone long."

VLADIMIR RESTED A cup of coffee on a tray and glanced at a dozen photos spread across the length of a glass table. The memories rose into the air like smoke. He had been a boy then and not yet begun the steep climb he attacked with such ferocity and viciousness that even the most hardened of Russia's criminal elite were shaken by it. He could not count the number of men and women he had killed, but he could count the millions his life of crime had reaped. He no longer concerned himself with vast real estate holdings, homes, and apartments spread throughout Europe and the United States. He ignored the expensive cars, the stunning women, and the lavish lifestyle such ways afforded him.

Now thirty-seven, for the past seven years Vladimir had been the undisputed leader of the Russian Mafiya. The frail boy who had trouble taking a full breath had grown into a proven power broker, deciding the fate of thousands. In his rise he had also amassed an impressive business portfolio. He was the first to set up a string of phony medical labs and clinics across Europe, utilizing them as fronts for profitable insurance scams that netted his organization roughly $1 billion per year. Through a network of middlemen, Vladimir owned several private security firms, installing systems in the homes of millionaire businessmen. This allowed him to see what they had of value and what his gangs could plunder without worry when the occupants were out of town.

His most lucrative dealings involved the drug trade.

He had established a successful working partnership with three Mexican cartels. These relationships enabled Vladimir's crew to move $1 million of cocaine and heroin through the world's pipeline per hour.

But on this day, on this early morning, with the glistening tops of the Swiss Alps close enough to touch, there was only one item that had Vladimir's full attention.

Vladimir "the Impaler" Kostolov was ready to begin the next phase of a plan he'd been constructing for more than a decade.

The plan that would cripple strong nations and wreak havoc with their financial institutions.

It would shudder the cores of national leaders, forcing them to make desperate moves.

It would lead to chaos, death, mass confusion, and despair.

It would bring the world to the brink of ruin.

VLADIMIR SAT BACK and watched as his cousin Alexander Zaverko shuffled onto the patio, his frail fingers barely holding onto a thick cup filled with hot coffee. Alexander, five years older than Vladimir, was one of his most trusted confidants and his only true friend. They had risen through the criminal ranks, side by side, until Alexander was stricken with stage four lung cancer less than a year ago, though he neither smoked nor drank. By the doctor's accounts, his cousin would be fortunate to live through the summer. Vladimir had doubts he would make it that far.

Alexander gazed at the photos spread across the table. "Have you selected one yet?" he asked, his voice barely audible.

Vladimir reached for one photo and showed it to his cousin. It was of a young man named Ali Ben Bashir. "This one would have been perfect," he said. "Sadly, he chose to be a martyr instead of a leader."

Alexander looked at the photo and nodded. "The bombing in Florence," he said. "Impressive work."

Vladimir slid a second photo across the table. "This one has the potential to be another," he said. "His name is Raza."

"Why him?"

"He's book-smart and street-smart," Vladimir said. "He has many reasons to be angry and that only helps fuel his passion to destroy. He's ambitious and craves power."

"Which makes him untrustworthy," Alexander said.

"They are *all* untrustworthy," Vladimir said. "But he has extra reasons to want to leave his mark. He was a student of art and at one point embraced the culture he now so much despises."

"What made him change?"

"He was rejected by a number of European universities," Vladimir said, "the majority of them in Italy. It seems they were at odds over his work. Raza thought himself a gifted painter and sculptor; school administrators thought otherwise. Raza looked in the mirror and saw Michelangelo; the administrators saw a meager talent, and a brown-skinned one at that."

"He turns his back on his own world, only to have . . ."

"The world he wished to enter turn their back to him," Vladimir said. "Ostracized in one, ridiculed in another—two necessary ingredients for a terrorist."

"How good is he?"

"Working on a small stage, he's done well," Vladimir said. "He's building a reputation, and that will only grow as he selects higher profile targets."

"Will he listen to you?" Alexander asked.

"None of the good ones can be expected to follow our orders," Vladimir said. "Which would make it a waste of our time to give them any. Raza will want our money and we will want him to kill and destroy. It makes for a sound arrangement."

"I wish there were enough time for me to see this one through to the end," Alexander said.

"As do I, cousin," Vladimir said. "But I will do my best in your absence."

3.

New York City

The meeting was held on the thirty-fifth floor of a downtown Manhattan office building.

The conference room table was covered with porcelain carafes, sterling silver coffeepots, and crystal bowls filled with fresh fruit. Three ornate chandeliers lit the room, the glow of their bulbs gleaming off the polished table and mahogany chairs. The floor to ceiling windows were bulletproof.

It was a landmark building whose halls were once populated by land barons and oil and steel magnates. It was a place accustomed to accommodating men of power, and I knew the ones I had invited to join me would feel at ease in here, impressed by the surroundings. They saw themselves as similar to those billionaires from an earlier century, so the parallel would not be lost on them.

I had food prepared by the finest chefs from every nation that would be represented at the table—from southern Italian delicacies to the freshest sushi to the finest French pastries. I had been around these men long enough to know they were appreciative of respectful gestures and put at ease by tastes of the familiar.

I needed them to feel comfortable as I pushed them to make what I knew would be an uncomfortable decision. My words had to be measured, my tone direct but not demanding. I would need to read the room quickly, watching for facial expressions, eye movements, and body language, to gauge each reaction. I had to anticipate concerns but never patronize or lie. I had to exert authority while being aware of the power each man at the table wielded.

I needed to convince a group of men who for decades were in full control of *everything* to join me in risking it all.

I was first to arrive.

I poured myself a cup of coffee and sat at a chair in the center of the table. I had requested the meeting three weeks earlier but given no details as to what would be discussed. Every one of the men scheduled to attend had offered condolences in the days following the deaths of my wife and daughters. They were hard-core crime bosses but they were husbands and fathers and had been knee-deep in a harsh business long enough to have suffered their share of loss.

I was the youngest of the eight.

My father, Mario, was a long-haul truck driver, a proud union member who put in heavy hours. He was a big man with a laugh as hearty as his appetite and he was always good company. My mother, Elena, was frail, and I never can recall a time when she wasn't ill with one malady or another. We lived in a two-story house in the northeast Bronx on a dead-end street. I attended a local Catholic school and was a weekend altar boy. I would smile when my mother would tell me what a handsome priest I would make, not wanting to shatter an illusion she shared with every other Italian-American woman in the parish. You could say I was bookish, spending hours in a back room in a small library that faced a supermarket parking lot, a pile of books by my side. I read the books boys my age would love—Sir Arthur Conan Doyle's Sherlock Holmes stories and the novels of Jack London, Rafael Sabatini, Victor Hugo, and Alexandre Dumas. On

Sundays, after mass, I would go for long walks with my father and tell him about the tales I had read during the time he was away. In return, he would tell me about the cities he had driven through and the small towns he had visited, spending nights in the cabin of his rig, the cackle of a portable radio the only company he required.

I preferred solitary activities, which I've been told is not uncommon for an only child. It is a habit that has served me well in the criminal world, a place populated by those who prefer to go it alone. I made a quick leap from checkers to chess and learned to compete against myself, using books about the masters of the game as my guide. It is a practice I've kept to this day, except now I use it to plan strategies and moves against a range of ruthless opponents.

I was a baseball fan, listening to the games during the season, anticipating the moves made by the managers of both New York teams, preferring National League ball to that played in the American due to the strategic in-game decisions required. I studied the stats in the morning paper, checked a player's on-base percentage against the opposing pitcher's hits-to-walk ratio, attempting to evaluate who had the greater chance to succeed, and look for reasons behind it.

I was a member of the school track team. I was a long-distance runner, choosing to compete against a clock as opposed to an opponent. I ran just about every day, regardless of weather. I loved the sounds of my sneakers bouncing off a dirt road.

With my father away, I spent a great deal of time with my mother. In the early evening, we sat in the living room and listened to the radio, tuned to an Italian station broadcasting news from a country she missed every day of her life. I would sometimes read to her from an assortment of books—some borrowed from the library, others in Italian, sent to her by relatives in Naples. I never understood the extent of her ailments and I couldn't guess at the pain she felt, but all I needed to know I could observe—my mother was sick and would never get better and I was there to offer comfort in any way I could.

It was a safe, simple existence, both within our home and around our neighborhood. I was too young to think much about what I wanted to make of my life, if there was indeed a place for me outside the Bronx. Few of the older kids from the area ventured far and all seemed to find work that required a uniform—military, police, fire, sanitation. I wasn't sure if that would be the direction I would seek, but I don't think I would have minded.

All that vanished the summer I turned thirteen.

On July 4 of that year, while other kids were in playgrounds or on rooftops waiting for the fireworks to begin, I was on the second floor of our home, at my mother's bedside, watching her draw her final breaths, her ravaged body giving in to the incessant demands of a disease without any quit. My father gripped one of her hands and I held tight to the other, listening as my mother strained to speak. "I'm sorry," she said in a painful rasp. "I'm so sorry." She closed her eyes and let her head tilt to one side.

My father was not an emotional man. The day after we buried my mother, the only woman he would ever love, he left to drive a sixteen-wheeler packed with oil drums to a factory in Missoula, Montana, expecting to return in less than a week. He left knowing I would be responsible enough to go to school every day and return home to a dinner left for me by our neighbor and my mother's best friend, Filomena. My father always treated me more as an adult than my years would indicate. There was a feeling of mutual trust between us that neither would betray. It's a weakness, I know, but one that can be forgiven between a father and a son.

On his return trip from Montana, somewhere on the curving roads of the Pennsylvania Turnpike, my father's truck swerved to avoid hitting two deer standing too close to the right-hand lane. The truck jackknifed and skidded for more than a quarter of a mile, the cabin crashing against the side of a guardrail, my father's body blasting through the windshield, landing head first against the base of a tree. He was pronounced dead at the scene, a victim of two innocent animals and a faulty seat belt.

But I knew better.

My father had driven those roads for years and knew of the large number of deer who congregated along the curves of that stretch of

76. He would always move his truck to the middle lane during that portion of the drive. He would downshift the rig, slow-riding the 150-mile stretch of road, knowing he was getting close to home. And my father was a stickler about safety, double-checking the engine and cabin, never pulling a rig on the road unless he was confident all was secure.

My father chose to end his life.

He had lived with the burden of my mother's illness for many years and now the weight of her death was more than he could bear and he brought it all to a close on a stretch of highway he had driven for over a decade.

And then I was alone in a large room, my father's sealed coffin resting a few feet away, surrounded by flowers and a prayer book. I wore the same dark jacket and slacks I wore for my mother's wake, sitting there in an uncomfortable chair in a foul-smelling room, having lost, in less than a month's time, the only two people in my life who mattered. At one point the door behind me swung open and I heard footsteps. I looked up and saw a man who resembled my father in feature and stature, though he was far better dressed and gave off an air of authority. He seemed to be the kind of man used to having his way.

He walked over to my father's coffin, rested a hand on the top and bowed his head. He stayed still for several minutes, then made the sign of the cross, turned, walked to a corner of the room and grabbed a folding chair. He stopped a few inches from me, popped open the chair and sat down.

"I'm Carlo Marelli," he said in a commanding voice. "Your father's brother and your uncle."

"He never mentioned you," I said. "Never told me he had a brother."

"We weren't close," he said.

"Why?"

"There's time for that later," he said, his dark eyes never moving from mine. "Right now, we need to talk about you and me."

"I don't know anything about you."

"And I know all I need to know about you," he said.

"Like what?" I asked.

"You're a smart kid with a bright head," he said. "You keep to yourself and don't let people you don't know get close."

"People like you?"

He smiled and nodded. "Especially people like me," he said. "At least for now. Until we get to a place where we know and trust one another, and that's going to take time. But if you agree, then you and me will have more than enough time to get to that point."

"How?" I asked.

"I want you to come live with me," he said. "I'll tell you up-front it will be a different life than what you had with your mother and father. And I'll also tell you right here and now, you won't be raised as a guest or a nephew I got stuck with. You'll be raised as if you were my son. On that you have my word. And that's usually good enough for anybody."

"Was it good enough for my father?" I asked.

Carlo stood, folded the chair and rested it against his side. "Okay, then," he said. "Most anybody. I know this came on you sudden so take time to think it over. But don't take too long. I won't hang around for the funeral; your father didn't want much to do with me when he was alive, find it hard to imagine he would want me to watch him get buried. I have a few meetings in the city the next day or so. Once those are wrapped up, I'll come find you and you can give me your answer."

"What if I decide no?" I asked.

"Then that's what you decide," he said. "I get out of your life as fast as I came into it."

With that, Carlo Marelli handed me the folding chair, patted me on the shoulder, slid his hands into the pockets of his tailored slacks, and walked out of the room.

In so many ways, my life was a straight shot from that funeral parlor to this boardroom.

4.

The first explosion rocked the Rome train station. It was 8:58 Monday morning. The blast came from a backpack left against the side of a water fountain by a chunky teenager in a Grateful Dead T-shirt, jeans, and a green windbreaker. He was out of the station when the bomb went off, timed to hit at the height of passenger traffic, a summer's blend of tourists beginning their vacation and Italians starting a week of work.

Fifteen minutes later a car bomb ignited in a quiet London middle-class neighborhood, a long street of row houses facing quaint shops, shuttered pubs, and a middle school playground jammed with children. The explosion sent the car—a late model Fiat 124—hurtling into the air, landing inside the second-floor den of a newlywed couple eating breakfast and planning a shopping excursion. They died instantly, the wife thrown against a wall, the husband left holding the remains of a teacup in a burnt and rigid hand. Six of the row houses were destroyed by fire, two of the shops and pubs suffered significant damage, and the schoolyard was now quiet.

TWO MINUTES LATER, 117 passengers boarded Lufthansa Flight 8142 from Frankfurt to Paris. They were mostly business commuters mixed in with a few scattered Parisians eager to return home. They were joined by an overweight man in a disheveled suit, a boarding pass in one hand, a copy of the King James Bible in the other. His manner was calm and he smiled often, as if being told a humorous story he alone could hear. He handed the woman at the gate his boarding pass, nodded his thanks as she slipped it through the readout and handed a portion back. He then followed an elderly couple into the walkway, gripping the Bible tighter, glancing at his watch and shutting his eyes for a moment.

He didn't wait for the flight to take off, nor did he walk to his seat. Instead, he stopped just short of the entrance to the plane, held the Bible with both hands and smiled at those around him. "You are a blessed few," he said to them, "for the Lord's might shines upon you on this day."

He then opened the Bible and set free the wired explosives.

VLADIMIR KOSTOLOV PRESSED a button on his cell phone and rested it on a coffee table, staring at the wide expanse of the northern Alps that bordered his mountain estate. He had orchestrated the first in a planned series of terror plots, three attacks in all. He took satisfaction knowing a certain degree of panic would set in among the Western nations' security networks, their primary focus on what all antiterrorist organizations fear most—the unknown. No group would call in to take credit for the attacks, and if one rogue group was bold enough to step forward, the full force of a number of national security agencies would be sent in search of the wrong enemy. Either way, Vladimir was at the controls.

Vladimir held the belief, one that permeated the higher echelons of the Red Mafiya, that where there was chaos there was profit, millions waiting to be made from massive unrest. International law enforcement would have no choice but to divert time and energy to capture the terrorist groups responsible for the acts of violence. That would leave his organization able to focus on their illegal activities free of concern from legal interlopers. With fewer eyes prying on his criminal network, Vladimir would be able to conclude a three-nation, multi-billion-dollar arms shipment to the Middle East, hundreds of cases of AK-47s and rocket launchers primed to make their way to the Yemen underground. He also had a seven-hundred-kilo shipment of heroin to move out of Pakistan, bound for European and American shores. His take from the completion of these two transactions would be several hundred million dollars.

Vladimir picked up the cell phone and punched in a four-digit code followed by a fourteen-digit international number. He gazed at the morning sun shining against the side of the mountains, making them gleam as if polished.

He said into the phone, "Begin the second phase."

5.

"You're asking us to take a risk that could cause us to lose what it took decades to build." The man across from me looked straight into my eyes. "Go all-in against crews that would rather die than cut a deal. And to what end? As it stands, they steer clear of us, we steer clear of them. Why stir the pot?"

The man was Anthony Zambelli, head of the Sicilian branch of organized crime, the Mafia. He had inherited the title and a temper from his father, Don Francisco Zambelli, the man credited with the invention of the double-decker coffin, the most convenient means of disposing of a body the mob ever devised. Anthony was, in many ways, smarter and savvier than his father, expanding their hold on the world's harbors to include cruise ships and luxury liners, allowing the organization to take in two dollars for every five spent on board. He helped expand our restaurant and casino holdings and turned the enforced sale of twigs of parsley into a $15 million a year operation.

Zambelli's initial comments surprised me. I came into the meeting thinking he would be the one in the group most willing to go along with my plan. Then again, maybe I would still turn out to be right about that. Anthony could be acting as my front-runner, asking questions he figured I came prepared to answer. I knew he had no love for the Russians or the Mexicans, and on the turf he ruled in Sicily anyone connected to terrorism was eliminated before the rumor could be confirmed.

I took note of his demeanor as he spoke. He was calm, not hostile, and if he had an inclination to push aside my plan, he would not have been able to keep a rein on his anger. He put up an aggressive defense, but while he questioned my plan he didn't discount it. He merely pointed out the inherent dangers.

"There is no 'later' in this," I said, looking at the men sitting around the table. "Not for me. Not for us. If we're going to act, the time is now. We might have waited too long as it is. We gave them space to grow. Maybe that made sense once. Not anymore. We might lose everything getting into an all-out war against them. That's a risk. But we lose everything if we don't fight them. That's a fact."

These were the most powerful mob leaders in the world—Jannetti from the Camorra sitting next to Kodoma of the Yakuza, and Qing, the Triad Dragon Head. The Israeli assassin squad sent Weiner, a former Mossad agent, and the French flew over old man Carbone, who seemed more dangerous now that he was battling prostate cancer. The Albanians sent Orto, the last link to the original Gypsy Kings, and the Greeks gave their slot to Big Mike Paleokrassas, as true with a knife as he was with his word.

They all had doubts about waging a war that in their minds was more about my thirst for vengeance than the need to protect their profit base.

In some ways we were run no differently than any multinational corporation. There really isn't much that separates an international organized crime council from oil conglomerates, hedge funds, and financial institutions. We're in the profit business, and all of us, on occasion, utilize methods frowned upon by those who live honest lives. Each of us has had days that end with blood on our hands, and not a single one of us—not gangsters, not legitimate businessmen—ever feel truly guilty about it.

"What is the cost of such an endeavor?" Qing asked, his manner smooth as ever.

"Financial or physical?" I asked.

"I would be interested in an answer to both," Qing said.

"Off the charts," I said, "on both. The Russians have enough cash to sustain a decade-long war, and the Mexicans aren't far behind. And we all know how they feel about leaving bodies in the sand."

"And these terrorists," Jannetti added, "live to die. And there's not one of us in this room can put a number to how many of them are out there waiting to pull a pin and take a trip to heaven."

"That's right," I said. "We would be on equal footing financially, able to match the Russians, Mexicans, and terrorists dollar for dollar. We have an edge on secondary sources—our street information, for example, is deeper and stronger than anything they have. Plus, we all have law enforcement contacts that work with us, especially when they know who we are going up against. But where we come up short—and there's no point in even guessing how short—is manpower."

"And you think there's no talking to them?" Kodoma asked. "Come to an agreement where their activities don't impact our businesses?"

"I don't think," I said. "I *know*."

"Vincent is correct," Weiner said, voice and manner relaxed. "You *can* talk to them, just don't expect it to get you anywhere."

"Look, everybody here is sorry about what happened to your wife and daughters," Carbone said, never one to shy from awkward moments. "And if it were my family instead of yours, I would do anything, *anything*, to get the bastards behind the job. If that's the reason, the only reason, you're asking us to go down into the pit, I think it fair we hear that from you right now, before we go further."

I had figured Qing and Kodoma would be up for my plan. The Triads and the Yakuza were organizations built on discipline, loyalty, and respect. They had disdain for any organization not designed in a similar fashion, which made them natural enemies of the Russians, Mexicans, South Americans, and terrorists. They were men of tradition and would expect one reason for my plan to be personal, since family members are held sacred in their cultures.

Carbone was a money whore. I could tell from the moment he sat down he would be opposed to a plan that brought with it risk to the bottom line of his outfit. I was also aware, as were others in the room, that his crew had a wink and nod deal with terrorists on his turf. He allowed them to use his areas as a base in return for monthly payments so long as there were no attacks perpetrated on sections he controlled. But I also knew Carbone was at the mercy of the Camorra and the Mafia, dependent on them for supplies and a pipeline into keeping his drug operations running. If they were in, he had to be, if only for the sake of appearances.

"It's part of it," I said. "To sit here and say otherwise would be insulting to each of you. But if it were only that, I wouldn't need any of you to do what needs to be done. I would take care of it myself. I don't lack the money, the manpower, or the stomach. So, if you think I called you in just for that, then there's a car waiting downstairs to take you back to your hotel or airport or wherever the hell it is you want to go. I don't need you to fight my battle. But this is a much bigger issue. This is about *our* war with them. A war that must be fought. You all know that. You knew it as soon as you were aware of the Russians brokering a deal with the terrorists. That is a line we cannot allow to be crossed. You wouldn't be who you are, wouldn't hold the positions you do, if you didn't believe that."

"Let's say, for sake of argument, we leave this alone, let them go about their business," Jannetti said. "How does that hurt us more than getting into an all-out war where numbers favor the other side?"

"Not to mention—again—the cost," Orto said. "If this thing runs as long as we think, both sides could end up fighting for nothing more than pocket change."

"That happens, we end up working for you," Big Mike said. "Right next to the other Gypsies, lifting wallets from tourists at train stations."

"They're hurting us now and have been for the last two to three years," I said. "You need to look deep into our budgets to find it, but the losses are there. We let it go the way it is or allow it to escalate, then soon enough you won't have to look deep to find the drop in profits."

"Please, let us talk about those costs," Kodoma asked. "Forget the money for a minute. I'm talking about manpower, disruption of distribution, upsetting the legal end of business. How much of a toll will that hit us with if we get bogged down in a war that will take years to resolve?"

"It will cost twice any number you have in mind," I said. "But I'm telling you that it will cost us triple that if we don't do anything to bring a halt to these crews now. All that damage you laid out, that's going to happen on its own if we let them continue to do business with us acting as if they're not even out there."

"You say you can't talk to them, but have you truly considered making a deal?" Orto asked.

It would be the Albanian to suggest we do business with terrorists and their financial backers. The Albanians were bottom-feeders, and in the past had no trouble brokering deals with groups that would give pause to the other criminal factions in the room. They never drew a line in the sand, not if there was a chance they could profit from those standing farther down the beach. At some point down the road, Orto would need to be handled. I had no doubt he would be the only one in the room who would pass my intentions on to the Russians. I glanced over at Big Mike and knew he was thinking the same thing.

Jannetti, red-faced and angered by the question, jumped in. "We do *not* do business with terrorists," he said. "I don't give a fuck if they pay us in barrels of cash. No one in this room deals with those pricks, not if they want to stay in this room."

"Look," I said, not wanting tempers to flare at a meeting I called, "if there was another way, a less costly way, I would pursue it. But there isn't. This is our only exit, not just to keep the businesses we have but to grow new ones. No one handed us a damn thing. We took what we needed, what we wanted, and we built from there. And we stopped anybody, big or small, who stood against us. So, sure, this is going to be a bigger battle than we've faced in the past. But we wouldn't be who we are if that kind of news made our legs tremble."

"Sounds as if you've made up your mind," Qing said.

I nodded. "If we want to keep what we have, this is what we need to do," I said.

"What's a win in this for us?" Big Mike asked. "It's not like we're going to do a full-scale wipeout, that's just not numerically possible. So how will we know if we won or lost?"

"No," I said, "you're right. There's no way we can kill them all. But we can regain our advantage. Put them on the defensive and leave them there."

"I don't need to hear any more," Weiner said. "In fact, I didn't need to hear any of what I heard. You ask me, this is a fight we should have brought to them ten years ago, when they weren't as strong, weren't as mobilized. But we bring it to them now, once and for all."

"Tell us what you know about our enemies," Qing said.

"There are 191 terrorist organizations operating around the world, spread across forty-two countries," I said. "Some are small—150 members, tops. Others have close to 200,000 in their ranks with thousands more offering secondary support. About 25 percent are kids willing to die for a cause they've been told to believe in. The rest have been fighting wars since they were old enough to hold guns. About 45 percent are from the Middle East, 40 percent are from Europe, the rest are USDA homegrown, from militias to neo-Nazis to biker gangs. They got the guns and the money and can move without worry from country to country."

"In Italy, they are making moves into high-end art," Zambelli said. "That's new turf for them. They hit home museums and hire out pros to help move the works out of the houses and into the black market. In less than seventy-two hours the art is turned into cash."

"In my country as well," Carbone said. "These terrorists don't know enough about that world to have gone into it on their own. They were guided there—by the Russians, would be my guess."

I noted how Carbone took Zambelli's lead and did his best to follow it. Carbone was an easy buy and I nodded in agreement as he spoke.

"The Russians give them access to the art world, to banks, to credit cards and to high-end weapons," I said. "The Mexicans buy their drugs and pay off the shipments with stolen guns. That's your real axis of evil right there."

"And the Russians and Mexicans, what do they expect to gain from all this?" Big Mike asked. "It's not like you can trust any of the terrorist cells. So *why*, is my question. Why are they in this with people they know they can never trust? What's the endgame?"

"Us," Kodoma said.

Kodoma could sway the room in my direction and had just begun to do so.

He had been the head of the Japanese mob—the Yakuza—for two decades now. He was a direct descendant of Yoshio Kodoma, the Yakuza boss who unified the various factions after World War II and made them a prominent criminal force in Japan and Asia.

Kodoma had fifteen thousand members under his command spread across forty-one gangs, all secretive and impossible to infiltrate. Together, the two of us had invested in dozens of American companies and had holdings in excess of $10 billion in legitimate enterprises. We then took that money, ran it through a series of shell companies, and funneled the profits back into the organization.

Kodoma controlled 2,500 banks worldwide, which made cash and wire transfers simple to complete, especially since money laundering is legal in Japan. He ran over three hundred gambling operations that netted the organization a yearly profit of $460 million. No one runs better gambling dens than the Yakuza. They initially began their operations by sponsoring underground tournaments of Bakuto, a card game similar to blackjack, with one distinct difference—if you lose a game of blackjack, you leave cash on the table; if you lose at Bakuto, you leave behind a finger, giving rise to the name Yakuza, which means hand-cutter. The Yakuza have even published a book called *How to Evade the Law*—which all members of the council are required to read. Kodoma gets a kickback for every book sold.

And if you control the money and the banks, the deck is stacked in your favor. I knew some in the room would balk at my plan, but it would be much more difficult for them to do so with Kodoma at my back. I could freeze any dissenters out of large chunks of my operation, costing them millions each month.

Kodoma could bring them to their knees by refusing to wash their money and oversee their gambling operations. I looked across the table at him and felt certain he was prepared to do just that.

"Close to two million Russians, we don't know how many terrorists, and have even less of an idea of the number of Mexicans," Carbone said, sitting rigidly in his chair, hands cupped around a glass of cold water. "That correct?"

"Pretty much," I said.

"So I'm hoping—we're *all* hoping—you have a plan to go along with your call to war," Carbone said.

"And it can't just be any plan," Jannetti said. "It has got to be one terrific, kick-ass plan. Because I am not eager to get into the trenches with these bastards just to have my ass handed to me."

"I have a plan," I said. "It's risky."

"Which means what?" Orto asked.

"Which means it's a great plan," Qing said. "Only risky plans have any chance to be great."

6.

Vittorio Emanuele Jannetti walked down the center of a crowded street of Spaccanapoli, the very heart of Naples, beside his confidant of more than thirty years, Alfredo Lambretto. Three burly body-guards walked several feet in front of them and two others followed close behind, all armed, eyes trained on the tourists and locals sur-rounding them.

"The kid's instincts are correct," Lambretto said.

He was a tall, thin man with a head of gray hair and a stylish beard. He had made it out of the hard streets of the most dangerous neighborhood in Italy—Forcella—and had the scars to prove it. He had risen from petty thief to become the Camorra's main enforcer, commanding a group of over five hundred. "If we are going to move," he continued, "now's the time. These terror crews keep grow-ing in number, and with Russian muscle at their backs it's only going to get worse. Until now I've been able to push back and keep them out of our business. But each day passes, it gets harder and harder to do."

"The all-out war Vincent has asked for comes with all-out risks," Jannetti said. "We see this through to the end and we'll be down by half, maybe more. And cash flow could become an issue if the fight lasts more than a few years. That may not be a concern to him, but it is to me."

"We started with nothing in our pockets but a gun, you and me," Lambretto said.

"We were a lot younger," Jannetti said, "and with all to gain and nothing to lose. And these new guys don't care about turf, running neighborhoods, bringing in cash. They just want to die, get to heaven and start the party."

"Maybe *they* don't care," Lambretto said, "but the Russians and the Mexicans care. And getting to heaven is the last thing on *their* minds."

Jannetti nodded. "I told Vincent to count us in," he said. "Not that I had much choice. Not only are we part of the council, we're part of the same family."

"You want me to run the operation?" Lambretto asked.

Jannetti shook his head. "I want Angela to take the lead."

"How you think she'll feel working with Vincent?" Lambretto asked.

"She's got Camorra blood in her veins, same as you and me," Jannetti said. "Vincent fell into this life, but she was born to it. This fight will give her a chance to show the others on the council she belongs at that table. Not just sitting in my seat one day. But sitting at the very head of the table."

Vittorio Jannetti was in charge of the Camorra, the Neapolitan branch of organized crime and one of the most vicious criminal outfits in the world. The group was established in the thirteenth century by a patriotic handful of citizens who decided they had seen enough abuse heaped onto the working poor by the powerful. They now number 3,500 members in Naples and New York, and are invested in the drug trade, fashion industry, construction, waste management, real estate, and the transport of toxic goods. They also control a wide portion of the European black market, which nets them $200 million per month.

Jannetti had entered the life as a boy, brought to the local Don when he was ten, a chronic truant with no patience for school. Jannetti lived in the heart of the Camorra power center and was delivered to them by his own out-of-work father. It was how the Camorra found their soldiers, taking boys from homes of men who owed them money or had nowhere to turn for help. They then raised the children as their own, placing each with a soldier's family, putting the child through school. If the boy excelled at math, he went to business school; if his forte was science, he became a doctor. Over time, the Camorra would place thousands of their children in legitimate businesses.

Jannetti seemed always to be in the middle of a street fight. He had a flash temper and went after anyone he considered to be in his way. He had few friends but many silent enemies, and was feared by any who crossed his path. He was also a skilled organizational leader and a master planner. And those abilities were put to good use by the older members of the Camorra. They realized they could always groom someone to be a banker, lawyer, or doctor, but a crew boss was difficult to find and nurture, and Vittorio Jannetti was a natural.

He was sent to New York in his early twenties and partnered with Carlo Marelli. Together, the two wove a violent path through the city's underworld, and by the time Jannetti was in his thirties, he and Marelli had risen through the ranks to control one of the five New York crime families. Jannetti had earned the respect of the Camorra power brokers and won a nickname that would follow him back to Naples, where he assumed control of his own men. He was called "the Cobra" because of the speed with which he attacked, launching an all-out assault when the enemy least expected, bringing a street war to an end when it had barely begun.

He had been married for a brief time to an American woman

from Birmingham, Michigan, who bore him one child, a daughter who lived in the States and made her living as a teacher. He had little time for either woman beyond gifts on birthdays and holidays.

His true love was the daughter he had by a mistress who died in childbirth. Her name was Angela, and Jannetti raised her in the Camorra way, teaching her the practices and traditions she would need to uphold if she were to replace him as the Naples crime boss. She was every inch her father's daughter and was known among the underworld as "the Strega," the Italian word for witch. Angela had taken to the name so enthusiastically that she had mastered the centuries-old practices of those women.

"You ready to move?" Jannetti asked Lambretto.

"I put everything in motion while you were in New York," Lambretto said. "Didn't think the council would give Vincent a thumbs-down."

"I gave him my vote, and we'll stay in this so long as it helps and not hurts us," Jannetti said. "Vincent lost his family so he's going to go into this hard. And while I feel bad about what happened, that's something he's got to deal with. It's his fight. Not ours."

"You think the other crews feel the same as you do?" Lambretto asked.

"Not everybody's heart is in it," Jannetti said. "The Gypsy, Orto, will be the first to fold. The Japanese and Chinese, they're all in, but who knows which way the French will go? The Greek will stick with us till the end. Still, Vincent can't risk even one bad move. They'll be on him in a flash."

"If he screws up, then some of the blowback can do damage to Angela," Lambretto said.

"Don't worry about her," Jannetti said. "She'll know what to do."

"When do we start?" Lambretto asked.

"Tonight," Jannetti said. "Send a team into one of the Muslim sections and have them find three on our target list. Drag them out of apartments, bars, mosques, wherever they are."

"Looking for information?"

Jannetti shook his head. "I don't care what they know," he said. "Throw them into the piazza and shoot them dead. Leave the bodies for their friends to find. That should get the ball moving."

"You want me to clear any of this with Vincent?"

"We never have before," Jannetti said. "Why start now?"

1.

New York City

I sat in the third row of an empty church, facing the main altar, partly hidden by the shadows cast by candles that lit the faces of the saints and the Blessed Mother. I was not a religious man but I sometimes hungered for the serenity of an empty church. I never prayed; I never confessed. I sought nothing more than a few moments of reflection.

So I arrived early for my planned sit-down with Vladimir Kostolov.

It might appear out of place for me to agree to a meeting with Vladimir, especially one that doesn't end with me taking him out. I had my reasons. First, there is the matter of respect. It's as true now as it was back in the days when Luciano would sit across the table from Dutch Schultz in the middle of a bootleg war. The time to worry is when a boss *doesn't* show at an agreed upon meeting. That's when you know bullets will fly.

It was also a chance for me to fill in some of the blanks on what I could expect. Now, I have a stack of ledgers on Vladimir's meetings with terrorists and the way he moves cash in their direction, but that only tells me so much. I need to sit across from a man, look him in the eye and get a sense of how deep he's willing to go in the fight. You can't get that out of a file folder. You get that by watching, listening not so much to what is said but what isn't, what your opponent is willing to risk and where he will draw the line.

It was unlikely that Vladimir had funded the attack on the plane. On the surface, it didn't seem a move he would make. There was little profit in it and the mayhem it caused was minimal. He would also need the approval of the Russian criminal federation to authorize an attack on a crime boss at my level, and no such meeting had taken place. If it had, word would have passed quickly through the criminal networks and I would have been made aware of it. Now Vladimir was never one to adhere to all the rules, but I had doubts whether he wanted to further risk the wrath of the Russian bosses this early in the game. Still, the loss of my family had sent me reeling, and despite my taking the controls and leading the charge into battle, I was not functioning at my best. That may have been the Russian's intent, and even though it went against the way he had done business in the past, I couldn't rule it out completely.

From his end, Vladimir was going to try to get just as much out of me. Our goals were the same—walk away knowing more than what we did coming into the meeting, while revealing little to the man on the other side of the pew.

By backing the terrorists, Vladimir had angered some of the older Russian crews. While they enjoyed the profits made off the chaos caused by any attacks, they felt it was in their best interests to keep their distance and let the bombers go about their business. Vladimir's move put the Russian mob at the same table as the terrorists, a place some in the old guard wanted to steer clear of. That kind of anger leads to resentment and ultimately to bloodshed, especially now, when Vladimir's actions put him at odds with the other orga-

nized crime syndicates. If he was feeling any heat from his own people, I could use that to my advantage.

"What is it with Italians and their churches?" Vladimir asked. "I
have always wondered."

"It's our first stop and our last," I said, staring straight ahead. "We
open with a baptism and close with a funeral. A full circle."

"Spoken like a believer," Vladimir said, sliding into the pew, sitting to my left.

"It's also a good place to meet, hear what a friend has on his
mind," I said.

"I know about the council meeting," Vladimir said, gazing at the
altar. "Your plan won't work. The others will realize it before you do.
But eventually you will come to the same conclusion."

"I doubt that," I said. "All these years, all those council meetings,
we somehow never come to the same conclusion."

"We are too big for you and the other gangs," Vladimir said. "My
men alone? Two million. The Mexicans? Another half million. And
not even the terrorists can count the number they have. You won't be
able to sustain the losses."

I turned to glance at him.

"I don't want to kill everyone on your side," I said. "Just those who
need to die."

Vladimir nodded. He shifted in the pew and turned his body
toward me. "You know what everyone calls you, right? The Wolf?" he
asked. "Do you mind it?"

"No," I said.

"It is a name that suits your talents," Vladimir said. "Track your
opponents, get to know how they think, behave, maneuver. Once you
have all the information you need . . . Except, of course, in your current situation. This time, even the mighty Wolf will be up against too
many sheep to do them much damage."

"What do you want?" I asked.

"I don't want anything," Vladimir said. "I came prepared to give.
Twenty percent of profits, out of my end. You and the others won't

have to pull a trigger. Just sit back, let us do our work, and get a big check every month. How you choose to divide it, I'll leave to you. You'll be making money, no losses, no war you cannot win. Plus I guarantee one more thing."

"What?"

"No harm will come to your son," Vladimir said. "You have lost enough. No fight is worth losing all those we love."

At the mention of my son's name, something inside me shattered. I looked up at the altar, then stood and faced Vladimir. "I don't want twenty percent. Or even that extra ten percent you would have thrown in if I had laughed at your offer. I don't want any of it. I wasn't looking to start a war. But I will be the one to finish it. That I promise."

"Your partners may not share your zeal," Vladimir said. "They should be told of the offer I made."

"They've been told," I said. "Your people reached out to *them* before our meeting was set."

Vladimir smiled. "And had they agreed to my offer?"

"I would still be here," I said. "Alone, if it came to that."

I stared at Vladimir for a few seconds and then made my way out of the long pew and turned to leave the church. I stopped after a few steps. "You know what it is I most admire about a wolf?" I asked, my voice echoing off the walls of the empty church.

"Tell me," Vladimir said.

"When he hunts his prey, he picks off the weakest first," I said. "One by one. He leaves the strongest for the end, when it's just the two of them, alone. And then he goes in for the kill."

Vladimir looked entertained. "Does he always win?"

"No," I told him. "But if he senses his pups are in danger, he will fight until his last breath."

I stood there a moment, hands in my pockets. Then I turned, walked down the aisle and out of the church, back into the blaring sunlight of a warm and humid day.

8.

Rome, Italy

The luggage carousel at Rome's Leonardo Da Vinci Airport began its slow circle around the cluster of passengers fresh off an Alitalia all-night flight from New York. The bags came out one at a time, watched over by a trio of airport personnel dressed in blue coveralls, one of them biting down on an unlit cigar. An American woman was trying to free a luggage cart from its slot while her husband shouted into a cell phone about a limo driver who was nowhere in sight.

Remi Frantoni stood to the side and watched the buildup to what he expected would eventually be full-blown chaos. He was careful not to lose sight of the attractive redhead in tight jeans and designer jacket, large backpack resting against the side of her left leg.

She was his target.

Remi was twenty-seven, six feet tall, and fit. He wore cream-colored cargo pants, a thin leather jacket, and brown desert boots.

He had two guns, both nine millimeters, nestled in holsters tucked under his jacket. He glanced at his watch.

There were seven minutes left.

Frantoni was the youngest member of Italy's antiterrorism unit, a group first formed in the 1970s when the country endured its own lengthy battle with homegrown terrorists, the Red Brigade among them. In that bloody decade, the terror outfits turned the streets, highways, and airports of Italy into avenues of slaughter.

Frantoni spoke four languages, was adept at weapons and tactics, and had a slew of street connections supplying information to keep him a step ahead of terror activity headed his way. He could break down the command structure of any known terrorist group working his corner of the globe, analyzing their mission and motives, helping narrow the target base.

But what Frantoni was most skilled at was spotting the face in the crowd, the one primed to do the most damage. It could be the elderly woman to his left navigating a carry-on with a handle that wouldn't budge. Or it could be the businessman under the large clock, the one in the wrinkled suit holding a leather satchel, initials embla-zoned in the center. Or it could be the middle-age priest leaning against a pole, hands in his pockets, black shirt one size too large for his slender frame.

But it wasn't any of them.

It was the redhead in the tight jeans.

Her body language was good, a little too good, giving off an air of indifference to the long wait for luggage, making a show that she wasn't in a rush to get anywhere. The backpack also was a tip-off. Not the fact that she had one, since practically anyone under the age of twenty-five getting off a plane had one. It was the way she carried it—or tried to. She made two attempts to get it on her back and each time found it too cumbersome a task to manage, resting it against her leg, always with the pocket side facing in. The backpack was not stuffed to the gills like those carried by others in her age group. Young adults treat them as suitcases and jam in as much as weight regulations allow. Instead, hers was thin and clean, as if it had been purchased the day of the flight. The redhead also gave off the look of privilege: she was clearly someone accustomed to having her bags, light or heavy, carried by other hands. And then, of course, there were the shoes.

A young woman of her background and breeding would have topped off the designer jacket and form-fitting jeans with a pair of fashionably expensive flats, or maybe a new pair of Nikes. She even might have gone with flip-flops, if she were seeking convenience. But it would be unlikely for her to choose a pair of Timberland boots.

The footwear was what first caught Frantoni's eye. It told him Rome was not her final destination. She was on the move to another city, a place where the terrain would be more hospitable to the boots she had chosen. They also would give her more traction in the event she needed to move quickly, to evade authorities or run clear from the heat and debris of an explosion. Frantoni was also aware that Timberland boots are a desired commodity among young terrorists, often given to them as gifts on the day of a crucial mission.

He pulled a BlackBerry from the rear pocket of his jeans, hit a button and waited through two rings. "If she reaches for her luggage," he said, "have them set off the fire alarm. Make sure they make enough noise to scare the hell out of the passengers. The more confusion, the better my chance to grab her before she can do damage. If it looks like I can't get to her in time or if she's holding a secondary device, take her out. Head shot only. If she goes down, she stays down."

Frantoni slipped the phone back into his jeans and walked toward the redhead. She had her back to him, eyes on a brown leather satchel snaking its way down the baggage wheel, inching within reach, her right hand poised to grab it. Frantoni brushed against her and smiled. "This is always the longest part of the trip," he said.

The redhead gave him the slightest of nods, attention focused on the satchel now less than a dozen feet away. He followed her eyes, turned his head, spotted the satchel and then looked back to the young woman. "Is that yours?" he asked.

The woman nodded.

"Allow me," he said, sliding toward the approaching satchel.

"I can manage," she responded in a firm voice.

Frantoni turned toward the woman, inches from her face. He grabbed her right arm with his left hand and held it. "I insist," he said, his voice taking on a harsher tone.

He held onto her, turned his body slightly, pulled the satchel off the carousel and dropped it by his left leg. "I also insist you not make any sudden moves. As fast as you think you can run, I run a lot faster. And I would prefer to walk you out of here than leave you dead on a filthy floor."

"Who the hell are you?" she asked. She was frightened but shielded it with an air of defiance. "What do you want?"

Frantoni moved close enough to kiss her and said in a low voice, "I need to know how you planned to set off the device. I need to know if there's a timer on it and if there's a backup, in the event something happened to you. Give me that in the next thirty seconds and there's a chance we'll walk out of here alive, along with everyone else in the terminal."

"What if I don't know anything about a device?" she said. "What if I don't know what you're talking about?"

"I'll kill you," Frantoni said. "And if I'm right about a secondary set-off and somebody else waiting to hit a switch, I'll die with you. Now, you may want that to happen. In which case consider it a victory for you and a loss for me."

The woman took a deep breath, her hazel eyes on Frantoni, still composed, with a trace of uncertainty crossing her brow. "What if I tell you what you want to hear?"

"We take the device and walk out of here," he said. "We go to my car and drive to my office. A bomb crew will take the device and you and I will sit. Have coffee. Talk."

The woman swung a few strands of hair from her forehead and smiled. "You might have the right device," she said, her confidence back, matched with a swagger he had not yet seen, "but you picked the wrong girl." She rested her head on Frantoni's shoulder and whispered into his ear, "I'm not the one supposed to set it off."

Frantoni released his grip on her arm and pushed her away. He scanned the faces in the baggage area, estimating the starter would need to be within fifty feet of the satchel.

"You have less than a minute," the redhead said, standing behind him, hands and arms folded across her chest. "That's not enough time to find the face you're looking to find."

"Unless I bring the face to me," Frantoni said.

"There's only one way to make that happen," she said, "and that's not in the good guy rule book."

He turned and faced the redhead, nine millimeter held low in his right hand. "I'm not a good guy," he said.

He raised the weapon and fired two bullets into her chest. The force lifted her off her feet, arms and legs spread wide. She landed with a thud against the hard floor, her head and back taking the brunt of the blow, lines of blood flowing out of both corners of her mouth, her eyes staring at a gray ceiling, red hair matted to one side.

She was dead before she hit the ground.

Frantoni wheeled around, surveyed the screaming crowd. Passengers were scurrying for cover, children shielded by the bodies of their mothers, the elderly collapsing to the floor, hands covering the backs of their heads. Frantoni grabbed the satchel in his left hand and ran, heading for the terminal exit, airport security in pursuit, screams and shots coming at him from all sides.

He was holding a satchel packed with heavy explosives in his left hand. Police snipers were stationed in the areas above the terminals, frozen in place, unsure of their next move.

And somewhere in the middle of the madness, a terrorist waited to press a red button and slaughter hundreds.

9.

New York City

I sat behind a desk, a hand-carved chessboard composed of characters from Sir Arthur Conan Doyle's Sherlock Holmes stories spread before me. I moved a pawn made to resemble a London bobby, sat back and gazed up at the still photo that filled the length of a fifty-two-inch flat screen. I was in the den of a four-bedroom apartment I kept in a Manhattan high-rise, staring at a face that belonged to a young man with short cropped hair; dark, penetrating eyes; and well-groomed brown beard. I had read through a thick file folder, now resting next to the board, filled with details both monotonous and monstrous. The young man was twenty-nine, born in Chicago, raised by relatives in Egypt and educated at Washington University in St. Louis and at Yale. He was the older of two sons, his father a respected chemist, his mother a social worker, both now living in a town house north of Michigan Avenue.

His name was Alshair Al-Madel and he was a chemical engineer by profession and one of the world's most feared terrorists by choice. A long list of biographical information ran down the left side of his photograph, but I didn't need to read it. I knew all I needed to know about him, the cause he believed in, the religion he embraced. Al-Madel had a small but loyal following of roughly two hundred men, all as educated as he was and equally as fanatical. He was well-funded, holding private bank accounts in Switzerland, Japan, and Saudi Arabia, three countries where banks are known to ask few questions. He traveled often and seldom slept in the same bed more than three nights in a row. He had a wife and two sons living in the suburbs of Cairo and a teenage mistress who occupied the top floor of a modest hotel on an island in southern Italy. But he spent the bulk of his time with a third woman, an American from Northern California, whose biographical information remained sketchy. All I knew about her at this point was that she had graduated from Northwestern with a degree in economics, worked for two years at a small accounting firm in New York, and met Al-Madel there. She became smitten with his charm, then his cause.

I sat back in the leather chair and looked at the chessboard. The crime bosses were right to question my desire to declare open war on the terrorists and their sponsors. It was difficult enough to go head-to-head with an enemy you knew.

Here, we would be up against thousands of young men who fit Al-Madel's profile, eager to die and take as many innocents with them as possible. They weren't after control of an operation or looking to come out of their gamble with a profit. Their victory rested in death, their spoils were the remains they left behind—in a schoolyard, a church, a crowded airport, crashing a plane through a building, or dropping vials of poison in the middle of a packed train. *How do you take down somebody whose goal is to be taken down?* Carbone, the French crime boss, had asked as we made our way out of the meeting. *If you come up with an answer, maybe we have a chance. If not, we're going to be knee-deep in blood for many years.*

Carbone wasn't wrong.

I had designed a road map I believed would lead to victory. But I felt there was still something missing. I leaned forward and moved my pawn in front of a Victorian-era version of a knight and looked up at Al-Madel's photo. There were too many of them. Too many Al-Madels spread throughout the world, each more eager to die than the next. I needed to figure a way to lessen the impact of such a numerical disadvantage. I would need to be three steps ahead of them at every play—detect their objective, break their plan, reach them before they could do damage.

And the only way for me to do this was to know who was calling the shots. Who was directing the Al-Madels of the world? If I knew for certain who that person was—or who those people were—and was able to anticipate the moves, then we had a chance.

The terrorist landscape was changing. It was no longer solely the realm of Middle Eastern fundamentalists, though they got all the attention. Each country had its own growing contingent, either disenchanted with the direction of their government or fueled by drugs and ready to right perceived wrongs. These free floaters would be the most difficult targets to pinpoint, because their faces could be any face, anywhere—from a neglected teenager in Ohio to an abused housewife in Budapest to a middle-age drifter in Norway. I would need to solve the riddle of a thousand nondescript faces.

I held the queen, debating whether to move her in direct line of a rook and a knight, anticipating the consequences of such an action to the second move, never the first. I knew Vladimir would utilize terrorists who did not fit the profile, promise them great wealth or financial security for their families.

His first move was obvious—keep the Colombian cartels in the loop, make them think they were more than shadows of the Mexican gangs who had grown so large that they now eclipsed their once more powerful adversaries. Together, the Mexicans, Colombians, Russians—and the terrorists they were exploiting—had enough manpower and financial resources to enter the profitable world of organized crime and disrupt the efficient operations that had long been in place.

We are at our best when we work in the shadows, Kodoma had told me.

From there we make millions, and few eyes look our way. If we are lucky, no one notices—and those who do are not upset we exist. To some people we are a threat and a scourge, to others a necessity. These Russians and their terrorist friends are not like us. They do not think of what we do as business. They do not believe in the shadow world. They choose to work under the light of day. To travel down that path is madness. But that is who we will be fighting—madmen. And if we are to fight them, it must be to the death. There can be no other way. If I bring my group in and join in battle with you, I will never accept a peace proposal from our opponents. Never. We fight until there is no one left to fight.

I moved the queen into position. She was surrounded and looked to be facing defeat. The first move would give her clearance. The second move would give her the upper hand. The third would lead to victory.

It was now time to play for real.

The first battle of our war would begin on this very day.

10.

Rome, Italy

Remi Frantoni ran out of the international arrivals terminal and into the sharp sunlight. He was followed by dozens of passengers and airport employees seeking refuge from the turmoil.

Remi crossed the walkway, dodging a bus and two taxis, feverishly looking for the one face he needed to find. He ran toward the parking garage, heading for the off-ramp, still holding the satchel, his police shield clipped to a chain and dangling around his neck, desperate to find a place to unload the bag where its explosion would do the least damage. As he ran, sweat streaming down his cheeks and across his back and chest, he wondered why it hadn't been set off yet, why the person with the device hadn't hit the button. An experienced hand would have detonated it in the airport, the second he saw the woman hit the ground. The device hidden in the satchel also eliminated any concern about a suicide bomber. That led Remi to conclude he was dealing with a trained recruit on his first mission; while it's not much of a task to set off a bomb in a terrorist camp under the eyes of seasoned killers, it is quite another to press the button in a crowded airport and watch hundreds of people be killed and wounded. The first murder is always the most perilous, even for a terrorist.

Remi stopped running, turned and walked back toward the scattering crowds. He was working on instinct now, a risk he was willing to take, one he really had no choice but to take. He could run with the satchel until the bomb squad arrived, but with traffic congestion and clogged roads leading out of the city, that could be ten, fifteen minutes away. And dropping it in a safer area, as far from the airport as he could find, helped only so much. There were roadways, garages, traffic, and hundreds of people walking in all directions.

Regardless of where he left the thing, innocent people would die.

He was close, Remi could sense it, feel it, willing to ride his hunch to the finish line. He inched forward, taking deliberate steps, glancing at the people running past, each one desperate to get as far from the airport as possible. In the distance, he heard the sirens, knew the bomb squad was close, knew his window to nab the terrorist was narrowing.

Remi smiled when he saw the young man standing next to a taxi stand, one hand in the pocket of a soiled blue windbreaker. He was rail thin with long brown hair and a cropped beard that did little to hide his youth. The boy was pasty white and seemed to shiver even under the glare of a warm sun. Remi crossed the walkway, sidestepping a Fiat 124 speeding toward him. The sirens grew louder, increasing the crowd's distress to a feverish level.

Remi stepped in next to the young man, one hand grabbing his free arm and holding it tight. "You can come out of this alive," he said to the boy. "We all can. All you need is to stay calm and hand me the device in your pocket. But do it slowly. Fast moves make me nervous."

"I'm not a fool," the young man said, struggling to regain his composure. "You'll kill me the second I hand it to you. And if you don't, the others who will be here will for certain."

"You *were* a fool," Remi said, catching the young man's British accent, reading him as well-bred and well-educated, another misguided missionary recruited into a battle whose motives he would never live long enough to understand, "when you agreed to step into this mess. Now you have a chance at smart. You can come out of this without blood on your hands. Take a look around. You see all these people? They can die because of what you do. Or they can live because of what you don't."

The young man took a deep breath. "I'm not afraid," he said.

"I know you're not," Remi said.

"I just didn't think it would be like this," the young man said. "I didn't think it would feel the way it does."

"You're not a fanatic," Remi said. He caught sight of a police van screeching to a halt in front of the terminal. "But you're down to seconds. Hand me the device and live, or set it off and die."

"You'll die, too," the young man said. "The other police officers. Hundreds of others."

"That's right," Remi said. "You are the one, the only one, who makes that decision."

The young man eased the device out of his pocket, gripping it in his right hand. He was sweating. Remi saw the control was crudely made, the kind he hated the most because something always went wrong with them. There were wires wrapped around a square box large enough to hold a wristwatch. Brown tape covered the detonator and there was a switch in the center of the box. The young man's thumb rested on the edge of the switch.

Remi took two steps back, placed the satchel next to his left leg and held his gun by his side. "What's your name?" he asked.

"John," the young man said.

"Well, John," Remi said, "seems you and I are in position, as are the snipers above us. But truth is, we're the only players here. Whatever happens will be because of what one of us does."

"What about me?" John asked.

"If you give me the device?"

John nodded.

"You'll be arrested," Remi said. "You'll be asked about the people who sent you here—names, locations, along those lines."

"Will I go to prison?"

"I don't know, John," Remi said. "But I know right now the only person dead in this is a terrorist, and that works in your favor."

Remi stared at the young man for several seconds and then holstered his gun, his hands inches from the device. "I'm going to help you, John," he said. "The ones who sent you? They were wrong about you."

"In what way?"

"You're not a murderer," Remi said. "If you were, you would have set off the bomb the minute I put her down in the terminal. But you didn't. You waited. You came out into the open air and waited, hoping someone like me would let you off the hook."

Remi put his hand on the box and eased it out of John's grip. He held it cupped in both hands and backed away, signaling with his head for the bomb squad members to advance. He waited as a unit rushed toward him from across the walkway, his eyes on John, who seemed relieved his ordeal was nearly over.

"You did well," Remi said to him.

"I know," John said, a smile spreading across his face. "Better than you, I would say."

Remi stared at John, followed the young man's eyes over toward an overweight man in a blue smock standing on the other end of the taxi stand. John looked at Remi and said, "I'm sorry I wasted your time."

Remi knew he had no chance to take down the overweight man, knew that his hunch had set him off course. He had gone for the obvious, the worst mistake a cop could make. He had narrowed his scope, and now it would not only cost him his life, but the lives of many innocent people, those he had been sent there to save.

Remi tossed the box to the ground, pulled his gun and aimed it at the overweight man in the blue smock.

He never got a chance to fire off a round.

The explosion was powerful, shattering glass and bodies as one, bringing an end to hundreds of lives on a sun-drenched day in Rome.

II.

Bridgehampton, New York

I walked with my son Jack along the shoreline of a quiet beach, the two of us lost in thought, ocean waves lapping at our bare feet. He was still reeling from the loss we had suffered together, and he would for years, I knew. Even so, he did his best to hide his pain.

"I'm sorry I haven't been around these last few days," I said. "There were a few things I had to do."

Jack nodded, eyes gazing at the rocks that dotted the shoreline. "Are you going to get them?" he asked, barely above a whisper.

I placed an arm around his shoulder and felt him ease in closer to me. "As many of them as I can," I said.

"Do you know who did it?" he asked.

I shook my head. "I need time to narrow it down."

"I miss them, Dad," he said, his voice walking the rope that separated childhood and puberty. "The other day, I thought I smelled Mom's sauce. I ran into the kitchen—"

"I miss them, too," I said, the words barely there.

I hadn't yet been able to allow my emotions to show, but I was close now to cracking. Exhausted as I was, I could not even think of sleep and played the pictures of what I imagined their final moments to be over and over in my mind, a torturous unending loop. I felt myself spiraling downward at a time when I needed to be at my best. I shunned my security detail, much to my uncle's dismay, spending time alone, planning a war and mourning a loss too unbearable to contemplate.

Yet at the same time, I had to ensure Jack's safety. As much disregard as I had for my own life, I made doubly sure to place my son in as contained and secure an environment as possible. He lived at the compound, which was manned by high-tech security cameras and armed personnel situated throughout the nine-acre property. He spent the bulk of his time with Uncle Carlo, still the most feared mob boss in the country. They ate meals together, played board games, went sailing on the Sound and fishing in the deep ocean, a small armada of bodyguards always nearby.

"Do you think it's your fault?" Jack asked.

I never hid who I was or what I did from my family. I didn't advertise it or go to lengths to explain it, but I didn't need to. They saw the guards stationed outside the house and on the perimeter of the property. They took note of my long absences and knew I was not a businessman out on the road. They didn't need to grasp the full weight of my work to figure it was outside the norm. Their understanding of my way of life was not based on anything I said or any action they witnessed. They just knew.

"Yes," I said. "But I would feel that way no matter who I was or what I did for a living. Just like any husband or father. It's not my job that causes me guilt. It's that I wasn't there to prevent it."

Jack was twelve and tall for his age. He was a good student, a better athlete. He loved sports of all kind except for golf. He was a fanatical baseball fan, absorbed in the most mundane statistical details, able to recite the hitting and pitching numbers of any player in either major league, from star to spot starter. He liked to read, and it pleased me to see him go beyond class requirements and seek out the books I absorbed as a child, finding in them as much pleasure as I once had. He also loved chess, as I did.

"Mom always worried about you," Jack said. "She never said anything, but I could tell."

That casual comment caught me off guard. I stopped and turned to face the ocean, waves still roiling from a storm. I was so focused on survival, on maintaining a criminal empire and pushing it to its furthest point of profit, mindful of the deceit and treachery around me, that I failed to detect the burden of fear I placed on those I most loved. My wife never voiced her concerns to me. I took it for granted that she not only was aware of the world I lived in but understood my position in it and was comfortable with both.

Again, I was wrong.

I turned to face Jack, who was now by my side staring out at the angry waves. "I didn't know," I told him.

"I didn't tell you to make you feel bad," Jack said. "I told you because I thought it was something you needed to know."

We stayed quiet for a few minutes, father and son. I wanted to tell him how badly I felt for both of us. That my biggest fear was I would lose him as well. Jack was the blade the enemy held over my neck, and I feared the worst.

That fear? It was both my sword and my Achilles' heel. My strength and my weakness.

"I think we've had enough ocean for one morning," I said. "You ready to head back?"

"You need to do some work?" he asked.

"No," I said, shaking my head. "I was actually thinking of finding someone foolish enough to challenge me to a game of chess. Can you think of anyone?"

"Depends on the stakes," Jack said.

"Cheeseburger, fries, and a shake to the winner," I said.

"Grilled onions and bacon toppings?" Jack asked.

"And extra pickles," I said.

"Game on, Dad," Jack said.

We turned from the slapping ocean waves and made our way up a sloping hill.

"Game on," I said.

12.

His name was Raza and he was my first target.

Some in the group thought I was taking a too cautious approach. They preferred sending out a small army of shooters to take down any terrorist working on their turf. But while that machine-gun approach would get our blood flowing, it wouldn't win us anything. We needed to focus on one powerful terrorist cell, work bottom up, to not only eliminate it but to learn how it functioned—how they move their money, make use of contacts, recruit suicide bombers, stay hidden from law enforcement. The more I knew about their operations, the more I could bring myself to think as a terrorist leader, the better equipped I would be to wage this war.

Raza was thirty-six and Ivy League educated. Born in Pakistan, raised in Iran, schooled in India and the United States. He spoke three languages, was fully funded by the Russians, and had more than three hundred followers, each willing to give his life at Raza's command. He moved often, though when he stayed in one place for longer than a week it was Rome, where he kept two apartments. He was armed with semiautomatic weapons and drove a bulletproof car.

Raza first surfaced in 1996 when he joined a group of disaffected Middle Eastern men, frustrated by what they believed was a breakdown of their way of life coupled with Western scorn for their religion. It was Raza who, over time, convinced dozens of angry young members that the only actions the West would respect would be violent ones.

He organized his first terror attack later that year, bombing a clothing store in London. That initial bomb was poorly constructed and did minimal damage, but Raza had made his first move and knew that with experience he would grow more proficient.

On the surface there seemed little reason for Raza to turn militant. He had degrees in both physics and art history and would have no trouble finding work if he desired. Young men with his educational background were always in high demand. The job offers included six-figure salaries and high-end perks. Raza also came from a family with money, and I found nothing in his profile to suggest he was a target of Muslim hate groups or had suffered in some similar fashion. While a student, he kept to himself. He seldom went to parties, preferring hours of quiet. He read hungrily, mostly nonfiction books dealing with spiritual healing and worship. He spent hours in museums absorbing the works of the masters, reading detailed biographies of each. Caravaggio was a favorite.

Raza was at once intrigued by Western culture and repulsed by it. He admired the work of Renaissance painters and sculptors, yet despised how art he considered to be precious had been turned into fodder for tourists, scoffing at the notion of the handiwork of the masters reduced to illustrations on bookmarks, notepads, calendars, and coffee mugs. He felt it better to destroy such works than to see them treated as trinkets.

It wasn't long before disdain turned into full-blown hatred. Raza believed he would never be fully accepted by Western countries. His appearance, his religion, his very name would keep him at a respectable distance, perceived at best as an unwanted stranger and at worst a threat to their safety. He had too often caught harsh looks when he ventured into a restaurant or café and was well aware of the concerns voiced by Europeans that young men like him were the reason there was such economic unrest in their countries, unacceptable levels of crime, and no jobs for their grown children.

They were surrounded by so much beauty, so many reasons to cherish their lives, but were too consumed by hate to enjoy the precious gifts that had been left them. So Raza grew to believe he had no other choice. He would give them even more reason to hate and would strip them of the wonders that graced their cities.

Raza moved quickly from that first bombing.

He placed progressively more lethal explosives in London, Madrid, Lyons, Bologna, and Budapest. He made use of everyday objects, from interiors of garbage bins to exteriors of church poor boxes.

And always, without exception, he struck on a weekend.

His death total numbered in the hundreds and he was soon on every antiterrorist watch list.

It was in the spring of 2008, outside a Madrid soccer stadium, that Raza was first approached by members of the Russian mob. The Russians were eager to expand the scope of his exploits and increase the frequency of his destruction. And they were willing to fund the damage, regardless of cost. The success of his operations over the next several years landed his name on Vladimir's watch list.

Initially, I didn't figure Vladimir to make a move in the direction of any terrorist, soliciting a bomber's help to bring about global chaos. He was a major crime boss operating on a level few gangsters get to see and there would be no need for him to bottom-feed and cut a deal with a terrorist.

But if such a move needed to be made, then Raza would be Vladimir's best choice—a man who kills neither for religious motive nor patriotic zeal, but for the sheer pleasure of bringing horror to the lives of others. And in the event Raza's goal was to accumulate wealth through death, to be a global player on an international scale—that would also be acceptable to the Russian crime boss.

Regardless of motive, Raza took advantage of Vladimir's largesse and was soon entrenched as one of the five most feared terrorists in the world.

He'd been marked for death by Israel's agency, the Mossad, and in the scope of the American CIA and British MI-5 for nearly a decade. Yet every attempt to capture or kill him had failed. Each foiled assassination added to the legend Raza had carefully built, while his network of sleeper cellmates became more difficult to infiltrate.

And now Raza was ready to play on center stage.

His series of successful bombings—as well as the difficulty agencies had in detaining or eliminating him—demanded large-scale brazen attacks. It would need to be a multitiered effort that would destroy major structures and leave thousands buried beneath the rubble.

Raza was primed for such a moment.

Vladimir's money and the terrorist's ego would demand it.

And I was counting on neither one to let me down.

I had no intention of having anyone infiltrate Raza's crew.

I had my reasons. Such an operation would take too long to set up, and once it was running the flow of information could never be trusted. Second, I didn't know anyone I thought could pull off this type of undercover plan.

And anyone I don't know, I don't trust.

My goal was to destroy Raza's network, leave it a smoking pile of dust. Everyone in his crew—from top down—would die. The move would announce the start of a war and make my intentions clear. Organized crime was an all-in business, and when we make a play, nobody walks and nobody talks.

So, for Raza I would need Angela.

I would need the Strega.

13.

Uncle Carlo took a sip of iced espresso.

"I gave my blessings on this war," he said, his once-strong voice weakened by age and illness. "But don't take that to mean I'd bet on it. Who knows how many council members will sit still for heavy losses over a long period of time? We're in the profit business, and if this war gets in the way, sooner than later those at the table will walk."

Carlo Marelli was the last of the great old school Dons.

He was a ruthless killer, a threat to anyone who challenged his rule. He ran a criminal organization that brought in $100 million a year in activities both legal and illegal. He was proud of what he had accomplished, building an empire from the ground up, having started out as a runner for the Chairman of the Board himself, Frank Costello, while still in his teens.

He had raised me as if I were his son, taking me into his home after my dad's death. He was a young widower then with two children—a daughter, Carla, and a son, Jimmy. Carla was fifteen when we met and made it clear she wanted as little to do with me as she did with the family business, a position that hasn't changed in the years since. Jimmy, on the other hand, was someone I grew to love. He is my brother and a trusted friend.

He was born with a degenerative muscular disease that confined him to a wheelchair and stripped him of the ability to talk and forced him to breathe through a small tube attached to an air purifier. But he was smart and stubborn and didn't allow his handicaps to speak for him. He read all the books in his father's library, earned degrees in music and art history, and, along with my father and uncle, taught me what he knew about chess—how to play it and how to apply it to my work.

Jimmy urged me to read a series of books and articles that exposed me to the useful skills taught by game theory. Nothing I've learned in life has helped me more. It has made it easier to think as an adversary would think, and has shown me how to outmaneuver my opponent by anticipating his next step.

Game theory also helps keep my father's memory alive.

My father loved to play cards and excelled at the Italian games of scoppa and sette bello. He enjoyed bocci, a game of chance, and chess, a game of skill. When I was very young my father would take me to watch him play with his friends. He would sit me up high—on a corner of a hutch or on a stool just above the players—hand me a prosciutto and mozzarella panini and give me a warm hug. "Watch and learn," he would whisper in my ear. "And try and guess the moves each player makes before he makes them."

Over time I mastered the games from my silent perch.

I learned you could minimize the risks in sette bello, similar to blackjack, by studying the habits of opposing players. In a game where any total above seven and a half means elimination, the more cautious route is often the safest. It is not, however, the clearest path to victory. I took note that players with the most aggressive reputations were the ones who took home the bulk of the winnings. They made it clear to the others they did not fear risk. Once that had been established, their need to take risks was minimized. They actually won the bulk of their hands by adopting a more cautious approach. It was the threat of a bold call that kept their opponents in check.

While I enjoyed watching the card games and took away many lessons from my hours spent in the company of my father and his friends, it was chess that intrigued me. There, across that board, a player had to consider three angles at once in order to enjoy success. He needed to be fearless and make a number of risky moves. He had to be able to gauge his opponent, anticipate not only his next move but, at the very least, his next two. And he had to know when best to play it safe, hold a position and stave off a strike until the moment was secure. It was a game of strategy that required skill and patience to ensure victory.

It was life played out across a checkered board.

Due to my father's work schedule, which kept him away from home for several days at a time, our chess games were played over the span of weeks. I would spend hours staring at the board, our pieces crossing over into the other's territory as I anticipated his next move as well as mine. My father was an excellent player but he was an even better teacher and he helped turn me into an unbeatable opponent.

After his death, Uncle Carlo took his place.

To him, chess was more than a game. It was a road map to how to run a crime organization—know your enemy, gauge his strengths and weaknesses, attack without mercy, and retreat only when absolutely necessary. Both brothers loved the game for entirely different reasons. My father played for pleasure. My uncle played to hone his instincts and keep them sharp, one more tool to help him stay on top of the vicious world he ruled. Over the years, I came to value the game for both reasons.

It wasn't a big leap to make the jump from chess to game theory.

It was Jimmy who first introduced me to the works of Emile Borel, the Godfather of Game Theory. By the time I was in college, I graduated to the lessons taught by Oskar Morgenstern and John von Neumann and spent a great deal of time devouring books and articles in the school library, usually late in the evening, a warm cup of coffee the only company I required. I learned how a significant number of world leaders grew adept at game theory and used its methods to maintain their power bases. In addition to offering all the benefits learned from chess—chiefly, how to read an opponent in order to propel him to eventual defeat—game theory extolled the zero-sum benefits of guile, deceit, and manipulation to help achieve the ultimate goal. Among our Presidents, no one was more practiced in the art than James Madison, who anticipated a friend's betrayal even before the first move had been attempted. The game plans of football coach Vince Lombardi and the mathematical genius of John Nash were nourished by game theory. In my world, Charles "Lucky" Luciano was said to be a proponent of game theory, as was the brilliant Meyer Lansky, the first certified genius ever labeled a gangster.

It made perfect sense for me to adapt the theory to our criminal undertakings. Gangsters like to keep rules simple, and when it comes to that there is nothing better. The most basic rule and also the most effective: deviate from the strategy of your opponent and you'll walk away with a win.

In recent years I've taken advantage of the anonymity of the Internet to stay sharp. I joined an online group where aspects of the methods are discussed and broken down. We seek each other's advice, make comments on another member's maneuvers, and attempt to solve potential challenges. In this company of seventy members, I am not Vincent. I am not the Wolf. I am not a crime boss. I am a faceless player in a group made up of investment bankers, housewives, attorneys, painters, and carpenters. I seek their guidance and they look to me to offer mine. In the safety of such a unique community I can be myself.

Face-to-face, however, there is no better partner than Jimmy. I speak to him every day, and while he can't respond, I can tell by his facial expressions if he agrees or is dismayed by my decisions. He is my anchor and I never finalize a deal or make a judgment without running it past him first. I am aware that if Jimmy, two years older than me, were able to function at full capacity, he would have been chosen to run our criminal organization into the twenty-first century.

"The threat is real," I said, looking back at Uncle Carlo. "Not just for the immediate but for the long haul."

"It's a good war to fight, I give you that," Uncle Carlo said. "Going to miss being part of it."

"You're in this," I said, "as long as I am."

"What did Jimmy think?" Uncle Carlo asked.

"Left a bio of George Patton on my desk with a note," I said, smiling.

"What'd it say?"

"Don't lose," I said.

Uncle Carlo chuckled as he pulled a cigar from his shirt pocket. He reached for a gold-tinted lighter with his initials engraved on the side and lit it, taking in a deep breath, ignoring the pain it caused his lungs. I had long ago given up any attempt to get him to quit his habits. "What do you need me to do?" he asked.

"First, in the event things don't go my way I need you to take care of Jack," I said, "the same way you took care of me."

"No worries there," Uncle Carlo said. "What else?"

"Talk to Jannetti," I said.

"About the Strega?" he asked.

I nodded. "He might balk at first," I said. "But once he gives it thought, he'll figure she's our best option against Raza."

"She's his daughter," Uncle Carlo said. "It might not sit well you asking to risk her life and his syndicate for a terrorist."

"He's never been shy about putting her in the way of a bullet."

"That was *him* sending her on those jobs," Uncle Carlo said. "Now it's you."

"Any more to it than that?" I asked.

Uncle Carlo rested the cigar against an ashtray and looked across the room at me. It was a look I knew, a staunch reminder that the wheezing, shaking old man was still one of the most powerful Dons in the country.

"Cut the shit, Vincent," he said. "When it comes to you and the Strega, there's always more to it."

I nodded and gazed out the bay window that looked down on the plush gardens of my uncle's Hamptons estate. "That was a long time ago," I said.

He laughed. "Jannetti and his crew are old school Camorristas. To them, we might as well still be in the seventeenth century. Their rules, their ways, they never change. You would *think* all these years later, especially in light of what happened, that would rest where it belongs—in the past. But on that, dear nephew, you would be wrong. Potentially dead wrong."

"Jannetti's been grooming her to take his place as head of the Camorra," I said. "He's been out in the open with that from the start. One day soon, Angela will be the only woman with a seat on the council. She comes through big in this fight, that will go a long way to making her acceptable to the others at the table."

"He may want more than that for her," Uncle Carlo said.

I looked at Uncle Carlo. "My seat," I said.

He nodded. "I've known him for too many years," Uncle Carlo said. "Jannetti sets his mind to something, he never lets go of it, like a dog with a bone. Angela's his legacy. Everything he does, every move he makes, is done with her future in mind."

Three years after my father died, Uncle Carlo sent Jimmy and me to Italy for a summer to meet the Dons on the other side of the ocean. It was there I first met Angela. We were the same age, and while I spoke a broken version of Italian and she managed a garbled form of English, we became fast friends and the three of us—me, Angela, and Jimmy—went everywhere together. Her father couldn't help but notice the affection she and I held for one another, but I was too naive to notice what signals I was sending the Don's way.

But Jimmy noticed, and one morning while we were having breakfast in the room we shared, he passed his notebook across the table. On the thin white sheet he had written a list of all the families he could think of—both royal and criminal—who had linked themselves together down the centuries through marriage.

"Why are you showing me this?" I asked.

He motioned for me to turn the page. When I did, I saw he had written down my name and Angela, linking our family with the Jannetti crew. "You're serious?"

From his look I realized it didn't matter if Jimmy was serious or not—what mattered was that Angela's father was likely very serious.

"Me and Angela talked about this, Jim," I said. "There's plenty of time for that. But right now we're just having fun. Nothing more to it than that."

Jimmy stared at me, watching as I finished my breakfast. He never mentioned marriage or Angela again.

We both knew I was in love with her. She was a teenager, as was I, but the woman she would become had already begun to take form. She had long golden brown hair and matching eyes and a smile like a camera flash. She had a quick temper and was not afraid to expose it, but she also was deeply generous to those she loved, and had a dark sense of humor. The attraction was instant—and, if I'm being honest with myself, eternal.

She was more at ease around boys and men than girls her own age. Even then, she was the daughter of a Don and understood the power such a designation held.

During that long, hot summer, the three of us spent our days and most of our nights together. We began our mornings at the beach, meeting friends, sunning ourselves on the rocky coast.

In the afternoons, while most of the town slept and the shops were closed, we ventured into the hills, cooled by the shade of pine trees and damp red dirt, staring at the various villas hidden from the city streets below us. The evenings were always the most fun. We danced in many of the local clubs, Jimmy at our table, watching as the two of us tried to break moves on a crowded floor.

Many of our nights ended with a gelato at a front table in an all-night bar overlooking the bay, music playing somewhere, fishing boats rocking against the tide.

When I got back to the States, Angela and I wrote often, each trying in vain to perfect the other's language. She also corresponded with Jimmy, whose command of Italian was superior to mine. It had been made clear to me by Jimmy and Uncle Carlo that Angela was being groomed to succeed her father. Maybe it was that reason that kept me from turning friendship into something more.

At that time, I still had doubts—which I kept to myself, didn't even share them with Jimmy—that the life of a crime boss was for me. Without feeling sure, I didn't believe I could move forward with anything serious, regardless of how I felt about Angela. And there was one other factor holding me back. Angela was a creature of Naples; she had no interest in making a move to America. And while I loved Italy and would always want to spend as much time there as I could, America was where I would work.

So I decided the best approach was for us to wait. And given our young ages, neither of us was in a rush to get married.

The senior members of the families were another issue.

They were eager for us to get going. Nothing makes old Dons happier than a merger. It would guarantee complete rule on both sides of the ocean for decades, consolidate power, and accumulate larger shares of the profits being generated.

It was Jimmy who pointed out one issue I had ignored.

If I married Angela and unified the families, only one of us would eventually be Don—there was no such thing as shared power. Many of the international syndicates would never put a woman in such a position. But the Camorra had no such qualms, making for a potentially uncomfortable situation.

It's not easy being a teenager in love, even in the best of circumstances. It is even more difficult when you put the pressures of organized crime into the mix.

"Why do you think she never married?" I asked Uncle Carlo, turning away from the window and walking toward him. "She's a beautiful woman and I couldn't have been the only one to take notice. She's got Gypsy eyes, and my father used to say a Gypsy could steal your heart, soul, and wallet all in the same day."

"She's powerful and deadly," Uncle Carlo said. "Most men shit their pants when they come across somebody like that. They can't handle the heat that comes with having her by their side. Toss in the drop-dead looks and for many guys a dream woman like Angela becomes a nightmare."

"Did you expect me to marry her?" I asked. "Would it have made it easier if we combined the families?"

Uncle Carlo took a deep breath. "You married who you were meant to be with," he said. "What it means for me doesn't matter. Not now, not then. I've never been one for arranged marriages. More often than not, they're more trouble than they're worth—easy as hell to get into, tough as shit to get out of. You and me have both been lucky and unlucky with the women we married. Lucky we found somebody we were crazy about and unlucky in that we lost both before their time."

I stared at my uncle. "I need her to go against Raza," I said. "There are other ways in, but she's the best option. She can get the information we need about his operation and then help me burn it to the ground."

"Let me talk to Jannetti," Uncle Carlo said. "He might be open to the notion of the two of you working together more than he might have been back a year or two."

"What makes you say that?"

Uncle Carlo shrugged. "You're single now. He might figure to play that card again. See if it comes up aces. Meantime, you get your ass on a plane and go see the Strega."

"It's a business deal," I said. "Nothing more."

Uncle Carlo shrugged. "Either way, she'll be good for you. Help get your mind straight and keep you on your game. And you can leave with no worries about Jack. Between me and Jimmy, we got him covered at every base."

I leaned over and kissed my uncle on the cheek and started to walk out of the room. "You know how she got that name?" I asked, turning back to face him, hand on the doorknob.

"She made sure everyone heard," Uncle Carlo said. "Invited half a dozen rival crime bosses over for a sit-down. She had a feast prepared, from baked clams to pasta with artichokes to steak pizzaiola.

And they ate it up like they were just let out of the state pen, every one of them."

"And they all died, right there at that table," I said, shaking my head, still amazed by the story. "Rat poison. Angela sitting at the head, sipping red wine, watching them drop one at a time. Overnight, with one meal, she helped her father take over the streets of Naples."

Uncle Carlo smiled. "Do yourself a favor when you're over there, would you?" he asked.

"What?"

"Eat alone," Uncle Carlo said. "You'll live longer."

14.

Paris, France

Raza and Vladimir sat with their backs to a setting sun, each holding a bottle of mineral water. They ignored the noise of the early evening traffic, the blared horns, the shouts from frustrated drivers.

"This should be the only time you and I meet," the Russian said. "It's how I conduct business."

"You've never done business with me," Raza said, his voice cool. "I like to know who my partners are before I complete a mission."

Vladimir gazed at Raza. He was impressed by the young man's confidence and manner but put off by his disrespect. Someone like Raza lacked the skill needed to reach the heights of the Russian syndicate. He might be a rising young power in terrorist circles, but in the bare-knuckle world of international organized crime he would be a low-end operator at best, a hired hand and nothing more.

Vladimir had gone over Raza's background with care, paying close attention to how he planned and executed his attacks. The young man was meticulous and trusted as few as possible. He had no entourage or circle of advisors. Raza worked with a small and efficient team, was brutal beyond measure, could be counted on to pull off daring attacks, and never showed remorse.

"I am not your partner," Vladimir said. "I have deposited $25 million in clean money into your accounts. And there will be an additional $25 million deposited three weeks from today. Since the money is coming from me to you, I believe it safe to consider you my employee."

"Is an employee entitled to ask questions?" Raza asked.

Vladimir shrugged. "I need these operations to go off without glitches. It was one of many reasons I chose you. I want each mission to make a statement, and you don't do that by putting bombs in a man's shoe or his underwear."

"Yet you seek no credit for the attacks," Raza said. "These will be high-end operations with hundreds if not thousands of casualties. That puts a bull's-eye on my back, one not even $50 million can erase. Now, I don't take issue with the bull's-eye. I wouldn't be doing what I do if I were concerned with such matters."

"What then?"

"The attention. These jobs will bring with them increased police presence and surveillance," Raza said. "That will make subsequent jobs more difficult."

"Are you up to this or not?" Vladimir said, growing impatient with the conversation. "Anyone can be a headline terrorist. It takes nothing more than dynamite and a ticking clock. I'm giving you an opportunity to be immortal. Isn't that what you want?"

Raza stood and glared out at the traffic. "And what is it *you* want?" he asked.

Vladimir stood and tossed his water bottle into a receptacle. "You have work to do and money to do it," he said. "Focus on that. But know this—if you fail me in any way, then that death you are so eager to embrace will be upon you in a most unpleasant way."

Vladimir walked off toward the center of the city.

Raza watched the Russian disappear into the crowd. He sat down, closed his eyes, and tilted his head toward a darkening sky.

15.

Northeast Yemen

The compound was well-lit and guarded, armed men and women walking the upper and lower perimeters, dressed in fatigues designed to blend with the bland landscape. All wore scarves or bandanas and had been in hard skirmishes since they were old enough to raise a weapon. There were forty guards in all, trained to fight to the death.

The compound—four small houses and one two-story structure—was the headquarters of Anwar Al-Sabir, the number two in Raza's terrorist organization and its main operator. He considered a bomb in a town square a waste of an explosive, preferring missions that called for catastrophic destruction.

Al-Sabir was also the man the group turned to when the goal involved a takeover of a passenger airline or cruise ship. It was said he wept with joy when he heard the news of the 9/11 attacks.

I needed to speak to Al-Sabir and find out what he knew of the flight that killed my wife and daughters. I needed to know if his prints were on the plan.

In order to do that, I had to get him out of the compound alive. Which would require killing the majority of his guards, capturing him, and getting him through hostile terrain. It was a job that required very little chatter; the fewer who knew, the better its chance to succeed.

That meant the plan had to be kept hidden from any of the organizations that signed on in the war against the Russians and the terrorists. I couldn't even bring it to the members of my own crew. My people were good, but they didn't have the skills such a mission would require. Besides, this job had to be done under mob radar, since I had gone to such lengths to tell all involved that the war was not a vendetta but a business move.

I was about to wage a war on two fronts and for two reasons.

If you know your history, you know such plans often end in defeat. From the Romans to Civil War generals to the Nazis, battles fought on dual fronts have low rates of success. But none of those undertakings had been waged for personal reasons. In none of those wars was there a single leader who went into battle because he had lost a family member. They went in because they were told to go in, or to further a cause, or some other vague purpose. At no time was any of it personal.

It is my strength and my weakness.

Which is why I called in my own group of assassins—four men and two women who had been part of my private team for nearly a decade. I recruited each myself, choosing them from the elite ranks of the military and intelligence arenas. I went looking for those who had seen heavy combat, hand-to-hand, street-level. I also went for those with a combination of academic excellence and street-smarts. I didn't want anyone eager to do the work only for the impressive salary and benefits I offered. I prize loyalty above all else and wanted these six to be beyond reproach in that regard. I needed them to be color-blind when it came to politics or patriotism. The work I had in mind would call into account neither. They had spent years training to do as they were told, and I was relying on that discipline. I also needed them to be a group of stone-cold killers bound by honor who would never betray me, no matter how seductive the offer.

It was no easy task and took three years to accomplish.

I logged thousands of air miles and talked to hundreds of contacts—from deep-cover intelligence operatives to mercenaries to some of the best assassins in the international organized crime universe. And before I contacted the six chosen for the job, I had extensive background checks done and psychological profiles drawn up. I left nothing to chance. I took the selection of my Silent Six as serious as any endeavor I had undertaken in my years as a crime boss.

They are the best at what they do and they do it only for me.

They operate in complete secrecy; no one is aware they exist. They are my invisible army, sent to make the impossible possible.

That is why, on this night, they were situated inside the walls of a compound in northern Yemen, ready to take out forty combatants and bring me a man I needed for a hard conversation.

The team was equipped with microscopic night-vision cameras strapped to their backpacks and the sleeves of their jackets. They also had high-def audio equipment wrapped around their gun belts. This allowed me to see and hear what they did from a penthouse apartment thousands of miles away. It was like watching a video game of my own creation, played before my eyes.

"We can make our move any time from here in."

It was the voice of team leader David Lee Burke. He was huddled in a corner of the outer perimeter of the compound, his muscular body coiled and braced.

"You have confirmation our guy is in the house?" I asked.

"Yes," Burke responded. *"Both from high-level intel and our own street informants. If he left here, he did it on a cloud. No one has seen him come out since he went in three days ago."*

"When he does come out, I need him to be breathing," I said. "Anything less and it's a burnt mission."

"Can't guarantee he won't take a bullet," Burke told me. *"We'll do our best not to hit him, but sometimes, well . . ."*

"A guy turns the wrong way," I said.

"Something along those lines," he said.

I liked David Lee Burke and always appreciated his candor and lack of airs. He was a decorated Green Beret, expert in hand-to-hand combat, and as close to a ninja warrior as anyone this side of the Yakuza. He was also a husband who had lost a wife to cancer, and a father who had buried a teenage daughter. A man who sought his comfort in the day-to-day skirmishes of war.

In my line of work we have associates we like and associates we pretend to like. We have more than our share of enemies and have forged alliances with factions from every part of the world. What we don't have are many friends outside the life, and that is one mob rule that will never change. But there were a few I knew I could count on, and David was in that small circle.

"It's time," I said to this man waiting at the other end of the world to kill as many people as he needed in order to bring back one man alive.

One I knew would bring me closer to the identity of the person who murdered my wife and daughters.

16.

East Hampton, New York

I sat in the brick-lined backyard of my uncle's main house on a bench beneath a weeping willow. Jimmy was at my side, his electronic wheelchair equipped with more devices than I would find in an airline cockpit. I caught the look of concern on his face as the morning sun warmed his already tan features. "You understand why this needs to be done," I said to him.

Jimmy nodded.

"Then you also understand how dangerous it will be," I said. "But we don't have a choice. Maybe we can put it off for a year or two, but what would be the point? We grow older and weaker and the other side bolder and stronger. The time is now. Win or lose."

There was no one I trusted more than Jimmy. I loved him as much as I did my own son. Jimmy, locked inside a silent world since birth, spoke to me in a way I could understand. As I said, if health had permitted, he would have been chosen to take the reins of the business. He had all the mental tools, and mettle.

Jimmy was by my side through the funeral mass for my wife and daughters, then sealed himself away and refused to see anyone for a week. My daughters loved spending time with him, and he doted on them and was the only member of the family my wife allowed to spoil them. He was the first one I went to with my plan, and I knew he would be there to guide me through the difficult days that would follow. In many ways, I thought of Jimmy as my secret weapon—the one person I could count on to stand beside me no matter how dark the tide.

"Is it the Strega?" I asked.

Jimmy nodded.

"You never trusted her," I said, catching the tilt of his head and the rise of his eyebrows. "But she's always come through for us when we needed her help. And we need her help now, Jimmy. This Raza is working out of her turf, and if we're going to wipe his plate clean, we need her."

Jimmy leaned his head back against the thick black leather of his chair and looked up at a clear blue sky. I had been in his company for a long time and could pick up on every gesture he made.

"Nobody rides with us for free," I said. "She'll want something in return. That doesn't make her different than any of the other crews. Nobody is in this because he thinks it's the right thing to do. They're in it because of the damage the terrorists and Russians will do to their bottom line. No different than us."

Jimmy lifted his head and gave me a hard stare.

"Right," I said. "Maybe it is different for me. It may take a while to find the truth, but I'll find it. I'll do whatever I have to."

Jimmy pushed his wheelchair closer to me, rested a hand on top of mine and squeezed it hard enough to hurt.

"You'll be with me, Jimmy," I said, "every step. Like always. I can't win without your help. That's why I want you on board with the Strega. When we move against Raza's crew, we need to be all-in."

Jimmy made two clenched fists and rested one on top of the other.

"We won't let the Russian out of our sight," I said, "just like he won't let us out of his. Vladimir has everything the terrorists need—money, the network, the weapons. He'll lay all that gold in front of Raza and demand loyalty."

Jimmy spread his fingers and placed them together as if he were in the middle of a prayer.

"That's right," I told him, standing and walking to the back of his wheelchair, my hands on the thick grips. "They'll play nice for a while, so long as Raza's crew comes through with some major hits. But it won't last. We'll see to that."

I turned Jimmy's chair around and wheeled him toward the main house. "We have to pick our spots with Raza," I told him. "When his missions start to go south, we need him thinking Vladimir might be the one botching up the works. That's where the Strega will help. Having an enemy she hates more than she hates us will make her willing to join our fight."

Jimmy shrugged and gave me a smile warm as the day.

"Fine, she doesn't *hate* me," I said, returning the smile. "She's angry at me. I spurned her—or at least she thinks I did, and with that temper of hers, that's all you need. But she despises Vladimir. And that's the card I'm betting on."

Jimmy looked away and up toward the house, his thick dark hair against the headrest. I could tell he still had doubts about getting involved with the Strega but I had his blessing.

I had doubts, too, but it was time to leave them behind.

17.

Rome, Italy

Raza and a rail-thin young man with a nervous laugh stood across the street from the entrance to Termini railway station, ignoring a heavy rain.

"You think he will go through with it?" the young man, Avrim, asked. "He was so anxious the other night I wondered if he was having second thoughts."

"He would be a fool not to have second thoughts," Raza said. "And it wasn't the notion of death that made him anxious, it was concern about whether we would send the money we promised his family in Pakistan."

"Why should he be concerned about that?" Avrim asked.

"Because sometimes I don't send the money to the families," Raza said.

This came as a surprise to Avrim and he didn't bother to hide that fact. "That is part of the holy bargain," he stammered. "It is why many of these men agree to surrender their lives."

"Are they choosing to die for our cause or to ensure their families will have plenty to eat and a place to live?" Raza asked. "A martyr, a true martyr, doesn't care about personal gain, either for himself or those he leaves behind. We have fed into this nonsense that giving up one's life for money is something to be admired, something noble. It is why so many of our missions end in failure. We send out the desperate, the mad, and the destitute to do our work. We should be sending out the determined and the inspired. They are the ones who will lead us to victory."

"You can be inspired and still have a family in need of money," Avrim said, reeling from the conversation. "Poverty doesn't make anyone less of a martyr. In fact, it is a driving force."

"If that is indeed the case," Raza said, "we have chosen the perfect martyr for this mission. He arrived at camp as penniless as an infant, not even a pair of sandals to protect his feet. We put in months training him, educating him in preparation for this moment. It will be the one time in his bleak existence where he might attain a degree of notoriety. I am the one who is giving him that opportunity. Now I ask you, what price would you place on such a precious gift?"

"I cannot place a price on the life of a martyr," Avrim answered. "That is for the martyr and his family to decide."

Raza nodded and checked the time on his BlackBerry. "Less than three minutes," he said, "before our lamb leads the innocents to slaughter."

"I left the car across from the park," Avrim said. "A nearby road will lead straight into the Via Veneto. From there we can be on the outskirts of the city long before the police arrive."

"You go if you wish," Raza said, eyes focused on the train station, Track 15 in particular. "Wait for me in the car. I'll be there soon after the explosion hits."

"You can hear it from the car," Avrim assured him. "The smoke alone will be strong enough to follow us for miles."

"I don't want to hear or smell it," Raza said. "I want to see it. See the blast go off, then wait for the screams and the panic. It will be in that moment that our enemy will understand what it means to live and suffer as our families have lived and suffered. That is what I need to see and why I will linger among them. I wish to feel the weight of their pain."

"You run the risk of being recognized," Avrim warned.

"I certainly hope so," Raza said, flashing a smile and walking several steps deeper into the main terminal.

18.

Naples, Italy

I stood on a large wraparound balcony staring at the serene waters of the Bay of Naples. Angela stepped in beside me to take in the view. She rested a glass of red wine on the marble countertop. "I've been looking at that bay since I was a child," she said, "and still I find comfort in its beauty."

"Not many places are meant to last forever," I said. "This might be one of them. I've always felt at home here. That's why I come back."

"Most people are afraid of Naples," Angela said. "But you never were."

I turned to her. "It was easy," I said. "I had a good friend teach me all about it."

Angela was a beautiful woman. She had long brown hair streaked blond by the summer sun. Her body was tan, sleek, and toned. She swam for an hour every day, either in the waters of the bay or in the heated pool of her villa. She had olive-shaped eyes and a smile that radiated feelings of warmth and comfort. She was educated and had a thirst for travel and adventure. She was the kind of woman some men spend their lives hoping to find. A woman beyond the imaginations of lesser men.

But to me, there was a part of her that would always be that pretty teenage girl who loved taking quiet walks on the beach, laughed at Terence Hill and Bud Spencer movies, and could prepare a feast of a meal out of a handful of tomatoes, red onions, and clumps of fresh basil. She was a terrible dancer but that didn't stop her from dragging me onto the floor of a local club to move to the beat of her favorite Italian bands. She taught me how to drive a motorcycle, putting me at the controls of her Ducati 999 and slapping the back of my helmet each time I grinded a gearshift. We went to our first opera together and we both fell asleep early in the first act and stayed that way until the standing ovation roused us. I stood next to her, gripping her hand in mine, as we both stared down at her grandmother as she took her final breaths. It was the first time I saw her cry—and the last.

I cared for Angela and maybe even loved her. And while she had earned my respect and that special place in my heart, I had always been hesitant to take our relationship to the next level. And, truth be told, I wasn't sure if she would have wanted me to move in that direction.

There was another part of Angela I had also grown to know well, and it was one that would give any man a reason to hold in check the affection he might feel.

Apart from her father, Angela was the most vicious gangster in Italy and one of the most powerful in Europe.

Vittorio Jannetti still held the reins of the Camorra, the Neapolitan branch of organized crime, but to those who did business with the outfit on a daily basis, it was common knowledge that his daughter was in the mix. Her voice was not only heard at council meetings, it was heeded.

Angela was in charge of recruitment and had a hand in investing the billions of dollars the Camorra earned each year through the sale of drugs, stolen high-end fashion, and the transportation and dispensation of toxic goods. Under her iron-fisted domain the Camorra controlled the European black market, an enterprise that netted the outfit a clean $200 million a month. Not too shabby a haul for a group first organized in the thirteenth century to protest the abuses of the working poor.

The Camorra recruit their personnel from children as young as six.

They exploit Naples to full advantage, thriving off the entrenched poverty of the poorest city in Europe, one with an unemployment rate over forty percent. They take boys from the homes of families who owe them money that can never be repaid. Many times, desperate parents seeing little hope for themselves and less for their sons bring them to the door of a Camorra captain and beg him to take in their child.

Over many decades, these children helped shape the foundation of Camorra power.

They are sent to the best schools, each chosen for the particular skill of the child. Down the years, this method has allowed the Camorra to raise a network of contacts unmatched by any crew in the international arena. They have insiders placed in any profession of note, able to supply them with whatever information is needed. To my way of thinking, this is the most powerful weapon a crime organization can possess.

Angela had degrees in world history and economics. She could speak with comfort and knowledge on a wide range of topics and was able to do so in any of four languages.

She also had a dark and sinister side that mirrored mine.

She was ruthless against any enemy, perceived or real. She would order hits on a whim, had a volatile temper, and was a proponent of the Camorra's preferred method of ridding themselves of opponents—strangulation.

I glanced at her now. She looked radiant, late afternoon sun highlighting her unlined face and a body that would quench any man's desires. I was also aware that beneath that beauty beat the heart of the most lethal woman I have ever known.

"How long has it been?" she asked. "Two years? Three?"

"Four," I said, aware that we both knew the year of my last visit to Naples, and the reasons behind it. "I came in for a meeting with government officials to secure cable operations. You were a big help."

"In Italy, a pretty face and a bag full of money will take you a long way," Angela said.

"What I need now . . . it's much more complicated," I said.

"This terrorist," Angela said, "was he involved in the incident with your wife and daughters?"

The question caught me off guard, which I'm sure was her intent. "Too soon to tell," I said. "But they live and work in a community, like us. If it wasn't him, he's in a position to know who it was."

"And is this why you want him taken out?"

"A piece of it," I said. "The major reason is to send a signal—to the terror groups and to the Russians."

"Why his group in particular?" Angela asked. "There are dozens of crews as big as his if not bigger working every city in Europe. We have our eye on four of them in Naples alone. Why does this Raza stand above them?"

"He's you and me fifteen years ago," I told her. "Ruthless. Willing to do what it takes. He's the one other terrorist crews look to, to see how far he will take the battle, how much damage he is prepared to do. If we wipe him clean, end him and his crew, it will tell the others we're all-in and are going to stay all-in."

"Vladimir lined his pockets," Angela said, "and gave him marching orders. We both know the Russian well. He doesn't let others spend his money foolishly. He'll watch every penny. If I agree to go head-to-head against Raza, then that will put the Camorra in the front of the line against Vladimir."

"Is that a problem?"

"I have 2,500 active in my crew," Angela said. "And I'm spread thin with that. Raza's numbers are hard to pin down but he can always find a fool willing to strap on a bomb. The Mexicans have more guns in one overseas shipment than you can find in all Naples. And Vladimir has ten times the active members we have and doesn't care how many die fighting for him. So, yes, I think we can refer to Vladimir as a problem."

"You're not alone on this," I said. "Every one of my guys, best I have, will be made available to you. I'll fund the entire operation and toss in an additional five million as a bonus. And let's not forget that you'll be fighting on home turf and no one knows this city like you do. That alone is worth a few million Vladimir dollars."

"I'll need more than money and manpower," Angela said, her voice still warm, but stiffening.

"Name it," I said.

"It's foolish to track a terrorist on foot," she said. "They do their planning by cell phone and rotate seven to ten different numbers. The best method to track Raza is with a digital GPS computerized system to monitor those cell numbers, tell me where they are, who they're talking to and about what. I'll need a system that can pinpoint time, location, and date and give me visual confirmation. I would like that system set up in a secure location and run by the best computer people you can find. If you can do that for me, you have a partner."

"I'll get you a system that can handle a dozen cell phones at the same time," I said. "And it will allow you to laser in on locations of as many as four people at once. It can be set up any place you choose in less than a week."

"How many techs to run it?" she asked. "It goes without saying, the fewer in on this, the more comfortable I feel."

"I'll leave that to the Greek," I said. "My guess would be no more than three rotating around the clock. Maybe a fourth on stand-by in case something happens. Big Mike will handpick the techs."

"I'll need your files and data on Raza," Angela said. "Everything, no matter how trivial—hobbies, favorite movie, what ice cream he likes."

"He's lactose intolerant," I said, giving her a smile, "so I wouldn't sweat the ice cream. But he likes licorice, black not red. With that tidbit alone you should be able to pin him down."

Angela gazed out at the city, a place she not only lived in but held sway over. She sipped her drink and stayed silent for a few moments. "What do you want, Vincent?" she asked. "I don't mean getting rid of Raza. That helps us all, and I'm with you on that. But when it's all over. What happens to you then?"

"I haven't thought it through that far," I said. "I suppose I'll take my son somewhere and try to piece together a normal life. I've never done it before and I'm no expert at what passes for normal, but I owe it to the kid to give it a shot."

"You're not a man who fails, Vincent," Angela said, her voice coated with affection.

"My wife and daughters are dead because of me," I said, words painful and measured. "I'd call that a failure."

"And you think if you were on that plane they would have survived?" Angela asked. "Or did you fail by letting them board that plane in the first place?"

"Any way you spin it, their death is on me. Now I have a son to protect. I won't fail him."

"This from a crime boss who has little use for bodyguards," Angela said. "Just because we run our business like a corporation, Vincent, doesn't make us CEOs. We're gangsters. That makes us targets. That goes for our families as well."

"I didn't see many guns guarding your front gates," I said.

"This is my father's city," Angela said with pride. "No one would dare lift a finger against either of us without expecting wrath to come down. Fear is my bodyguard. But I live under different rules than you do back home."

"What else do you need?" I asked.

"Just one thing more," she said. Angela put down her glass and walked toward the interior of the palazzo.

"What?"

"Buy me dinner," she said, glancing at me over her left shoulder, "a very expensive dinner. I know just the place."

"I bet you do," I said.

19.

The pieces of my plan were falling into place.

I would work in alliance with Angela, a brutal blending of the Camorra with my New York outfit, the Silent Six tossed into the sauce. The other crews were each given specific assignments—the Yakuza would put dents in the financial pipeline of the terror networks, focusing primarily on Raza's organization; the Triads were to steer terror outfits clear of our core businesses and ensure they made no inroads in the Asian marketplace; the Marseilles mob would supply me with street intel gathered from the dozens of Muslim gangs working in their city; the Mafia would wreak havoc with the gun and drug shipments sent out of Mexico to be sold in European territories; the Israelis' assassin team would target key Russian gangsters, selecting the elimination of high-end bosses, all of whom had close connections to terror groups.

My focus would be on Vladimir and Raza.

Like I've said, it's not that different from a chess match.

The first steps appear unimportant, movements of convenience or opportunity. It is not until later, deep in the heat of battle, that the vanquished realize how cruel and purposeful those first moves had been. That's what I expected the elimination of Raza and his crew to be—a winning first play in a long and difficult fight.

Taking Raza down would show the other crews that Vladimir could be made to taste defeat. I know many of the organizations, despite the tough talk and bluster, feared the Russians. My allies were envious of the piles of money they accumulated, the manpower at their disposal, and the difficulties that existed in infiltrating their ranks or brokering an arrangement with them. The Russians made their working model clear from day one. They are quick to break their word and have nothing but contempt for other members of the organized crime world.

They are convinced it is their destiny to rule, with all factions reporting to them. And they see no better way to ensure such a take-over than to partner with terrorists. It was a bold move, forging an alliance with ideological murderers. In the short run, neither group—the Russians or the terror outfits—entered into the partnership seeking profit. Terrorists, from their end, are determined to set straight the world in their own demonic fashion, slaughtering as many innocents as they can. The Russians thrive on chaos and confusion and are willing to bankroll the terrorists. In the process, the structures that have been in place and which have held firm for decades would be sure to collapse.

Then Vladimir intended to step in and fill the void.

"It boils down to organized crime against disorganized crime," Frank Tonelli once told me. "For my money, give me organized crime any day. At least with those guys I know the playbook, the rules. These other guys . . . they're in it for the kill, pure and simple. That scares the hell out of a guy like me, and I don't scare easy."

Tonelli was a retired detective, considered one of New York's best. Back when he was a young cop, he often butted heads with my uncle. Over time, despite being on opposite sides of the table, they developed a mutual respect. In their winter years that respect evolved into friendship. They were similar in many ways, and it would not be an odd occurrence for me to turn to either for advice, often on the same subject.

I had a strong feeling Tonelli would hate my plan but see the logic behind it. He knew law enforcement could not defeat the terrorists on their own, despite the legal and manpower advantages. He understood that sometimes you needed to live beyond the reach of the law in order to bring down those who walked its edges. He had been a cop for too long not to frown on such a notion, but he was also a realist and understood the brutal capabilities of the enemy I was circling. And he knew that enemy needed to be stopped.

I considered him a useful resource, someone I could turn to in a pinch and who would provide me with a name, a background, the address of a safe house or a police connection in a foreign city. I never pushed to get information that would cause him to break the law. All he required in return was to remain in the shadows, keep the business end of our relationship private, and never be put in a compromising position. There were dozens of men and women like Tonelli to whom I could turn in time of need. It was one of the early lessons my uncle embedded: if I were to survive as a crime boss, I would need lifelines that extended beyond the borders of the mob.

The more trusted confidants I had, the longer my reign would last. Now, to my way of thinking, there is a major difference between a trusted confidant and a friend. A confidant expects something in return for information; a friend expects nothing.

The ability to tell the difference between the two can keep a man in my line of work alive for a long time.

Trusting no one and suspecting everyone may not be the way to lead a balanced life, but that applies only to the civilian world, not the criminal. A great crime boss must live his life on the seam. There is little room for mistakes, no hedging a move based on a hunch.

I normally prefer to go into my battles alone, but with this fight, going it alone would have been a plan destined for failure. And while we're on the subject, I may not like to have bodyguards, but that doesn't mean they're not there. You just can't see them. Not just true of me. It's true of any top-tier mob boss. You want to *see* bodyguards, find yourself a movie star or a model. They pay good money for a show of force. The best bodyguards are the ones you never see, an invisible army that doesn't materialize until they're needed. I may walk alone. But you can bet your life—and it will be *your* life—on this one fact: I am never alone.

I find comfort that the rules I apply to my plans date back centuries and were once used, with various modifications, by the crime bosses who preceded me—from the Mafia's legendary founder, Giuliano, to Joe "the Boss" Masseria, to Frank Costello, to Lucky Luciano. These mob bosses took calculated risks, eyes to the future. These were the men I emulated and studied, adapting their lessons to a world that was changing, shrinking, a world that would become something not even they could imagine.

There is one more element essential to achieving victory against an opponent as imposing as the one I now confronted—the utilization of enemies.

An enemy is as crucial as any friend or ally. His motives vary depending on who sits on the other side of the table. In the case of the Russians, the Mexicans, and the terrorists, my chosen enemies were members of the Colombian drug cartels.

They were once kings of the cocaine trade and among the most feared gangsters in the world. Now they were standing outside the candy store, faces pressed against the glass, looking in with envy and anger. Their power was reduced by increased law enforcement scrutiny, rebellion in their ranks, and bold maneuvers by their rivals. The Mexicans had been making a concerted effort to go after the Colombian end of the action since the early 1990s and the Colombians did little to prevent the takeover. They had grown weary, tired of the chase, drug lords too rich or too drugged up to put up much of a battle. They had failed to plan for the future and made an error fatal to any gangster—in truth, fatal to any businessman who seeks to stay on top: they assumed they would always be the leaders. But there is always someone else waiting to move in, take over, and toss the current boss aside.

That's where the Colombians now sit, stripped of power and assets, biding their time, rebuilding their resources, eager to move against the Mexicans and regain their premier standing in the multi-billion-dollar drug trade.

I can help them achieve those goals, which would make me an important component in their success or failure. By doing so, I would be turning a potentially lethal enemy into a criminal element fighting on my side.

All they need to do is accept the proposition I make them.

A long war with the Mexican gangs would cut deep into the drug pipeline that is a major source of income for all the criminal factions involved, including my crew. The syndicates would be willing to sustain a loss of income for a certain period. But as the drug flow slowed and demand increased, their patience would wear thin and their allegiance to the battle would weaken. If I got the Colombians to step in, they would fill the drug vacuum and ensure the bottom line would hold. In return, I would supply them with cash and legal cover in their head-butt against the Mexicans. Two enemies would then have no choice but to wage war against a mutual foe, forming an uneasy partnership that would benefit both.

It is the way of the world.

20.

New York City

Michael Paleokrassas, head of the Greek cartel, was one of the most important members of the international crime syndicate. He was a tall man, in his early thirties, muscular and always tanned, regardless of the time of year. He had a relaxed and easy manner and never showed signs of a temper. But he was first-rate with a gun, better with a knife, and just plain deadly with his hands. He was a man of his word and respected by all factions of the underworld.

Michael was also a digital genius.

I made my first deal with him fifteen years ago and have since grown to trust him more than anyone outside my inner circle. He was one of Jimmy's long-distance computer buddies, and when he was in town would come by the house and together the two would spend hours playing chess or video games.

It was the Greek who developed the sophisticated software for us to use in our business—from running background checks to eyes on the ground to tracking devices. He was our syndicate's Bill Gates, only heavily armed and ready to kill to preserve his business interests.

I ordered two Camparis and a plate of biscotti. We were in an outdoor café in downtown Manhattan, street traffic crawling its way through the morning rush.

Mike rested his large hands on the small table. "How you holding up?" he asked.

"Every day's the same," I said. "Mostly bad."

"Time will help with that," the Greek said. "A little."

"I need more than time," I said. "I need a lot of people to die."

The Greek nodded. "I'm with you."

I slid a folded piece of white paper across the table. "Let's start by cloning those cell numbers," I said. "I'd like to have visual as well as audio on each. Link them to one another. I need to know who talks to who, where, and when."

The Greek picked up the piece of paper and slipped it into the left pocket of his blue jacket. "How far back?"

"Three months before the attack on the plane," I said. "You can give me the before in one batch. Moving forward, I'd like to see daily reports. Can you make that happen?"

"Money's not an issue," the Greek said. "Neither is capability."

"What is?"

"The terrorists change cell phones on a daily basis," he said. "If they're working on something big or think they're being monitored, that can go as high as three times a day. The Russians not so much, only because they hardly speak on cell phones. They have other people in other locations do the talking for them."

I sat back and waited as a young waitress placed the two drinks in front of us and the plate of biscotti in the center of the table. "Can you overcome that?"

"Not easy," the Greek said. "But every system has a crack. Just need to find it."

"You work this alone or you need a team?"

"A team would be a help," the Greek said. "But given the circumstances, I'll work with John Loo on this if that's right by you. He's as good as I am and has a horse in the same race."

"Kodoma's nephew," I said. "Being groomed for the top spot. The more we involve the Yakuza in this, the better our chances."

"I've had my eye on him for a while," the Greek said. "John's the real deal. Smart, ruthless, and loyal. Reminds me of you in some ways. Solid guy to have on our side."

"I don't want anyone else to know about this," I said. "We need to run silent and deadly."

The Greek sat back and smiled. "They can clone our phones as easy as I can clone theirs," he said. "These days secrets don't last long."

"I'll cover you on that end," I said.

The Greek picked up on my intended meaning. "We can't kill everyone, Vincent," he said.

I pushed back my chair, stood and dropped two twenties on the table. I looked at the Greek. "We can try," I said.

"We might want to start with the two on the far corner trying real hard to make us think they're not looking our way," he said.

"There are two more on the other end of the street," I said. "Been on me since I left the apartment."

"So they had two tailing you," Big Mike said, "but those first two were here waiting for us. Which means they knew where you were meeting me."

"Let's take a walk," I said.

We stepped onto the sidewalk, late morning pedestrian traffic light, and headed farther downtown. Big Mike stood to my left, taking the outside position, the first to be targeted if the ones on our tail made a move. "I didn't tell anyone I was meeting you," he said. "And no one asked where I was going."

"No one on my end, either," I said. "Jimmy's the only one who knows you're even in town."

"But here we are," Big Mike said, "four on our tail, two in place before we even got here. I don't think they showed up working off a guess."

"Let's walk to a friendly street."

"Lead the way," he said.

We headed west, away from the chic boutiques and high-end coffee shops that had sprouted up in recent years, turning right and left until the streets got narrower, with even fewer people, the sidewalks hemmed in by thick cobblestones. The four men were still following us, forced by space to be even more conspicuous, tossing aside any doubt that Big Mike and I were the intended targets.

We were in the middle of a street filled with tenements and old-world storefronts selling fresh fruit and pastries. It was a street that had fought against the crush of the modern world, resisting the lure of the developer's money. I knew everyone on this block and everyone knew me. I stepped off the sidewalk, walked to the center of the street and turned and faced the four men. Two were to my far left, the other two on my far right, all standing a short distance away from the corner. Big Mike stood next to me and slid his hands into his pockets. "Looks like they got us right where they want us," he said.

"Looks like," I said.

We stood for a moment that must have felt like an hour to the four men who held their positions, confident but confused. A car appeared behind them and blocked off entry to the street, four burly men swinging open doors and stepping out. Within seconds three more men emerged from tenements and storefronts, closing in on the four on our tail, freezing them in their place. I walked with Big Mike by my side down the center of the street toward them, slowly, our eyes on each one, Russian muscle sent on a mission that was now doomed to fail.

We passed the four men, saw the look of the inevitable on their faces, and turned at the corner, walking uptown now, the sun warming our backs.

21.

The lead wolf in a pack never attacks without learning the habits of his prey.

He forms a thirty-mile radius when tracking an adversary, following him from dawn to dusk. He learns an opponent's eating habits and sleep patterns. He gauges how long the other can go without food, whether he can sleep under open sky or needs shelter, whether it is best to attack when he is alone or part of a group. It can take as long as three hundred miles for this information to be gathered, but the wolf is a patient creature, confident that once he is primed for the kill he will succeed.

A wolf can attack at any time, though he prefers darkness or morning fog. He moves with silent steps and controls his breathing as he draws closer to the target. While tracking his prey, the wolf can go for days without food, water, or shelter, his whole being focused on the hunt. If the wolf suspects a trap, he steps back and lets the oldest wolves take the most visible positions. He lurks in the shadows, watching for movement, senses on alert.

Once the wolf attacks, he does so with a ferocity that is frightening to witness.

He does not move in to wound or slow his target. He is there for only one purpose—to kill. He destroys his victims without hesitation, his body awash in blood and bone, oblivious to screams and cries for aid. The attack is over in a matter of minutes, and the pack rushes in to gnaw on the remains of the carcass as the lead wolf steps back, his breath coming in shallow spurts, taking in his surroundings and savoring the conquest. He watches as the younger cubs walk in a circle around the kill site, wiping away the markings of the older wolves, leaving behind as little evidence as possible. Yet at the same time making it clear to anyone who came upon the blood-soaked scene that this was the handiwork of a wolf.

The lead wolf stands away from the pack, watchful for a counter-attack, mindful of his surroundings. He is already plotting when and where to strike again, a restless leader who never tires of the chase.

I have been fascinated with wolves since I was a boy.

I can remember reading the books and stories of Jack London, and while the wolves were almost always adversaries in those tales, he wrote about them with respect and affection. He admired their courage and their ability to withstand the harsh blows of the elements and still survive. I read books about them and would see photos of them in *National Geographic* magazine, always impressed with their strength and stamina. Sometimes I dreamed of their steel-blue eyes.

They were eyes that sent a clear warning to any enemy looking to do them harm. I came to view them as creatures from another time, animals following their own code of conduct, killing out of need or when threatened. They trusted no one but those in their pack and even then were on guard against the possibility of betrayal.

In the world in which I was raised, the ways of the wolf kept me alive.

I had put in place the pieces needed to track my prey.

I had the Greek and John Loo locking in on their communications.

I had the Yakuza on their money trail.

I had the Strega following their movements and learning their habits.

I had the Silent Six primed to destroy their field operations.

It was time to attack an opponent who dared to step into my lair and destroy what was most dear to me. I was ready to hear them plead for their lives and beg for a forgiveness that would never come.

Ready to leave them ruined, shredding them to the bone.

Ready to taste the kill.

II.

"If you are going through hell, keep going."

—WINSTON CHURCHILL

Naples, Italy

SUMMER, 2013

"I was left an envelope with twenty euros and a note telling me where the bag was and when I was to pick it up." The man was in his early thirties but looked older because of a thick beard and ill-fitting clothes. He was French by birth but had spent the last five years living and working as a sales clerk in a low-end clothing store in Naples. He was single and had been dating a woman from Forcella for two years. He had no criminal record, rented a two-room apartment above the shop where he worked, and had no credit cards or driver's license.

"Where is the bag now?" I asked.

"I left it where I was told to leave it," the man said, "in the lobby of the Excelsior Hotel, mixed in with the luggage of arriving guests."

"That's as much as you know?"

"That is *all* I know," the man said. "I swear it."

"You their regular courier?" I asked.

"This was the third time," the man said. "Instructions are always the same, the money, too. Only locations change."

"You part of the cell?" I asked. "Or in debt to them?"

The man shook his head. "My father," he said in a low voice. He spoke English, colored with traces of a French accent. "Back home. He's ill and hasn't been able to work for the last six months. He borrowed money to help pay for food and rent. He thought they were friends. They weren't."

"They never are," I said.

"Are you going to kill me?" the man asked.

"How many more runs you need to make before your father's debt is cleared?" I asked.

"Three," the man said. "Then my father and I will be free of them. That's what they told us."

"That won't happen," I told the man. "You'll be left with two options. You keep working for them, doing whatever they ask. Or they kill you and your father."

"I must believe them," the man said. "What else am I to do?"

"I need a name," I said. "The contact that first approached you with the offer. And I'm going to need it now. If I get that, maybe I can help you out of this situation. I don't, the answer to your earlier question is yes. I will kill you."

"I need to protect my father," the man said. He was wet with sweat and had trouble catching his breath. I knew the look on his face: he was staring into the void of total despair.

"Your father will be killed, whether you help me or not," I said. "He's of no use to them. There's nothing I can do about that. You, I can still help, but only if you tell me what I need to know. Right now, that's the only decision you have to make."

The man looked around at his surroundings. Oak barrels filled with wine dominated the four sides of the large room. There was a small wooden table in one corner, large espresso pot and two porcelain cups at rest in the center. He was tired and frightened and unsure of how his ordeal would end. I leaned against one of the oak barrels. He looked at me with eyes that welled with tears. "Your men killed everyone at the compound," he said. "Everyone but me. Why? What makes you think I can be of use to you?"

"I told them to bring out one," I said. "They brought you. So think on this hard but don't take too long. The next words I hear from you will decide whether or not I chose the wrong guy. Now, who is it that contacts you?"

The man lowered his head. "He is someone from back home," he said. "We were both at university together."

"His name?" I said.

"Kazmir," he said, trembling as he spoke. "He heard I was in financial difficulty and told me he could be of help."

"Who does he work for?"

The young man shook his head, droplets of sweat dripping down to the cracked wooden floor. "I never asked and he never told me. I figured the less I knew about the people involved the better."

"Kazmir works for Raza," I told him. When I moved a few feet closer, he looked up with pleading eyes. "Kazmir was recruited shortly after he finished his studies. As were others at your university."

"I was never political," the young man said. "It's not a path I cared to follow."

"Yet here you are," I said, "willingly or not, walking down that path."

"I had no choice," the young man said.

"You do now," I said.

"What is it you want me to do?"

"The other times you were used as a courier, was it always a bag you were given?"

He nodded.

"How soon after the drop did the bombs go off?"

"I left them during morning rush, with the confusion of people checking in while others were trying to check out," he said. "Both explosions went off in the early evening."

"How much damage?"

"There were many bodies in both locations," the man said.

"And no police link back to Raza?"

"He wasn't looking for credit," he said. "He seemed to be trying out different types of explosives."

I smiled at the man. "You see," I said. "You do know much more than you think. You knew there were bombs in the bags you left behind. You knew when they were set to go off and where best to leave them where they would go undetected for hours. And you knew there would be people, innocent people, who would die because of the bags you left behind. That makes you much more than a courier. That makes you an accomplice to murder."

The man stayed silent. I'm sure he knew that any words spoken from here on would fall on deaf ears. I reached into my jacket pocket, pulled out a small black-and-white photo and showed it to the man. "Is this your father?"

He nodded, confusion doubling down on his fear. "Who gave that to you?"

"You're going to go back to the Excelsior," I said, "and you're going to find that bag you left and take it out of there."

"And bring it where?"

"Back to Kazmir," I said. "Back to the man who gave it to you. Bring it to where he is waiting for news of the blast and have it go off there."

"But then I will die as well," the man said.

"Throw it in, walk it in," I said. "That's your call. So long as that bomb goes off close enough to Kazmir to kill."

"And then?"

"Then you and I are finished," I said.

I watched the man stand on unsteady legs and walk toward the door leading out to the street. He turned to look at me one final time. "Who are you?" he asked.

When I said nothing, the man opened the door and walked out into the heat of a summer day in Naples.

David Lee Burke stood next to me. He had spent his time in the cool shadows of the room, silent and unnoticed. "I have two on him to make sure he does as he's been told."

"He'll do it," I said. "Taking orders is all someone like him understands."

"If he survives the explosion?"

I looked at David. "He won't," I said. "Make sure of it."

23.

Rome, Italy

"We need to work on a much larger scale," Raza said. "No longer be content with dozens, sometimes hundreds of bodies. We must think in the thousands. We have always had the cause. Thanks to the Russian, we now have the money."

"We also have many more eyes on us," Avrim noted. "And they are not hindered by law. They make up their own laws. So far, they have proved to be very disruptive."

"That's because we have allowed them to be," Raza said.

"What do you propose?"

"It is time to destroy places the enemy holds sacred," Raza said.

They were inside the Borghese Gallery, standing in front of Caravaggio's *Boy with a Basket of Fruit,* Raza admiring its detail and colors. "The fruit looks real enough to taste," he said with admiration. "And the boy's features resemble skin more than paint. But it is the darkness that shrouds the work that always catches my eye. He was a master of darkness."

"Have you selected a target?"

Raza nodded, glancing at the work from a different angle.

"I've been told the American has partnered with the crime organization in Naples," Avrim said. "They seem to be led by a woman."

"The Italians are such romantics," Raza said, a small smile creasing his handsome features. "Only they would allow a woman to lead them into battle."

"She has a lethal reputation," Avrim said.

"She is strong in her city, on her streets. Outside of that, she is a housewife."

"We shouldn't underestimate her."

"I underestimate no one," Raza said, staring now for the first time at Avrim, his anger apparent. "But she is a gangster put in a position of power because of birth, not accomplishment."

"Unlike the American, she has lost no family in the struggle," Avrim said in a calm voice, eager to settle Raza's flash temper.

"Not yet," Raza said.

"I must tell you," Avrim said, "I have concerns about our situation. Some of the men in the cell have voiced similar worries."

They were walking now, stopping every so often to gaze at a painting. "Tell me your concerns," Raza said.

"We expect to be a target of the police and the governments against whom we have chosen to wage our battle," Avrim said, keeping his manner calm. "But these others present a more difficult challenge. They are criminals. No government would go to the lengths they will. They are without rules."

"As are we," Raza said. "They die seeking profits. We die seeking paradise. A subtle difference."

"They have killed some of our men on sight," Avrim said. "They raided one of our compounds and killed all but one—and him they took prisoner."

"Do you fear them?"

"Yes," Avrim said. "Especially the Wolf."

"Why the Wolf in particular?"

"Unlike the others, he has two reasons to want us dead. For business and for revenge."

"Why is it you think he has targeted our cell?" Raza asked. "I'm sure I'm not the only one who has made a deal with the Russian."

"He may believe we had something to do with the loss of his women," Avrim said. "Or he might think we can lead the way to the ones who did."

"I don't care what he believes," Raza said. "The criminal organizations were going to go after groups like ours sooner or later. When it comes to their business interests, they trust no one to do their dirty work. They are no different than us running their operations."

"Do you trust this Russian?" Avrim asked.

"I have known you for years, Avrim," Raza said, "and I barely trust you. I have no reason or desire to trust our financial benefactor. He is nothing more to me than a bank. Once that need diminishes, we rid ourselves of him as well."

"I trust you, Raza," Avrim said, walking with the terror leader toward a first-floor bookshop. "I would give my life for you."

Raza stopped and smiled. "And one day I will ask you to do so. But for today, we shall enjoy a delicious lunch. After which, we will spend the rest of the afternoon in church."

"Church?"

Raza picked up a copy of *Caravaggio's Roma* and strolled toward the cashier's counter. "Don't worry," he said. "*We* won't be praying."

24.

New York City

"Took a while, but we were able to break into their cell phone system and clone three of their active numbers," Big Mike said. "Keep in mind that's three out of a possible rotating dozen, with four new ones added every week to ten days."

"Can you get visuals along with the pickups?" I asked.

"On some," Big Mike said, "not all. These guys are slick. They use three different numbers at three different locations to relay one message. They talk in their own code that's hard to break down. Gets even harder, if not impossible, when they start to talk in their own lingo."

I sat back and stared out at the churning waters of the river. We were sitting on a bench in Hudson Park in Chelsea, the skyline stretched out behind us, the sun warming our faces. "How many?"

"In the cell?" Big Mike asked. "Or on the calls?"

"Both."

"From near as me and John can tell, he's got about a hundred regulars stretched out across Europe, mostly in Italy and England, don't ask me why. Out of that number, maybe five to no more than seven are in on the phone rotation."

"The rest get the messages relayed verbally or through intercepts?" I asked.

"Pretty much," Big Mike said. "Boil it down, it comes off as a simple operation. The higher-ups, starting with Raza, come up with the plan. They relay it to the second tier and from there it rolls downhill. The least important guy in the chain is the poor bastard who straps on the bomb and is sent to do the job."

"Have you picked up Vladimir on any of the calls?"

"Not a word," Big Mike said, shaking his head. "Either he wants to keep his distance and is giving them free rein to do what they want or he is keeping track of operations in a way we haven't figured out yet."

"What have you got so far?"

"Raza's smart," Big Mike said. "He works without a pattern other than each job is bigger than the last."

"It's all a big game to them," I said. "This cause they claim to have, this mission they're on, it's all bullshit. It's about the chase and killing as many people as they can as quickly as they can."

"There's no end game and we shouldn't waste our time looking for one," Big Mike said. "Vladimir's angle is easy to figure. We were in his position, we might well be doing the same thing. He's exploiting a weakness in order to make his foothold stronger. He's making a gangster move. What these other guys are doing is not as easy to figure."

"You have a read on their next target?" I asked.

"Not yet," Big Mike said. "But we're getting closer. It's going to be big, though. That much I can tell you."

"It's going to be a cultural site," I said. "Hitting the World Trade Center, that was a shot at our financial core. The next big one is going to go for the heart. And that means Europe. Italy, most likely."

"Is that why you went in deep on this with the Strega?"

"That's a big part of it," I said. "This first battle is crucial. We take down Raza, wipe out his crew and clean out his cash flow, then our allies will step up. I need a win out of the gate, Mike. You and the Strega give me my best chance at that."

Big Mike was one of the toughest men I knew, and balanced that with being one of the most thoughtful. He was part of the new wave of organized crime bosses who grasped that the twenty-first century would be a turning point for our way of doing business. He always seemed troubled that the other groups were not as quick to grasp the obvious. "You think we can be as ruthless as they are?" he asked. "These guys have no boundaries. They'll use a kid as a decoy or a target. You can be five or fifty-five, makes no difference to them. You're in their way, they take you down. For my money, if they have any edge at all, there it is."

"I know," I said. "There are things they do we would never consider."

"But not the Russians," Big Mike said. "They found themselves a perfect partner with that crew."

"We just have to be smarter and sharper, and a whole lot luckier," I said. "There are things we're going to have to do we're not going to be happy with. But no war comes without a heavy price."

Big Mike stayed silent for a few moments, taking in the view. "You've paid a big enough price already," he said.

"I've doubled the security on Jack," I told him. "He's my primary concern. Did it in ways he wouldn't notice. He's been through enough without having to walk around with guys with guns shadowing his every move."

"I'm not worried about Jack," Big Mike said. "He's a good kid and he'll come out the other end of this in one piece. We'll all see to that. My concern is you."

"There's no need to worry," I said. "I'll be fine."

"You're eager to get into a fight," Big Mike said. "And you've tossed caution aside. Now, you always went your own way when it came to safety issues. But this time there's a different feel to it."

"I want them dead, Mike," I said. "And if putting myself in harm's way helps me achieve that, then that's what I'll do. It's a risk I have to take. For me, there is no other choice."

"And *I* need you alive," he said. "And so does Jack. The Wolf can take all the risks he wants. Jack's father can't."

Big Mike reached into his jacket and pulled out a small black cell phone. He handed it to me. "You need to contact me, this is what you should use. Call or text, doesn't matter. They don't have anyone who can clone it. I'll get one to the Strega and to Jimmy as well."

"How come they can't clone it?"

"Because *I* can't," Big Mike said. "And neither can John. That gives it the Good Housekeeping seal of approval."

I took the phone and slid it into my shirt pocket. "You flying back tonight?" I asked.

"Got a plane waiting at Teterboro," he said. "Should be back home by early morning. Unless you want me to stick around for the meeting with the Colombians."

I shook my head. "They're a suspicious bunch," I said. "They might flake if I show up with someone they weren't expecting."

"Think they'll play along?"

"Think so," I said. "The Mexicans have taken a big piece of their pie and they are desperate to get back in. I can help open the door. In return, they keep the Mexicans busy while we focus on the terrorists and the Russians."

"They strong enough to take on the Mexicans?"

"Not long-term," I said. "But they'll buy us enough time to slow the gun supply going out and disrupt the drug flow coming in. Makes it one less thing we have on our plates."

"Watch your back in there," Big Mike said. "I don't like that crew."

"No one likes them," I said. "But if they can help us, then we'll make good use of them."

"And once we don't need their help anymore?"

I turned to Big Mike and rested a hand on his right shoulder.

"Then we kill as many of them as we can and take over as much of their business as we need to take."

He nodded. "Can't wait for that day," he said. "Be nice to get back to taking care of business. It's a lot nicer and cleaner."

"And a lot more profitable," I said.

25.

Florence, Italy

Vladimir and Raza walked down a quiet street, the harsh currents of the Arno roiling just below them. Neither was pleased to be in the company of the other.

"We cannot afford to be seen together," Vladimir said. "I was under the impression I made that clear."

Raza glanced down at the river, walking closest to the edge of the redbrick wall, street traffic drowned out by the rushing waters below.

"I need to ask you a question."

"Then ask," Vladimir said.

"How much bad blood is there between you and the American gangster?"

"What makes you think there is any?"

"He's been on me since I partnered with you," Raza said. "My men see strange faces wherever they go. Money transfers have been delayed or rerouted. Three of my cash couriers have been robbed at gunpoint. I thought our partnership would make my life easier. Instead, it's painted a bull's-eye on my entire organization."

"There was no need for anyone to pay attention to you before," Vladimir said. "Your prior targets were enough to bring you to my attention, but none of them placed you under a scope. With a higher profile comes higher risk."

"Is he hunting me to get to you?" Raza asked. "Or does he suspect me to have been involved in the attack on his family?"

"Does it matter?" Vladimir said. "He's on the chase and he won't stop until he's stopped."

"The woman, too?"

Vladimir nodded. "Individually, each would pose a threat. I imagine they will be much more of a danger as a team."

"Many will die before my task is completed," Raza said. "These two will be lined up next to the other bodies."

"How many targets have you lined up?" Vladimir asked.

"As of now, two," Raza said. "Perhaps three."

"You're being coy," Vladimir said. "I despise that."

Raza shrugged. "I supply the bombers and choose the targets. You supply the finance. That was our arrangement. Our *only* arrangement."

"Remember the objective," Vladimir said. "The body count is secondary to me. What I need is chaos, and the fear that follows."

"This will give you that in abundance," Raza said, his words coated with arrogance. "We will both get out of this mission what we sought going in."

"We'll know soon if your actions are equal to your words," Vladimir said.

Raza stopped, turned and glared at Vladimir for several seconds, struggling to maintain his composure. "I can show you one of the potential targets," he finally said. "If you want."

Vladimir shrugged. "I would much prefer to enjoy a long lunch. Alone."

Raza watched Vladimir turn back toward the Ponte Vecchio, disappearing into a crowd of tourists clogging the path to the jewelry center of the city. He shook his head and smiled, realizing that the Russian had no intention of letting him live past the completion of his mission. He was merely a gateway to a goal, and a piece of evidence that needed to be discarded before anyone would look to see if there was a connection between the two.

Raza remained unfazed. He had entered into an agreement with the Russian to fund his attacks, bring them to a level no terrorist could contemplate.

He also knew there was no room in his world for gangsters. They were adversaries, nothing more. These were men and women hardened by the battles they had waged to reach the top of their professions but softened by the demands of family and allies. They lacked the dedication to bring terror to the people, the ability to be free of emotional bonds. They had no cause to fight for and their only concern was the profits they could earn for themselves and their organizations. That desire would take them far in battle, but not far enough.

The taste of victory would belong to him.

It was his destiny.

26.

New York City

"You've been quiet," I said to Jack, holding his hand as we crossed West 57th Street, making our way to the theater district for an afternoon matinee. "Feeling okay?"

"I'm good," he said, "just thinking."

I smiled. "About what?"

"Maybe I shouldn't tell you," he said.

"Now that you put it that way," I said, concerned about what was on his mind, "you have no choice but to tell me."

"You keep secrets," Jack said. "Why can't I keep some, too?"

"Tell you what," I said. "Fill me in on one of your secrets and I'll do the same with one of mine."

Jack crinkled his brow and narrowed his eyes. He was a handsome boy and had many of his mother's mannerisms, which were both painful and wonderful to see. "How about you go first?" he said, not bothering to stifle a giggle.

"Dads always go last," I said. "Especially when it comes to secrets."

"Says who?"

"It's in the dad book of rules," I said, "which you only get to read when you become a dad."

"I think you just made that rule up," Jack said.

"Maybe, maybe not," I said. "But until you can prove otherwise, you go first."

"I'm worried, Dad," he said.

His serious tone caught me short. The boy was only a few months removed from losing his mother and sisters in the most horrific way he could imagine. I had sent him to see a therapist I trusted, which helped as much as that sort of thing ever helps. Jimmy took him under his wing and in a few short weeks had Jack playing chess at an advanced level. They almost never missed a Yankees home game and Jimmy made sure Jack and his friends not only had a good time but were heavily guarded as well. He also made sure none of the boys—and especially Jack—noticed the extra security. I had entrusted David Lee Burke with the security hires and he brought in top-level pros as adept at not being seen as they were at protecting their charge.

But I knew I'd been away too long. I was deep in the weeds of the job, but at the expense of time with my son, my only remaining child.

"What about?" I asked.

"You," he said in a voice barely audible above the heavy midtown traffic.

We turned left on 52nd Street and stopped in front of a hot dog cart, a middle-age man working the wagon, ignoring the steam coming up from the tins and warm coal fire near his waist. "You still like your pretzels hot and with plenty of mustard?" I asked Jack.

"Yep," he said, "same as you."

"Give us two," I told the man, "the darker, the better. And two cold bottles of water."

Within seconds the man handed us each a hot pretzel covered with yellow mustard followed by two sweaty bottles of Poland Spring. He palmed a fistful of thin napkins and passed them to me. I dropped a twenty on the slot next to the mustard and nodded my thanks. "Keep the rest," I said to him.

Jack and I stood against the wall of a large office building, eating our pretzels, drinking our water, and watching the faces of the crowd rushing past us. "They always taste better off the cart," I said. "Better than at a ballpark or at the Garden."

Jack nodded as he wiped a line of mustard from his lower lip. "Mom liked them, too," he said. "Remember?"

"I remember," I said.

I swallowed a long cold gulp of water. "I don't want you to worry, Jack," I said.

"Mom worried," he said.

"I know," I said. "And I told her what I'm going to tell you. I may not have been the best husband or father. I may not have always been there when you guys needed me to be. And I'm sorry for that."

"Mom was always cool about it," Jack said. "It bothered Paula and Sandy a lot more, I think. They missed having you around. Me, too."

I closed my eyes for a moment, the pain of the truth spoken as sharp and as sudden as the blade of a knife.

"I did my best, Jack," I said, holding my composure, not wanting to expose the boy to my grief and guilt. "You need to believe that."

"I know, Dad," Jack said.

"But where I never come up short, where I never drop the ball, is with my work," I said. "I am very good at what I do and there's no need for you to worry about me when it comes to that. I can take care of myself and I will take care of you. I went against my gut with Mom and the girls and let them talk me into something I felt wasn't right. That will never happen again. Nothing is going to happen to you. You have my word on that."

"But something can happen to you," Jack said.

I nodded. "It's the world I live in, Jack," I said. "But it's a world I know well, and I've survived in it for a long time. It's going to take a lot to keep me from coming back and being with you."

Jack stared at me. The pretzel and the water were long since finished and his small body was shielded by the shade of the imposing building. We ignored the passersby and bumper-to-bumper traffic. None of that mattered now. It was just the two of us.

"You have my word, Jack," I repeated. "You will be safe."

Jack held the look for a few seconds and then put his small arms around my waist and hugged me. I bent forward, lifted him into my arms and held him close, as tight as I could. "I love you, little man," I whispered into his ear.

"I love you, too," he whispered back.

"We good?" I asked.

Jack nodded.

I put him down, his right hand buried inside mine, and we started walking toward the theater to see a matinee of Jack's favorite Broadway musical, *The Book of Mormon*.

"You know who does need to worry?" I said to him.

"Who?"

"Your Yankees," I said. "No bench, weak outfield, no A-Rod, old rotation, even older bullpen. Maybe you should think about rooting for another team."

"I never worry about the Yankees, Dad," Jack said, shrugging aside the teasing. "They're gonna be fine."

"Okay," I said, "then you're worry-free."

27.

Naples, Italy

The restaurant at the heart of Forcella was half filled with late evening diners. The four young men at a corner table relished the fine food, drinking more than their share of high-end red. They grew louder as the wine continued to flow, on occasion even drowning out the middle-age woman in a form-fitting dress singing Neapolitan ballads from a small stage next to the bar a few feet from the narrow entrance.

Two men sat at the bar, quietly nursing glasses of Fernet Branca with ice and a lemon twist. The taller and younger of the two, Luigi Manzo, was in his early thirties and a member of the Camorra since his late teens. In that time, he had worked as a runner, a driver for Don Vittorio Jannetti, and as a loan collector, up to his current position as one of the Strega's most trusted triggermen. In his free time Manzo collected vintage Fiats and portraits of the streets of the toughest and poorest city in Europe. He was trim, hard-wired, and slow to anger but quick to act.

The man next to him was older and calmer but equally as dangerous. His name was Bartolo Vinopianno, but he was known to all the locals as Brunello, due to the fact that he owned a piece of a vineyard in the North that produced his favorite wine.

Manzo gazed up at the large clock above the bar and noted the time. "Lock the front door," he told Brunello. "We don't want any late night arrivals. Have the waiters let the ones at the tables know it's closing time. And do it without attracting attention."

"All of the tables?" Brunello asked, catching the eye of the head-waiter.

"All but one," Manzo said.

"And what are we going to do with that one?" Brunello asked.

"Offer them an after-dinner drink," Manzo said. "And leave the bottle."

"I was wondering when she was going to make her move," Brunello said. "At least they got to finish their meal."

"That's when she's at her best," Manzo said. "After dinner."

Within fifteen minutes the restaurant had emptied. The departures were evenly spaced out and seemed nothing more than a normal end to an evening meal at a favorite local restaurant. The four men at the corner table, immersed in their drinking and storytelling, barely took note of the patrons leaving. They were probably younger than they appeared to be, aged somewhat by the full beards on three of them and a scruffy growth on the one with the loudest laugh and high-pitched voice. The clothes didn't help either—knockoff designer jeans topped by wrinkled J.Crew long-sleeve T-shirts and ankle-high boots with worn-down heels. They barely acknowledged the waiter as he placed four frosted glasses in front of them and a bottle of Limoncello in the center of the table. "With our compliments," the waiter said.

"Clear out the staff," Manzo said to Brunello. "She'll want to be alone with them."

"You're not worried they'll pull a gun on her if they feel cornered?"

"These are not the guys who strap on guns," Manzo said. "These are the ones who strap on bombs and blow themselves up. That's all they know. But tonight they are bomb-free."

Brunello made eye contact with the headwaiter and gestured for him to leave, along with the kitchen staff. The waiter nodded and walked through wooden double doors into the near-quiet kitchen.

"Make a pot of fresh coffee," Manzo said. "Bring out a large cup and leave it on the table to their left. Then, take a seat on the other side and keep your eyes on all four."

"You'll be here?"

"I'll be where she needs me to be," Manzo said.

Brunello started to walk toward the back, stopped and turned to face Manzo. "I always forget," he said. "How does she like her coffee?"

Manzo smiled. "Dark and bitter," he said, "just like you."

ANGELA JANNETTI STOOD next to the table and smiled at the four men still talking and drinking. The bottle of Limoncello was now empty, and the weight of the drink along with the bottles of wine that preceded it were taking their toll. Their voices were hoarse, their words slurred.

"I hope you enjoyed your dinner," Angela said to them.

They looked up at her and smiled. "Are you here to dance for us?" one of them asked.

"Not the way you like," Angela said.

"Maybe you can do more for us than dance," the oldest said, wiping his mouth with the back of his right hand. "Something we would all enjoy."

"If there's any fun to be had here tonight," Angela said, "I assure you it will be on my part."

"Who are you?" the one with the scruffy growth asked.

"You're sitting in my restaurant," Angela said, tossing a quick glance toward Brunello. "In my neighborhood, in a city I control."

The four men chuckled. "Is that supposed to scare us?" one asked.

"It would," Angela said, "if you were bright enough."

"I'm afraid to disappoint you," the oldest said, his voice coated with anger. "But where we come from, we fear no one, especially a woman."

"That's a mistake," Angela said.

The thin blade slid down Angela's right arm and her fingers wrapped themselves around the black handle, gripping it tight. She kept her arm down low and stepped closer to the table, standing now between two of the men, a smile still on her face. "Are any of you armed?" she asked.

"We would be as stupid as you think we are if we answered that," one said.

She moved with professional speed. Lifting the head of the man closest to her, she swiped the blade across the length of his throat in one rapid movement. She let the man go and watched as he fell flat against the table, the white cloth and the wood floor now coated with his blood.

She moved behind the dying man and kept her eyes across the table at the other three frozen in place. She didn't blink as the bullet from Brunello's weapon tore a hole through the eye of the young man with the scruffy growth, killing him instantly.

Manzo stood behind the two remaining men, Brunello keeping his place at a nearby table. Angela stepped around the two dead men, her eyes on the ones across from her, walking with a confident stride. "As you can see, there are some similarities between my group and yours," she said. "We have no trouble shedding blood to find answers to our questions."

"You didn't ask any questions," one of the two managed to say. "You just talked about our dinner."

"I'm asking now," Angela said. "You are members of Raza's cell. There is much street talk about an attack here in Naples and somewhere else in Italy in the coming days. I would like to know where and when those attacks are to take place."

"You will kill us whether we tell you or not," the more brazen of the two said. "So why should we tell you anything?"

"Because there are many ways for someone to die," Angela said. "Quickly, as you have just witnessed with your two partners. And then there is the other way. Your choice to make."

"We are not high-ranking members of the cell," the other man said. He was young and frightened. "There is only so much information we have access to, and none of it might be any help to you."

"I'll decide that," Angela said, "as soon as you tell me what it is you do know."

The younger man glanced over at his friend and waited until he looked his way. "We have no choice," he told him. "Tell her."

"I will tell this Italian bitch nothing," the man snarled. "And neither will you, coward."

Angela looked up at Manzo and nodded. Manzo wrapped a thin, double-coiled rope around the angry man's neck and braced his right knee against the wooden brackets of the chair, keeping his prey in place. The man's hands rose in a meek attempt to avoid the inevitable, his lower limbs trembling, thin lines of white spittle running down the edges of his mouth. Manzo's strength was too large a hurdle to overcome, his skill far exceeding his target's abilities to fight him off. It took less than twenty seconds to snuff the life out of the terrorist who only minutes ago was savoring the last of an excellent Italian meal.

Angela waited until the man's body slumped in his chair and Manzo pulled his rope off his neck and placed it back in the front pocket of his jacket. She then looked at the remaining terrorist. "It should be easier for you to speak to me now," she said.

The young man scanned the three dead bodies surrounding him. His hands shook and the lines of his face trembled. His eyes were rimmed with tears, more out of fear than sorrow.

Angela looked at Manzo. "Get him a glass of water and something strong to drink," she told him. She kept her eyes on the young man while Manzo went to the bar.

"Do you intend to kill me even if I tell you all I know?" he asked.

Angela watched as Manzo rested two glasses in front of the frightened young man. "Drink," she ordered. "Don't be concerned about dying. Just tell me what it is you know."

The young man lifted the water glass and drained it with one gulp. "We are never told specifics," he said, resting the glass back on the table with a shaking hand. "We don't even know the target until the morning of the attack. At best the night before, if the bombing is to occur in the morning."

"What are you told?"

"Very little," he said. "Rumors mostly."

"Such as?"

"There is quite a bit of talk of cultural sites," he said. "Some think that means a church or perhaps a museum. There are a few art books around the compound and we've been encouraged to read them. Most are picture books, others biographies."

"Which artists?"

"From the Renaissance, mostly," he said. "Raza spends a great deal of time in museums and churches. He is as consumed with the artists as he is with his own mission."

"Any artists in particular?"

"Michelangelo is one he mentions frequently," the man said. "And he worships Caravaggio. I have heard he sees many similarities between his life and that of the artist. He fancies himself a painter, and when he paints he copies Caravaggio."

"Why are you in Naples?"

"Again," he said, "we're not told much beyond where to go and where to stay while we wait for the order. We arrived here two days ago and this was our first night out of the safe apartment."

"You and your friends were celebrating," Angela said. "It seemed more than a simple night out. Or do I have that wrong?"

The young man paused and reached for the glass of wine given him by Manzo. Angela leaned across the table and held the man's hand in place. "Talk now," she said. "Drink later."

"I don't understand," the young man said, though the sudden shift in his body language confirmed that he realized the severity of the situation he was now in.

"I'll make it clear," Angela said. "Where were you and your friends supposed to go tomorrow morning?"

The young man drew a deep breath, hesitating, unable to stop his body from shuddering as if he were standing on a cold street corner instead of a warm restaurant. "The port at Margellina," he said.

"Where in the port?"

"The ticket counter," he said. "There would be someone waiting with four duffel bags and four tickets. One for each of us."

"And then what?" Angela asked, though she could already guess the answer.

"We were to each board a different boat to the islands and to Sorrento," the young man said.

"Do you know what would be inside the duffel bags?" Angela asked.

The young man closed his eyes and nodded.

"This time of year, early in the day, start of a weekend, those boats would be packed with people," Angela said. "And you and your friends were ready to kill them all, yourselves included."

The young man didn't answer. He just stared at the woman glaring down at him. Angela released the hold she had on his hand and stepped away from the table. "You will meet with the man with the duffel bags tomorrow," she said. "You will tell him your friends are running late, tell him in a convincing manner. Understood?"

The young man nodded.

"Did they tell you how long before the bombs in the duffel bags would be set to explode?"

"Thirty minutes. They want enough time for the ships to load and head out to sea. They also took into account the fact that the boats never leave the port on schedule."

Angela exchanged a look with Brunello, who nodded, stood and walked toward the front door, pulling a cell phone from his pants pocket as he moved. She watched him leave the restaurant, relocking the door as he slammed it closed, and turned her attention back to the young man. "Were the four of you sharing a *pensione* room?" she asked.

"Yes."

"No one else?"

"No."

"The owner of the *pensione* or anyone who works there, are they involved?"

"No," he said. "Just the four of us. We spoke to no one else."

"You'll spend the night here," Angela said. "There's a cot in the basement. There will also be two men down there to make sure you don't oversleep."

"What will happen tomorrow morning?"

"You will die," Angela said, "just as you planned."

28.

Rome, Italy

"We need to divert his attention," Raza said.

He was walking between Avrim and a somber man named Santos. Tall and slender, Santos carried himself with a manner that gravitated between confidence and arrogance. He held a walking stick in his right hand and an unlit cigar in his left. He had not been back to his home country of Mexico since he was a teenager, spending long stretches in the capitals of Europe, London and Rome his primary bases. He was an old school arms dealer who started as a teenager when he supplied stolen weapons to Germany's lethal Baader-Meinhof crew. In his mid-twenties, he married a woman who was one of the original members of the Italian terror group, the Red Brigade, losing her to a police shootout in a small town south of Salerno. He remained a high-end dealer throughout, his position never wavering, regardless of which networks rose and which fell. Santos was at his happiest when he was sowing seeds of torment.

He currently was the point man navigating the supply lines of weapons from Mexico to the cells. He was the most dangerous gun-runner in Europe and had done business with all the major players in the rapidly growing terrorist community. They trusted him and often sought him out for advice and counsel.

"How much damage has the Wolf caused?" Santos asked.

"We get all our funding from the Russian," Raza said. "Our other avenues have been sealed off."

"You can thank the Yakuza for that," Santos said. "The dirty money flows through them and they decide if it comes out or gets lost in the wash."

"There is little information coming from America," Raza continued. "Either nothing is going on worth mentioning or there's a lid on information getting out."

"So far, nothing that sounds insurmountable," Santos said.

They crossed against traffic walking toward Piazza Navona, a short distance from the balcony where Mussolini once stood and addressed the packed square. Raza nodded in agreement as he looked out at the blend of slow-moving tourists and even slower-moving locals making their way to a variety of destinations.

"I'm not worried," Raza said. "The Italian criminals have always been a problem for us. The same is true for the Japanese and Chinese organizations. But we never needed their help in the past and there is no reason to think we'll need it in the future."

"Then why not ignore the American now?" Santos said. "Why go looking to light a fire under his ass?"

"He's targeting me," Raza said.

Santos stopped by a fountain and rested his back against its lower base. He looked at the crowds for a few moments and then turned to Raza. "You're saying it's personal?"

"He's made it personal," Raza said. "I had no idea who the hell he was before this started."

"But now you do know who he is," Santos said.

"I need to give him something to worry about besides me," Raza said.

"I would think twice before getting into a head-to-head with a guy like the Wolf," Santos said. "He didn't get where he is because he looks good in a suit. He's got weight. And he's tag-teamed with the Camorra. In most places that would double his weight. In this country, it triples it."

"I'm aware of the risks," Raza said.

Santos nodded. "His family's been touched already," he said. "Which is why he's chasing your ass in the first place. You think a guy like him would have made a war move if his family was in one piece?"

"I don't know his reasons."

Santos wanted to keep his relationship with Raza, with any terrorist, no deeper than a business transaction. Santos regarded himself as someone who chose a life of crime for no reason other than to make cash in fast fashion. He didn't strap on a gun and deal drugs and arms for any cause other than financial freedom. He even viewed the two prison stretches he served along the way as instructive, investing the time spent in lockup learning how to be a master of his trade. Santos could never understand the mentality of a terrorist, martyrs willing to die in the name of a religion he found as corrupt as any he had encountered. But he happily took their money and offered free advice if asked, though he was certain it was a waste of breath since he had yet to meet a terrorist who didn't think his way was the only way.

"Take careful steps, friend," Santos said to Raza. "The Wolf is no Wonder Bread wop. You're not going to see his face splashed on a newspaper doing a slow walk to the courthouse. This guy and the Italian woman and even the Greek play in a whole other league. Major league."

"You fear him?"

"I wouldn't push it that far," Santos said. "But I would say he has earned my respect."

"You ever go up against him?"

"Not yet," Santos said.

Santos moved away from the fountain and walked toward the north end of the piazza, Raza by his side. "Some in my line of work hate the idea of wars," he said. "I'm not one. In fact, I wish there were more of them. The more different crews go after each other, the more guns and ammo they'll need and the more cash finds its way into my pockets. So go at it. And if it happens to bring some trouble my way, so be it. Comes with the turf."

"But you have no interest in who wins and who loses?" Raza asked.

"This ain't a ball game," Santos said. "And I make no money by rooting for one group over another. You get beat by the Italians, then I move my wares to the next wannabe Bin Laden who waves money in my direction. Nice, clean, simple. No emotions, no cheering section, no ties to any group or any person. That's up-front, and I've never hinted at it being anything deeper than a deal. Everyone I do business with, you included, is just another paycheck."

Raza nodded. "This last load, is it enough to last me a few weeks?" he asked, not doubting Santos's position.

"That depends more on you than me," Santos said. "I would guess yes, but I have no idea what your plans are and how much action you expect to go up against. I would ballpark it that even under heavy fire and with one or two major jobs in the works, you should have enough. But like I said, the Wolf may have plans that will cut into your supply."

"That happens, how soon can you restock?"

"Depending on needs and what the demands are elsewhere, I can refill your tank in about a week," Santos said.

They walked in silence for a few moments, neither one at ease in the company of the other. "You think I'm in over my head against the Wolf?" Raza said.

Santos shrugged. "You never heard me say that," he said. "It depends on who's more on his game. What I was trying to say is that whoever comes out of this breathing don't mean jack shit to me. I'm not doing this to make friends, Raza. I'm in this to make money."

Raza stared at Santos. The Russian and Santos were cut of one cloth, each out for himself, looking to expand or preserve his power. The Wolf was out to avenge the death of his family and validate his concerns that terrorists would erode the financial structure of organized crime. Santos was a gun merchant without loyalties. The Russian was a money source with an arsenal of men and weapons at his disposal. He was intelligent and ambitious. The same held true for the Wolf.

But despite these hurdles, Raza believed that if he were able to go through with his plans, he would become the most feared man in the terrorist world. And that was his goal.

His only goal.

"I promise you, Santos," Raza said, "by the time my work is done, you will be a richer man than you already must be."

"Music to my ears," Santos said with a wide smile.

29.

Margellina, Italy

The sea was choppy, waves splashing over the edges of the pier, workmen in wool shirts and blue pants standing in clusters waiting for the next hydrofoil to pull into port. It was 9:25 in the morning and already the harbor was packed with anxious tourists lugging bags, locals wanting to get home, and businessmen heading for a day of work on one of the many islands serviced by the ships that moved in and out twenty hours a day.

The lines clogging the ticket windows were thick and noisy and lacked any sense of organization. Behind thick glass windows emblazoned with stickers, boat schedules, and tour signs posted in three languages, the stoic faces of the ticket brokers stared out above the crazed throng in front of them toward the congested traffic just beyond the stone barriers separating street from port.

A middle-age man with a thin brown beard stood off to the side, watching the chaos with indifference, smoking an unfiltered cigarette and wearing a gray jacket two sizes too big for his svelte frame. Four black duffel bags rested by the sides of his soiled brown desert boots, each one zippered and taped shut. He wiped at his brow and glanced at the time on the small blue cell phone he clutched in his right hand.

"You must be Dal." The voice came at him from behind. Startled, he turned and glanced at the young man standing inches away from the duffel bags.

"Are you . . . ?" The middle-age man hesitated, reached into a side pocket of his jacket and pulled out a small, folded piece of white paper. He opened it, gave a quick look at what was written on it and then gazed back up at the young man. "Are you Pandi?" he asked.

The young man nodded.

Dal looked around the port area, concern etched on his brow, lines of sweat running down the sides of his cherubic face. "Where are the others?" he asked. "You were all to have come together."

Pandi smiled and shrugged. "Too much wine and too little food," he said. "I woke them before I left. They should be here within minutes."

"I don't care how much they drank," Dal said, heat and tension giving way to anger and frustration. "You were supposed to be here together. Those were the instructions."

"We have plenty of time," Pandi assured him, eager not to draw attention, looking at the throng of people around them, wondering if there was a way he could escape and die as he intended and not how some woman and her thugs planned it. "They have prepared for this day for months. There is no need for you to be concerned."

"I will lose my concerns the second I see their faces," Dal said. "And if I don't see those faces in the next five minutes, I will make a call that will be bad news for both of us."

"I told you they *will* be here. I mean it," Pandi said, his voice cracking ever so slightly, the strain of the moment no longer easy to disguise.

Dal stiffened when he felt the barrel of the gun push against the center of his back. Brunello stood behind him now, a thin black leather jacket folded over his right arm hiding the gun from view. Dal could feel Brunello's warm breath on the folds of his neck and glared at Pandi. "You betray us?" he said. "You are a fool if you think this will save your life. No one can save your sorry life. You could have died with honor. Instead you will die of shame. As will everyone in your family."

Brunello leaned in closer to Dal. "Take two of the bags and then turn when I turn." He tilted his head toward Pandi. "You take the other two," he told him, "and we walk together toward the black car, the one right behind the taxi."

"What if I refuse?" Dal asked.

"Then the boy will take the four bags to the car," Brunello said, "while you lay here on the pavement choking on your own blood. If you want to die brave and in public, makes no difference to me. But that decision needs to be made now."

Dal hesitated, staring at the crowd, larger and more agitated than when he first arrived at the port only minutes earlier. He took a short breath and then bent over and picked up two of the bags, waiting as Pandi quickly grabbed the remaining two.

"To the car," Brunello said. "And walk like you mean it."

Manzo held the back door of a Mercedes sedan open as they approached. "The both of you and the bags in the backseat," he ordered. Brunello jumped in behind the wheel, engine idling, and waited as Manzo slid in next to him. Brunello looked up at a traffic officer standing in front of the car, nodded, and was waved into the congestion of the wide cobblestone street.

"How much time?" he asked Manzo.

"Fifteen minutes," Manzo said, "assuming the rocket scientists laid the timer and detonator in correctly. Otherwise, we all get to meet the virgins this morning."

"I hope not," Brunello said. "I haven't had a coffee yet."

Brunello navigated through the Naples traffic with practiced ease, shifting gears, dodging slow-moving buses and Vespas, edging away from the luxury end of town. Manzo shifted slightly in his seat and looked at both Pandi and Dal. "Your boss is going to be pretty pissed when he finds out you put to waste all those expensive explosives," he said to them.

"He will make sure you die because of what you are about to do," Dal hissed, his voice a blend of fear and arrogance.

Manzo smiled. "We all will die," he said, "as you both will soon find out."

"Terrorist bastards," Brunello said, his cheeks red, his body tense, the fingers of his right hand gripping the gearshift, his anger no longer contained.

"What is it?" Manzo asked.

"My niece, Rosa," Brunello said, "my sister Anna's oldest."

"What about her?"

"She takes those boats every morning," Brunello said. "Found herself a job in one of the hotels on Capri. These two had their way, she would have died in one of those explosions."

"She was lucky today," Dal said. "But there will come a day when she will not be as lucky."

Brunello made a sharp left against oncoming traffic, barely avoiding a fast-moving Fiat and a scooter, and sped down a narrow side street, swerving when he caught sight of a free-roaming Jack Russell walking against the stone walls of the old homes lining the block. The tires of the sedan held steady riding the cobblestones, but still there was enough bounce inside the car to cause Manzo concern. "You might want to think about slowing down," he said to Brunello. "We have no idea how well these bombs have been wired."

Brunello shifted gears and brought the sedan to a gradual halt in the middle of the empty street. "You're right," he said. "You know how I get when the blood goes to my head."

Manzo nodded. "We got less than ten minutes," he said.

Brunello shifted the gears to neutral and slid his right hand into the side pocket of his leather jacket, pulling out his Beretta, a silencer attached to the barrel. He turned and pointed the gun at Dal. "First things first," he said, his eyes on Dal, his words meant for Manzo.

Brunello pulled the trigger three times, careful to avoid going anywhere near the duffel bags resting beside Dal's legs. The first two bullets landed in the center of the terrorist's chest. The last one hit to the left of his upper lip.

Dal died instantly, his eyes open and staring at the moon roof. Next to him, Pandi lowered his head, trembling like a straw doll left out in a harsh wind, and threw up on his pants and the two duffel bags braced against his slender body.

"That was not on the program," Manzo said.

Brunello took a final glance at the dead terrorist and turned, re-holstered his gun, and moved the car forward, keeping it in second gear, turning at the first corner. "He was going to die anyway," he said after a few moments of silence.

"Seven minutes," Manzo said. "It's up here on the left."

They were now in an abandoned area of Spaccanapoli, a neighborhood divided into seven sections, each leading into the heart of the city. Brunello made one final turn and was now facing the water again, only this time he was far removed from any tourists heading to the island of Capri. He brought the car to the edge of a dilapidated pier and left the gear in neutral, engine running.

Manzo turned to look at Pandi. "This is where we get off," he told the young man now completely resigned to his predetermined death. "You seem like a good kid. Not like the dead prick next to you. But you made this choice, not us."

"I don't fear death," Pandi managed to say.

"No worries, then," Manzo said. "You drown or are blown up. Either way, you get your wish."

Brunello and Manzo leaned against the trunk of the sedan and pushed it over the edge of the pier. They watched as the car did a slow sink into the murky water, the top sheen a blanket of slick oil, grime, and splintered chunks of wood.

"You sure the bombs will go off underwater?" Brunello asked as he and Manzo began to walk from the pier.

"We'll find out in three minutes," Manzo said.

The underwater blast shook the pier, sending rowboats flailing through the air. Two massive waves hooked over the pier and onto the sand-drenched cobblestones, washing away decades of soot and stain.

"Where'd you leave our car?" Manzo asked.

"A couple of streets over," Brunello said. "Found a spot near that place used to be a butcher shop. The one Mario's cousin let us use when we first got started."

"Do you believe any of that?" Manzo asked.

"Any of what?"

"What the terrorists believe," Manzo said. "That when you die you'll find seventy-seven virgins waiting for you in heaven."

"I got news for you, Luigi," Brunello said. "I don't think there are seventy-seven virgins *anywhere*. Not in heaven, not in hell, not on earth. If you're lucky, you might find yourself one. But I hate to think what she must look like."

30.

New York City

I looked at Jack through the glass separating the terrace from the living room in the penthouse apartment. He was sitting on the hardwood floor tossing a tennis ball to a bullmastiff puppy he had named Hugo. The dog, only four months old and already close to a dozen pounds, was a gift from Angela, who stood next to me on the terrace, smiling as she watched Jack and Hugo take pleasure in each other's company.

"You know a pug would have been just as nice," I said to her.

"Maybe," she said, turning to look at me. "But they don't have the royal bloodlines and the history our bullmastiffs do."

"They also won't grow to weigh as much as a middleweight boxer," I said.

Angela laughed. "Look how happy he is," she said, nodding toward Jack. "They'll be good for each other. And the dog will help keep him safe. Bullmastiffs defend to the death the ones they love."

"I remember," I said. "It took a month before the two you had left my side whenever I came to visit that first summer."

"They're slow to trust," Angela said. "We could all take a lesson from them."

I turned to look out at the view of downtown Manhattan, rays of sun bouncing off the polished windows of the tall buildings that formed the skyline Truman Capote once called a "diamond iceberg."

The war against the terrorists was less than a month old.

The Yakuza and the Triads were doing their part—squeezing the institutions that funneled money into the terrorist pipeline, some of them corporations we had done business with for years. Eastern European and Middle Eastern money that for decades had been sent to Japan to be cleaned and turned legal within twenty-four hours instead disappeared without a trace, days later finding its way into organized crime coffers. No one was better at this than the Chinese and Japanese syndicates. They had been handling organized crime funds since the midpoint of the last century and did so in stealth fashion, keeping track of millions of moving dollars stretched across at least a dozen syndicates around the world. Despite the daily avalanche of money coming in and then just as quickly leaving the country, not a single notation that was put to paper could be deciphered by any law enforcement authorities. The clean dollars were then invested in dozens of legitimate enterprises that not only expanded our power base, but made it that much easier to conduct the illegal end of the business. That ability to access funds without fear of exposure was one of the main reasons we thrived through the tail end of the twentieth century and the first decades of the current one. If you can't link us to money, it is almost impossible to link us to crime.

The two Asian syndicates had quickly put a dent into the terrorist money supply. I estimated it would take another month, six weeks at the outside, to drain the well in such a manner that the only cash finding its way into their hands belonged to the Russians. I wanted their money to flow unimpeded into terrorist accounts and allow Big Mike, John Loo, and their computer team the opportunity to crack their intricate code system and find out who the main money men of terror networks were and if they ever operated in tandem. Once a paper trail was established and I knew for certain it was accurate, I would have associates spread that information to trusted allies in law enforcement, both in the States and Europe, and let them help with the heavy lifting. I knew such a maneuver would bring a smile to Uncle Carlo's face. "What difference does it make if your opponent goes away with a bullet or with a judge's gavel?" he once told me. "What's important is, he goes away. And the less the trail leads back to you, the better."

I was betting that the combination of the two cash drains would eventually lead to a backlash against the terror networks, banking on the fact that no one likes to see their money disappear without substantial returns. It was as true for a criminal organization as it was for a hedge fund.

Once they had their system in place, Big Mike and John Loo were able to clone hundreds of terror cell phones and monitor their activities on a daily basis. They then matched the numbers, tossed them up on a large monitor, and without leaving the comforts of a downtown Athens office, knew who was calling which number and how often. With that information, we were able to establish links between the various cells and do a breakdown as to which were working together and which chose to fly solo. This helped me with a general overview of the terror landscape. With that key information in hand, I burrowed deeper toward my first target—Raza.

He was an impressive young man, the unlikeliest of terrorists, and as I have come to learn, the unlikeliest often turn out to be the most dangerous.

He listened to classical music when planning an attack and had built an army of several hundred willing to die at his command. There were no women in his cell. I found that curious, since leaders of such groups actively recruit women because they are not easily pegged as suicide bombers by authorities.

If I were counting on Raza to make a mistake or a judgment error, I would never bring him to ruin. He had already shown he was too smart to commit either. To defeat him, I would need to continue to strip away his forces, dig even deeper into his financial reserves, interrupt his weapons flow, and get into his head. Make him think I was out there, close by, anticipating his every move, aware of his plans, capable of shutting him down at any point in the process. I would need Raza to believe that regardless of what moves he made or planned, I was already two ahead and ready to close him out.

As for Angela—standing next to me on the terrace, pouring herself a glass of chilled wine, looking radiant in a strapless yellow summer dress, warm sun beating down on toned muscles and tanned skin—she had more than done her part. She had sent her Camorristas as far north as Florence and given clear orders to target kill all known terrorists operating in major cities. Working in league with David Lee Burke and members of his Silent Six team, she then focused her attentions on Raza and his network. She showed no mercy, accepted no excuses, and didn't bargain deals with terrorists. "I had heard about her and her operation," David Lee Burke told me one evening in Rome. "But the talk doesn't do it justice. It is cold, relentless, and final. When the Strega marks you for death, the only thing left is to pick out a headstone."

The Strega struck quickly and harshly.

In one Naples neighborhood alone, her crew eliminated eight men who had been rumored to be involved in sleeper cell activity. In Rome and in Florence her group foiled two Raza attacks and had stopped the bombing of the tourist boats in Margellina. Her methods were ruthless and she showed no mercy to any suspected terrorist. She operated under the centuries-honored code of the Camorra—kill all in your path and leave behind nothing but blood and ruin.

She was living up to her reputation as the most ruthless mob boss in Europe, and I was happy to have her working on my side of the field.

"Has he given the dog a name yet?" she asked.

"Hugo," I said. "He's in a Victor Hugo and Alexandre Dumas phase. I did manage to talk him out of naming him after one of the Musketeers."

"Sometimes the apple does fall close to the tree," she said, smiling. "I recall you being in such a phase yourself. One, if my instincts are correct, you have yet to outgrow."

"Jack's noticed the heavy security detail I put on him," I said. "And he's not too happy about it. What boy his age would be? Maybe Hugo will help him ignore what's going on around him and let him be a kid again."

"Give that dog some time, Vincent," Angela said. "Watch him grow and then watch how he will not only know where Jack is but will be aware of who surrounds him, who is a friend, and who is a threat. I've seen it myself. Those two dogs of mine you mentioned? They saved my life on more than one occasion. My father told me each dog was worth six of his best bodyguards."

I nodded, my back against the brick wall of the terrace, my eyes on my son. "He'll also have a friend," I said.

"He's his father's son, Vincent," Angela said, turning to face me. "He can handle anything thrown his way."

"I hate leaving him for such long periods," I said. "Jimmy fills the void most of the time and my uncle does, too, but it's not the same as having a father around."

"Maybe being alone isn't such a bad thing for him right now," Angela said.

"You've been busy rattling Raza's cage," I said, eager to shift the topic to business. "I would imagine by now he's sniffed out who it is that's bringing havoc to his plans."

"My guess is he'll focus more on you than me," Angela said.

"Why?"

"You're the bigger name," Angela said. "And all terrorists, whether they admit it or not, are headline hunters. He gets me, he might get a few headlines in the Italian papers. But if he brings down a wealthy American, mob boss or not, he's sure to get a lot more attention."

"We're slowing him down," I said. "But we're no closer to nailing him or finding out what he has in mind for his major attack."

"We know more than we think we do," Angela said. "We know, for example, that the big job will be in Europe, most likely Italy. He's building up to it. That job we foiled, the one in the port, would have been his biggest attack to date."

"Did anyone in your crew pick up anything we can use off that train station bombing?" I asked.

Angela nodded. "A sketch pad," she said. "Not the kind an art student would use. This one was leather bound and expensive. They're sold in the high-end shops along the Arno in Florence or by the Spanish Steps in Rome."

"How does that link to Raza?"

"Not sure that it does," Angela said. "But similar books were found in two of the safe houses we've hit. It might have been left behind by mistake or it might be just coincidence."

"None of that was in the police files," I said.

"And none of it will be," Angela said. "One of my men got it from one of his police contacts. It's in our files now."

"What was in the sketch pad?" I asked.

"Some charcoal drawings," Angela said. "Bad replicas of works by Michelangelo, Caravaggio, and Raphael. Again, the same as was found in the safe houses."

"It's worth checking out," I said. "Have our guys run Raza's photo past the shop owners in both cities, see if it lights a match. He loves Renaissance art, and if he's a terrorist eager to leave his mark, why not destroy what you love?"

Angela nodded. "It troubles me we're finding members of his cell too fast and too easy. They practically lead us by the hand to the jobs they're planning. Raza is smarter than that. He's better than that and he thinks bigger than that."

"Which tells you what?"

"That we've been fed sacrificial lambs," Angela said. "Put out there for us to follow and then foil, giving us a sense of thwarting his goals and bringing havoc to his organization."

"While he is far from the scene, planning the big attacks," I said. "He's working out of our sight, without any worries we are on to his game."

"I knew coming into this, Raza was a clever young man," Angela said. "The question then becomes is he more than just clever? Is he as devious as we like to think we are?"

"He could well be," I said. "Or it could be Vladimir working as he works best, in the shadows, calling the shots."

Angela walked over to the glass table in the center of the terrace and pulled back a soft leather chair. "It doesn't matter who is calling the shots," she said after several moments. "Maybe they've been playing us or maybe not. But this major attack is going to happen soon and it's going to happen in my country."

"Why are you so sure?"

"There are no signs of Raza's crew anywhere in the States," Angela said. "And he would find it difficult to set up an operation from scratch. Too many eyes on the ground for him to operate in any sort of comfort zone."

"What else?"

"He likes to devise his plans and take his meetings in museums," Angela said, talking as much to herself as she was to me. "It serves a dual purpose, allowing him to meet and discuss finance and operations in public places and feeding his love of Renaissance artists. He can accomplish that more easily in Europe than he can in America."

"And he recruits out of Europe," I said. "That may be a trust factor more than anything else, bringing new people in who were recommended by those already in his circle."

"That's part of it," Angela said. "But he has never attempted to set up a footprint in this country. I don't think it's on his radar, at least not yet. There would be no point. He's a young man looking to make a name in the terror world. If he executed an attack here, no matter how well planned and how destructive, it would still leave him under Bin Laden's shadow. In Europe, he has the terrain to himself. If the attack were big enough, it would grab all the attention and put him at the head of the terrorist line. If he's going for the big hit, Europe will be where it will happen."

"If he's not looking to copy Bin Laden and risk being compared to him, he won't go after financial sites," I said. "That leaves cultural landmarks."

"Which feeds right back into his passion for art," Angela said. "Makes perfect sense."

I nodded and stepped in closer to her. "If you wanted to make your mark, make a statement and blow up a cultural landmark in Italy, killing as many people as possible in the process, what would you hit?" I asked.

"It would have to be someplace that would shake Europe to its core," she said, "as 9/11 took America's breath away. I can think of half a dozen places that would have such a powerful effect—the *David* in Florence, the Duomo, the Leaning Tower, Vatican City, the Colosseum, the Grand Canal in Venice."

"How secure are all those places?"

"The Vatican is pretty tight, but with crowds coming in every day by the thousands, it would not be difficult for one or two wired terrorists to slip in," she said. "The Galleria and the rest of them would be a cakewalk. They are big on camera surveillance, but you have a bomb strapped to your chest, you don't care who sees you walk in."

"And Raza's notion of a cultural landmark could differ from ours," I said. "We could have our eyes on Rome or Florence and he could be targeting Pisa or Milan. We can't afford to be wrong on this. There's too much at stake."

"Raza's been planning something this big ever since he got into the terror business," Angela said. "And if he's half as smart as we think, he feels by now he pretty much has it gamed."

I nodded. "And he'll keep the plan to himself until he has to put it out there for his crew. Not even Vladimir will be told, even though it's his money Raza is playing with. He's got it figured out. Except for us. There was no way for him to imagine we would step into this. It won't stop him but it might give him pause."

"If that's true," Angela said, "that he wasn't planning on drawing the attention of the syndicate, then maybe he wasn't the one who targeted your family."

"We'll find out in due time," I said. "And that starts with getting our hands on Raza."

Angela pushed her chair back and stood. "I'll spend some time with Jack," she said, walking toward the glass doors, "and then I'll fly back to Italy. If we're going to stop Raza, there's quite a bit of work still to be done. And it would help if we doubled up the crew we have on Vladimir."

"I'll have that done by tonight," I said. "I'll fly out day after tomorrow. I promised Jack I would take him and Hugo to Central Park. And I need to talk to Jimmy."

"Give my love to your silent consigliere," she said as she walked into the living room. "And tell him if he ever tires of taking care of you, I have a villa waiting for him in Naples."

"Thank you," I said. "This would be much harder to accomplish without you."

Angela turned and gave me a smile. "You can thank me later," she said. "After they're all dead."

31.

I sat on the clean cut grass of the Great Lawn in Central Park, under the shade of an oak tree whose limbs had seen better decades. Jack and Hugo rested on each side of me while Jimmy sat in his wheelchair, parked atop the tree's roots. It was late afternoon and the sun was bright and warm, the sky a blinding blue. Jack looked up at me and then at Jimmy; the smile on his face hadn't changed since he first saw Hugo pop out of the cardboard box Angela handed him earlier that day.

"Angela gave me a list of the foods he should eat and treats he can have," Jack said. "She also told me if I trained him right, he would listen to me and be the best-behaved dog anyone could ever have."

Jimmy nodded and held his hands out wide. "That's right, Uncle Jimmy," Jack said, "and be the biggest dog anyone could ever have."

"You watch after him and he'll watch after you," I said. "You'll be partners."

"Just like you and Uncle Jimmy," Jack said.

I smiled. "Except Hugo will outweigh Uncle Jimmy by forty pounds and eat three times as much."

The bullmastiff had a gray coat with touches of white around his face, neck, and sides. I could tell from his wide puppy paws that he would grow to be a large dog, but even now, after only a few hours with Jack, you could see how protective of the boy he would grow to become. The puppy seemed keenly aware of the activity around him—the kids tossing Frisbees; the middle-age man up against a chain-link fence playing a soulful tune on a trumpet, couples laying next to one another, young men sitting on folded towels, deli sandwiches in hand, sneaking in a few quiet moments from a hectic day—but he kept his gaze on Jack, taking in his every move, learning my son's mannerisms and adapting to the sound of his voice.

"You think Uncle Carlo will like him?" Jack asked.

Jimmy made a gun motion with one hand and pointed at Hugo with the other.

"Jimmy's right," I said. "Uncle Carlo will be the one to teach Hugo to shoot a prowler rather than bite one."

Jack stood, grabbed a tennis ball out of one of the rear pockets of his jeans and showed it to Hugo. "You think it'd be okay if I tossed a ball with him?" he asked.

"As long as you don't mind him chewing it to bits in about ten minutes," I said.

I watched my son and the puppy play for a few moments and then turned to Jimmy. "I'll drive Jack and Hugo out to the house tomorrow morning," I said. "He's all excited about taking the dog to the beach and hanging out with you. He's not keen about me being away again but he loves being out there with you and Uncle Carlo, and even more so now that he has a companion."

Jimmy made a few hand gestures, calm and assured in his manner, only his eyes radiating concern.

"That sounds about right," I said. "I want the house covered in and out, but not to such an extent that Jack feels penned in."

I looked back to see them at play, Hugo gnawing away at the tennis ball, Jack sitting by his side, petting him and speaking to him in a low voice.

"Check out everyone, Jimmy," I said. "Even kids he's had play dates with in the past. Take nothing for granted. If Raza is going to make a move on Jack, he'll try anything."

Jimmy moved his hands back and forth, a bit more agitated than before.

"I know you can handle it," I said. "I just want to make sure I have every base covered. I can't lose him, too, Jimmy."

Jimmy's gestures softened and I reached out a hand and rested it on one of his. "If Raza's got to go through you to get to Jack, then I got nothing to worry about. I know."

I leaned against the tree and looked out. "The gun guy Raza is using," I said, "the Mexican, Santos, doesn't much care where his money comes from so long as it comes. We can offer him twice what Raza is paying, plus he doesn't have to hand us any weapons."

Jimmy took out a notepad, scrawled a few lines on a thin piece of paper and handed it to me.

I read it and handed it back. "We might not need to touch Santos," I said. "Once this is finished and we take Raza down, we hand the Mexican over to the Colombians. They'll be glad to take care of him."

Jimmy dashed off another note.

I read and shrugged. "The Russians have been quiet," I said. "The older bosses are not as keen as Vladimir on working with the terror crews. They might be sitting tight to see how this plays out. If there is as much money in it as Vladimir says, then you'll see them move—and fast. Until then, there's no reason for them to do anything other than wait."

In that sense Vladimir and I were in a similar situation. I knew I still needed to make a convincing argument with some of the leaders of the other crime syndicates that my idea of a declared war would turn out to be worthwhile. While they agreed to start the war and help fund it, many were content to keep their distance and monitor the situation. A few groups—the Yakuza, the Triads, and the Greeks, with Big Mike taking the lead—had done more than their share. The others were sitting back, doing their due diligence, weighing the cost of war versus the loss of revenue brought their way by the terrorists.

If we focused strictly on criminal activities, the terrorist situation would not be as big a concern since it would have little impact on our profits. In truth, we would see an uptick in the sale of drugs and guns, have even more free rein in the sex trade—especially in the distribution of low-budget porno movies—and increase the demand for loan shark money and bookies to work the sports end. It would also enable us to tighten our control over the international movement of counterfeit currency, taking in five clean dollars for every false one sent out.

But our legal investments would be subject to substantial losses. Our vast worldwide real estate holdings, including hotels and casinos, would suffer if terrorist attacks curtailed travel to those areas. Since the 1980s, organized crime had taken control of most of the world's airports, and we took in $650 million a year in lost luggage items alone. We were deep in the financial business pool, silently owning everything from multi-billion-dollar hedge funds to board control of four major banking institutions. Name any business you can think of and we were not only in it, odds were better than even we controlled the levers and made the bulk of the decisions.

And that is where terrorists could cause us to lose millions, if not billions. These legal enterprises relied on stability, and terrorists— and their Russian allies—brought only chaos. The illegal operations were accustomed to ebbs and flows in profit margins. The legitimate operations, needing to respond to the demands of an appointed board, operating under the intense gaze of legal authorities and, in many cases, subject to investors and stockholders, had to function in a clean and calm business environment. The risks taken there had to bring in more money than was laid out. Acts of terror brought havoc to such stability.

I watched Jimmy make several gestures, moving his fingers slowly so I would understand the shorthand version of conversation we had perfected over the years.

"You're right," I told him. "We've wounded Raza's network, but only enough to let him know we're looking in his direction. It gave us the time we needed to put our pieces in place."

Jimmy looked at me, his usually cheerful face now a determined mask of defiance and strength. He balled his two hands into fists and slapped them together several times. I stood and rested my hands on his shoulders, bending down to meet his gaze. "Yes, it's time to let Raza see how hard we play," I told him.

Jimmy's face muscles relaxed and his upper body was no longer tense; he was satisfied we were headed on a course he approved.

"We still have time," I told him. "Let's put it to good use."

He smiled. I moved his wheelchair out from under the shade of the tree and pushed him toward Jack and Hugo, both deep into a game of fetch on the Great Lawn. I stopped and watched as my son and his puppy rolled in the grass and chased one another under the glare of a hot sun. Jimmy turned his head and looked up at me. "No one gets close to them while I'm gone," I told him. "I don't care if it's a UPS guy. No one. If they do, you give the order and end them right then and there."

Jimmy opened his left hand and ran his right index finger across the veins on his wrist.

A blood oath.

32.

Toronto, Canada

We sat at a large table in the back of the dining room in the Sutton Place Hotel. I had a small stack of folders and sealed manila envelopes piled on my left, a glass of ice water close to my right elbow. Around the table were the members of my Silent Six team, David Lee Burke beside me. Also in the group were Big Mike Paleokrassas and John Loo, who had been working on loan to us from the Yakuza. Files and spreadsheets surrounded Big Mike and John.

This was a special crew of trained assassins in our company:

Jennifer Malasson, not yet thirty and already with a dozen kills to her name, as lethal with a knife as with a rope.

Robert Kinder, thirty-five, an Iraqi war veteran and one of the military's most proficient snipers.

Franklin J. Pierce, twenty-eight, named after the former President, a martial-arts warrior, adept at killing with either hands or feet.

Carl Anderson, forty-one, a former government chemist who could poison an opponent a dozen different ways.

Beverly Weaver, thirty-two, the only member of the group to have worked in law enforcement—a bomb unit in North Carolina. She was the munitions expert of the team.

Burke kept the Silent Six functioning as a unit and was the one charged with making the key decisions once the team was out on the field.

Burke had been in Special Forces and served some of his time in Italy, and he was looking for a second career that would incorporate the skills he had acquired in nearly a decade of service. He was not the type who would find satisfaction working as a consultant in a war zone or locking down security concerns for high-end corporations. He was a man born for battle and was at his best when the fight looked its bleakest.

I'd been in the middle of my first European venture, sent overseas by Uncle Carlo to see if I could broker a truce between the Camorra and the Casalesi, a branch of the Neapolitan mob that decided they were due for a bigger cut of the money flowing into southern Italy. When my attempts at a peaceful resolution failed, stronger and bloodier measures were called for. Burke came aboard to help in what eventually turned out to be a brutal three-month war, with heavy casualties sustained by both sides.

During that skirmish, Burke had shown a natural ability to lead and an unquenchable thirst for battle. He was also loyal and had proved trustworthy on enough occasions to put that matter to rest. Soon after the dust had settled, the bodies buried, and a truce arranged, I asked him to come to New York and hired him. He was to put together a team, work under everyone's radar, and report only to me. When the group wasn't needed, they were free to live where they pleased, as long as they stayed clear of trouble, took no freelance work, and had a solid cover for how they earned their money. They were each paid high six-figure salaries, with Burke taking down one million a year plus expenses. I wanted each to be beyond reproach, not open to an easy bribe or tempted by better offers elsewhere. While I trusted Burke, he would need to recruit team members that he could hold to the same standard. He went out and filled the specific needs the group required, and so far they had never once failed me. This, however, would be their biggest challenge to date. I knew before I spoke a single word that not all of them might make it out of the hell I was about to send them into.

It was a fact that would soon become apparent to everyone else at that table as well.

I pushed the folders aside and watched as Burke took one off the top, then gave it to Weaver, the team member closest to him. I sipped some water and waited until all the folders had been passed before speaking.

"Those are your targets," I told them. "There is background information on each and you will get more from Big Mike and John before you leave. These are all kill-shot situations. We're not looking for information. We don't want to know who else is involved in their network. We just want them dead."

"Any concerns about collaterals?" Kinder asked.

"That can't be avoided," I said. "When these guys are on the loose they like to hide in the company of women and children. I would prefer to keep the casualties to a minimum, but do what needs to be done to bring down the primary."

"You each have eighteen names spread out across a number of countries," Burke said to the group. "I'll work up a plan as to who goes where and when. Needless to say, expenses are not an issue. Getting the job done is the priority."

"We on a clock with this?" Malasson asked.

"In a way," I said. "You have a lot of ground to cover and a lot of targets to take down, and I understand all of that can be time-consuming. Under normal circumstances you would have three to four months to get the hits lined up."

"Under *these* circumstances?" Pierce asked.

"Two to three weeks," I said.

"Some of the higher level targets will have extra layers of protection," Burke told them. "I think we save the more difficult ones for last and knock off the easier hits first. That's how I'll map it out. But if you see an opening for one of the bigger names on your list, you catch a break somewhere down the line, do not be afraid to deviate from the plan and go after the hit. Understood?"

Each member gave him a knowing nod, glancing at the names and the brief biographical sketches of their designated targets. I let them sit quietly for a few moments and then looked at Big Mike and John and gave them the green light.

"You won't be alone on this," Big Mike told the group. "Some of you may know me or John by reputation. Which, at this point, is as it should be. But from today on, think of us as your best friends. Before you leave here you will have cell numbers on each of the faces in your folders. You will also have their last known addresses, their favorite restaurants, where they meet up with friends for a game of cards and where they meet when it's time to plan a new terror attack."

"We have cloned all their existing numbers," John Loo said. "But as each of you knows, these guys change numbers like we change shirts. That should not be a concern. When those numbers change, you will be sent the new ones as soon as we have them. The time lapse won't be long."

"Terrorists keep at least five phones active at any one time," David Lee Burke said. "How can we know the one you cloned is the one we should follow?"

"Our crew monitors conversations on all the phones in Raza's network," Big Mike said. "We know everything that's said on every call, but what we send to you is essential information only from the most prominent of the lines."

"Still, it's not close to being an exact science," Weaver said.

"We're not claiming it is," John Loo said, not at all on the defensive. "We can get you in close, give you access to ongoing conversations, and narrow down location sites. The rest is up to you."

I glanced at Big Mike and nodded. He was as impressed as I was by John, who looked like a younger version of his uncle, Kodoma, the head of the Yakuza, and had many of the same mannerisms. He was tall, his dark hair kept long, strands occasionally covering a thin, handsome face highlighted by a set of charcoal eyes that took in everything but revealed little. He showed no emotion as he spoke, relaying the facts as he knew them, and was the only one at the table dressed in a suit.

"The combination of the information that's in the folders plus what's being supplied to you through the cloned phones should be enough to get you within the target zone," I said.

"You want anyone brought back?" Anderson asked. "For information, leads to other cells?"

"They all die," I said. "Every name on that list."

"What about intel we might find from the kill site?" Burke asked. "Should we make the grab or leave it?"

"If there's time, take anything you think can help in any way," I said. "Destroy anything you can't carry out. The fewer footprints you leave behind, the better."

"How much firepower can we expect in return?" Malasson asked.

"Raza is going to be expecting some heat," I said, "just as we expect some from him. What I'm counting on is that he won't look for it to be this big and this fast."

"What about the Russians?" Pierce asked. "They putting manpower into this along with their money?"

"Nothing heavy as yet," I said. "But Vladimir is not a sideline guy. He likes to control the action. If he sees Raza's crew taking heavy casualties, he won't hesitate. He'll send in as many guns as he needs to slow it down."

"Sounds like we have ourselves a job to do," Burke said. He patted his folders into a neat pile and watched as the other members began to do the same, ready to bolt the room and head out for a mission from which some of them might not return.

"There is something I need you to bring me," I said. I waited as they all eased back into their seats and focused their attention on me.

"What?" Burke asked.

"A name," I said.

"We pick up a lot of chatter on the cloned phones," Big Mike said. "Three-quarters of it is useless bullshit. Sometimes they slip up and talk about a job being planned or a recruit coming in, stop chatting in code long enough for us to break it down and figure it out."

"So you want the name of a recruit?" Kinder asked.

"No," I said. "I want the name of a traitor."

"It's still fresh information and we're still trying to piece it together," Big Mike said. "But we think there's someone on our team doing business with Raza or Vladimir or both."

"From your crew?" Burke asked, turning to look at me.

"Too soon to tell," I said. "I also don't know how deep into this they are, but the fact that the other side feels comfortable enough to talk about it on cells is a serious problem."

"Just general chatter or something deeper?" Burke asked.

"What we've picked up so far is mostly location talk," I said, "where we might be heading, where we might be staying. The only names mentioned have been Big Mike's and mine."

"And if any of you are curious—and you should be," John Loo said, "Mike and I have been checked and cleared."

"Anyone you suspect?" Burke asked me.

"Until I know who it is," I said, "I suspect everyone not in this room."

"If my team gets closer, I'll make sure they pass it your way," Big Mike said. "But I think the better shot is squeezing one of the higher-ups in your folder to get what you can out of him."

"If you do get a name," I said, "don't call it in. Bring it in. I don't want to risk giving him a heads-up."

"Does he get put on our target list?" Malasson asked.

"No," I said. "He gets put on mine."

33.

33

Florence, Italy

Raza stood in the center of the large hall in the Galleria gazing up at the massive sculpture of Michelangelo's *David,* completed when the artist was only twenty-six. The room was crowded with tourists taking photos, students taking detailed notes, children staring in wonder.

"It is a work of beauty," Avrim said.

He was just to Raza's left, nestled between a cluster of Asian students staring intently at the imposing sculpture and a well-dressed American woman in her mid-twenties leafing through a photo history of *David,* a black Sharpie clutched between her teeth.

"And in a few weeks time? Who knows?" Raza said. "It could end up as damaged as it began."

"But I thought—"

"That this would be our decoy," Raza said, quick to finish Avrim's thought. "There still may be truth to that. It does make a certain sense to have anyone intercepting our calls—the police, other groups, Vladimir, the American—to have them think this is our target and deploy their resources here, leaving us free to do our damage elsewhere. But then, it might also make sense to ruin not one site but two at the same time. If that were to occur, then I would truly have left my mark."

Avrim looked up at *David* and then in a lower voice said, "Do we have the resources for such an undertaking? Or for that matter, the manpower?"

"What we lack, we will be given," Raza said.

"The job you have planned is massive, and on its own will make our enemies shiver," Avrim said. "It is brilliant and will do for us in Europe what Osama did to America on September eleventh. Do you really see a need to expand the operation?"

"Bin Laden brought down *both* towers," Raza said, "though I'm sure one would have had the same emotional impact. We walk in his footsteps. This is a plan he would have embraced. It will bring fear to our enemies and leave them in such a state of confusion they will think we can attack at any time from any place. They will finally believe there isn't anything of theirs we hold sacred."

"There are security cameras in every corner of the room," Avrim said, walking now with Raza around the large statue. "And armed guards at the entrance."

"They can have as many cameras as they wish," Raza said. "Once a bomber is in the Galleria, the mission is all but complete."

"And the guards at the front gate?"

Raza shrugged. "All they see are long lines."

"So you would think of doing two attacks on the same day?"

"Would be poetry, no?" Raza said. "Look around you. Look at the faces. They are left speechless by such a magnificent work of art. Think how they would feel if it were no longer here, taken from them forever, as if it never existed? They will never recover from such an emotional loss. Never."

"Have you anyone in mind, should you choose to go in that direction?" Avrim asked.

"I knew who it would be before I envisioned the plan," Raza said.

"I also knew he would embrace the assignment because he will be doing something that will always be remembered."

"Has he been told yet?"

Raza looked at his friend, smiled and rested an arm around his shoulders. "Not yet," he said to Avrim.

34.

Naples, Italy

Santos crossed against heavy traffic, heading for the small coffee shop, eager for a bitter espresso and two—maybe three—fresh pastries. There was a time when he had been in great physical shape and worked out daily, running five to seven miles regardless of weather or which city he happened to be in. But those days were firmly in the rearview mirror. Now, there was nothing he liked better than a good meal and the occasional romp with a high-end woman. Those things, and watching his portfolio grow into the mid-seven figure range. He slid a hand into the side pocket of his blue windbreaker and pulled out a twenty-euro bill. He was less than ten feet from the café's entrance; he could taste the harsh brew on his tongue.

The years of steady success and the safety he felt working in Europe had rusted Santos's street antenna. Otherwise he would have noticed the black sedan, engine idling, parked in front of the café. He would have seen the two men in leather jackets sitting at an outside table, pretending to read the morning papers. But Santos had made the biggest mistake a man in the business can make—he'd begun to think like a civilian.

The sedan's door swung open to block his path. The move startled him and caused him to drop the bill to the curb.

"Get in and make it look like it's something you want to do," I said. I didn't move from my seat in the back, but my voice was loud enough to be heard.

Santos held his ground and peered in. "Sounds like a piss-poor idea to these ears," he said.

"You think dying on the street is a better one?" I said. "If so, I go on my way and the two at the table behind you take it from there. Your call, but make it now."

Santos looked at the two men in leather jackets, their newspapers now resting on the table.

He took a deep breath and then slid into the backseat next to me.

"Pick up your money and close the door," I told him, nodding at the bill on the curb.

He did as told, and I nodded to the driver. We eased into the early morning traffic.

"You know who I am?" I asked.

"You're not looking to sell me a car, know that much," Santos said, a trace of a Mexican accent still there, despite the years spent living in Europe.

"You run guns and ammo," I said.

"If I could run, I wouldn't be in this car," Santos said. "But, yeah, somebody fed you right. I move arms. Move them to your side if you put up the cash."

"For the moment, I don't care about any of the other terror outfits on your payroll," I said. "I only care about one. Raza's crew."

"They bought about five dozen crates and paid the freight in cash," Santos said. "But you knew that before I got in the car, which, by the way, is a nice ride. You put four gold hubs on this piece and you got yourself a top-of-the-line skirt chaser."

"I'll mention it to my mechanic," I said.

"You want me to stop selling to his crew?" he asked. "That why you breathin' hard in my direction?"

I sighed. "They don't get their guns from you, there's always somebody else ready to sell to them. You keep moving whatever it is they ask you to move. And the money you make from them stays where it is now—in your pockets."

"So what do you want?"

"I want you to come work for me," I said.

We were off the side streets now, out on the autostrada, the driver, a handsome young man in his mid-twenties with thick dark hair and skin the color of leather, settling the sedan in at a steady ninety kilometers an hour, following the signs that led to Salerno.

"You know who Raza's gunrunner was before he reached out for you?" I asked.

Santos shook his head. "Mexicans never put their nose in somebody else's soup. I'm like your army before they found religion—don't ask, don't tell," he said. "I just take jobs as they come."

"He was a Colombian named Carlos Mendoza," I said. "For a while he was pulling in big money working the terror circuit, Raza's group included. They paid cash and the guns were costing him nothing. It seems he had a connection in Iraq, one of our soldiers looking to get more out of the war than a free ride home. So stolen guns made their way to Raza and others like him and thick wads of cash found its way to Mendoza and his bosses."

"Seems like a good deal for all hands on the deck," Santos said.

"It was," I said, "and it could have stayed that way for as long as Mendoza had the guns and the terrorists had a need."

"So what happened?"

"It seems guys who do business with terrorists—guys like you, Mendoza, others—have a short shelf life," I said. "That's because guys like Raza only trust people for so long, especially those not loyal to his particular cause."

"They killed him?"

"They didn't stop with him," I said. "They cleared them all out—his transporter, his banker, the soldier in Iraq, Mendoza's wife and two kids. Each shot dead at close range. That's their way of letting you know the partnership no longer seems to be working."

"It's harsh, give you that," Santos said. "But we are in a harsh business. And what was bad for him turned out good for me. Everybody in my *famiglia* owes me too many pesos to count, so the more that get dirt-napped, the lighter my load."

"How much you taking in running weapons for Raza?"

"Terrorists pay a higher freight than what somebody like you would be charged," Santos said. "Risk factor is higher, more eyes on their movements, longer transport distance."

"Save it for your accountant," I said. "All I want to know is how much?"

"I clear about $175,000 if it's a simple drop," Santos said. "Nothing more than guns and ammo. Price climbs when they start to toss in explosives and high-end items."

"How long have you been feeding him?"

"He came on my radar about a year, maybe fourteen months back. Figure five, maybe six shipments in all. One more on the way."

"You deal with him direct?"

"Why you asking all this shit?" Santos said. "I mean, where you want to go with this? Don't think an OC hombre big as you gets wrinkles worrying about whether a low-rider like me keeps breathing. That were true, then me coming in with you and double-dealing Raza ain't exactly laying out a safety net under my Mexican ass."

"I'll pay you $250,000 a month. In return, all I need to know is what Raza is asking you to get him and when and where it's coming in," I said. "I cannot keep you alive, not when you're that close to him. And frankly, even if I could, I doubt I would. If you go down, then I make the same offer to the runner who replaces you."

"So I walk on hot coals for a quarter a million a month," Santos said. "Say that works for one, maybe two hauls. He's no moron, Raza, sharp as a farmer's machete, from what I can tell. He catches on it's me feeding you? All that extra money you throw my way gets me is a nice coffin and a top-tier mariachi band. And he *will* catch on."

"It's a short-term job," I told Santos. "Either I make sure of that or Raza will. But whatever happens, you walk away with money from both ends without having to expend yourself."

"Raza ain't the only terrorist I ride the rap with," Santos said. "Word gets out I was doing a double tap, my business on that end dries up."

"That's your concern, not mine," I said. "Won't be the first time you played one side against another. I have a feeling you'll figure a way to work it out."

"I take a pass on your offer," Santos said, "what happens then?"

"I'm not talking to you because I'm lonely," I said. "You pass on the offer, that's your business. My driver will drop you off at the train station. You make your way back to Naples."

"No bad blood?"

I shook my head. "But I can't promise Raza won't know you and I had a conversation, and he might be curious to know what it was about," I said. "What takes place from that point will be between you and him."

"So, I read it right, you puttin' out a take-it-or-leave-it deal?"

I glanced out the window at a clear view of miles of well-tended farmland, the occasional stone house dotting the landscape. "We're about ten minutes from Salerno," I said. "I'll need an answer by the time we get there."

"No need for a ticking clock," Santos said. "I'm in."

I kept looking out at the passing countryside, farmland now giving way to row after row of vineyards, a line of workers tending to the grapes, a sprinkler system keeping the ground drenched. These lands had been harvested for centuries, the only intrusion being attacks from outside forces. I imagine there is a certain serenity that comes from living a safe life. Working the land, waiting through the seasons as the crops ripen and then die.

"The car will stop across from the station," I said. "The trunk will be open. Inside will be a backpack. Belongs to you. Your first payment is in the pack. There's also a number in there for you to call when you have information to send my way. Learn the number and burn the paper. If anyone but you uses that number, it would not be good if I found out about it."

Santos nodded. "Do you need my number?" he asked.

"I have your number," I said.

35.

Paris, France

Vladimir sat in an ornate chair admiring the massive lobby of the George V Hotel, from the crystal chandeliers to the marble floor to the oil paintings hanging on the walls, resting within faux golden frames. He had always admired French taste, its shameless excess. Their upper class had a unique style, whether it was clothing, jewelry, cars, or the way they decorated their homes. But he also admired the way they didn't publicly flaunt their wealth, unlike his fellow Russians, who flung cash around as if it were a day away from being outlawed. He saw the behavior as crude and dangerous, since nothing attracted unwanted attention like the flashing of large sums of money.

"The Wolf is moving much faster than we originally anticipated," Klaus Marni said.

Marni was one of two men sitting across the table from Vladimir, each having vodka on the rocks. He was one of Vladimir's most trusted advisors and a dependable assassin. He had turned to petty crime at a young age and soon came to the attention of Klensko, a gangster known for turning street money thousands into legally earned millions. Klensko organized the best of Russia's young thugs and brought them into his ranks by offering high-end salaries and a percentage of profits. "He acted like a CEO of a major corporation," Uncle Carlo told me during one of the late night talks we had as I was being prepped to take over the reins. "He paid them enough money not to bolt to other outfits and gave them input into the day-to-day dealings. You had to compare Klensko to anybody, it would be to Luciano."

It was Klensko who put Marni together with Vladimir, and the two proved a formidable and lethal combination as they rose through the Russian criminal ranks at a rocket pace. And it was Marni who brought the third man sitting at the table into their crew. Ruslan Holt was a Canadian-born street orphan who bounced around a number of European cities as a teenager before making his way to Russia with a fake passport after a drunken argument in a London nightclub left two men dead and Ruslan's prints all over the crime scene. He thrived in the Russian underworld, where the police could be ignored and he could operate with impunity so long as he remembered to kick back a portion of any profits he earned to the local bosses in his district.

The three men, sitting in the safe confines of one of the finest hotels in the world, were now in control of nearly forty percent of the vast Russian criminal organization. They had risen through the ranks together, gathering profits and disposing of enemies at an alarming pace, brushing past the old guard and bringing fresh vitality to the Russian criminal landscape, thriving even in a chaotic new world order where the Soviet Union became a distant and forlorn memory. From the beginning they had set their sights on dominating all of organized crime, not just the vast and extremely profitable Russian end. The growth of terrorism and the declared war launched by the various branches of the criminal universe was the opening for which they had patiently waited for decades.

"He's doing what we would do in his place," Vladimir said. "He knows that to wait for a terrorist to make the first move would be catastrophic. He is looking to take the fight out of him even before the fight begins."

"At that, he might succeed," Holt said. "But the other organizations were lukewarm to his war proposal, giving their consent more out of respect than anything else. They are helping him, but from a distance."

"That's why he teamed up with the Strega," Marni said.

He was in his forties, though his thick gray hair and beard gave him an older appearance. He was an expert marksman with both a handgun and high-powered rifle and was a workout fanatic, spending as much as three hours a day lifting weights and pounding a treadmill.

"Nothing can interfere with the terrorist's plans," Vladimir said. "If he fails, so much will be wasted."

Holt shrugged. "He's good."

He was the physical opposite of Marni, preferring food and wine to sweating inside poorly ventilated gyms, his body soft and round, covered by oversize shirts and jackets. He was, at thirty-six, a year younger than Vladimir and in charge of the rough end of the organization, skilled at planning assassinations and kidnappings that ended with the ransom secured and the hostage left for dead. He also oversaw the $3 billion a year sex trade, making buys or organizing lifts of girls as young as twelve and selling them on the lucrative underground markets of Asia and the Middle East. Any girl not sold into sexual slavery would either be killed or doled out to Russian pimps to work the streets of their districts.

Of the three at that small table, Vladimir was the most feared and respected in organized crime circles.

Marni was admired for his business skills and ability to spot on-the-rise talent. He was trusted within the Russian mob and wielded an impressive international Rolodex crammed with names on both sides of the coin—criminal or legitimate.

Holt, instead, was hated by any who crossed his path. He had been targeted by international law enforcement for a decade, and each time either the charge wasn't strong enough to hold up in court or the witness disappeared within weeks of his arrest. Russian outfits steered clear of him unless they had no choice but to work a deal. No crime boss had anything good to say about him, and weren't shy about expressing their disgust.

"But having the two Italians on his ass? Might be more than Raza can handle," Marni said.

"Has he asked for help?" Holt asked.

"He has only asked for financing," Vladimir said. "And as you can tell if you've been reading the papers, he's put at the very least a portion of that money to good use."

"We are paying him for more than a few newspaper and magazine headlines and a mention on the evening news," Marni said.

"The chaos I hoped to see happen is already taking place," Vladimir said. "Terrorists have been emboldened and the attacks that have taken place this summer have put a major dent on tourism and all that flows from it. The press has taken note, and when they write about it, the public reacts. These days fear spreads at a much faster rate."

"Does Raza have anyone who would know how to take the Italians down?" Holt asked.

"There are syndicates who cannot take on either one," Vladimir said. "Both?" He shook his head.

"But terrorism relies as much on luck as it does planning," he added. "Raza has the element of surprise in his favor. No one outside his inner circle—not the Italians, not even us—has knowledge as to where he plans to strike. As much as I despise being kept in the dark, it is the best part of Raza's plan. By keeping everyone unaware of his intentions, he maintains his advantage."

"What if he no longer had to worry about the Italians?" Holt asked.

"That would benefit Raza," Vladimir said. "On the other hand, it might rally the other crime organizations to make a move, as it would suggest to them an existent threat. And we are their first and only suspects."

"So?" Holt said. He shrugged his shoulders, his designer labeled clothes wasted on his bulky physique.

"I'm not eager to do battle with every crime outfit in the world, Ruslan," Vladimir said, always quick to lose his temper when pushed by his old friend. "At least not yet."

"That's assuming every group we're thinking about will jump into the fight," Marni said, adding logic to Holt's argument. "So far only a few have shown a taste for this war. If the Italians were out of the way, they might decide maybe now's not the time to go all-out. Let the dust settle, see how deep the terrorists cut into their action before they make their move."

"You know it upsets me to agree with Marni," Holt said, "but he has a good point. And there is the fact that if they do indeed get eager for battle, they would do so knowing it would be against us— not a few hundred terrorists. That might give them pause."

Vladimir sat back in the plush chair, gazing at a portrait of a soft-faced duke from centuries past. "If it is to be done, we need to eliminate both at the same time," he said after several moments. "If we choose one over the other, the survivor will come after us with all the force they can bring."

"They see each other, no?" Marni asked. "My understanding is they are close."

"It would need to be in a public place," Holt said. "Her home in Naples is as secure as a military compound. And on his own grounds, the Wolf is virtually untouchable."

"Where do they meet when they get together?" Vladimir asked.

"Hotel suites, usually," Holt said. "Heavily guarded. When he's in Naples, they meet at her house. The Wolf has several homes and he's hard to pin down. Makes it a point to move around quite a bit, more so since his wife and daughters were murdered."

"He has taken her out to dinner on a few occasions," Marni said. "I've read that in one of the files we have on them. The Strega owns several restaurants, mostly in Naples, a few in Rome. If they venture out for a meal, my guess is it would be at one of those locations."

"They both disdain bodyguards," Vladimir said. "Is that still true now that they've joined forces?"

"They may not like them, but they have them," Holt said. "The Strega has two men who never let her out of their sight. Where she goes, they go, and they only make an appearance if there's trouble. She feels invulnerable in Naples, but these two have been around her since she was a teenager, and her father insists they be her shadows."

"And the Wolf?" Vladimir asked.

"His son is heavily guarded night and day," Marni said. "As are his homes and offices. As for himself, he only appears to go it alone. At least from the few times we've seen him out in public. The only time he seems to be guarded is when he is with his son. But we all know from our own experience the best bodyguards stay invisible until it's time to draw a weapon."

"They are partners now and will need to meet more frequently," Vladimir said. "If, as you say, the Strega believes no one will make attempts on her while she is in Naples, then that might be an ideal place to make our move."

"How soon before Raza's plan is put in motion?" Marni asked.

"The most recent cash infusion he requested was the largest and the last," Vladimir said. "So, two weeks? Three?"

"Then we need to make the attempt on the Wolf and the Strega within ten days," Holt said. "The crime bosses would need to regroup and decide how to proceed, but by the time they come to a decision, Raza will have done his damage."

"Take them both out," Vladimir said, "first opening you have. Send only our best assassins, but keep it a small group. They will need to move at a moment's notice."

"We could bomb one of her restaurants," Holt said. "Eliminate the risk of a shoot-out."

"I want proof of death," Vladimir said. "So will the other criminal organizations. Only a bullet gives us that."

36.

Naples, Italy

"The police may have found something of interest," Angela said.

"Is it solid?" I asked.

Angela shrugged. "It came from a detective in Rome," she said. "It's not another case to him. He's invested. Like you."

"Like me?"

"Had a younger brother on the force," Angela said, "pretty good with arrests and smoking out terrorists. He was killed a short while back at the airport in Rome."

"The bomb outside the terminal," I said. "That was one of Raza's jobs, about the time he made his deal with Vladimir."

We were in a corner booth in one of the oldest restaurants in Naples, Mimi alla Ferrovia, a short distance from the courthouse. Every American President since Dwight Eisenhower had eaten a meal there, and their photos, along with those of countless politicians and movie stars, adorned the walls.

Angela had wanted to go out for dinner and didn't need to convince me. We were in her city and her two top gunmen were somewhere nearby, ready to pounce at a moment's notice.

A waiter approached and opened a bottle of an expensive red wine. "Just for the lady," I said to him.

"Bullets are what kill, Vincent," Angela said. "Not wine. And you're too much of a gentleman to let a lady drink alone."

I glanced up at the waiter and nodded, watching him pour two full glasses after Angela brushed aside the request to taste it.

I stared across the table, the room lit by soft lights and candles, and for an instant Angela looked like the girl I met that summer long ago, a beautiful teenager with a wild heart and a city at her beck and call. She was in a tight black skirt with a matching top. Her thin pearl necklace glowed in the candlelight.

"This cop . . ."

"Luca Frantoni," Angela said. "His brother, Remi, was the one who tried and failed to take down the suicide bomber in Rome."

"Has he given you information in the past?"

"It's not what you're thinking," Angela said. "He's not on our payroll, or anyone else's. He passes on information if he thinks it will help him get closer to nailing someone, in this particular case Raza. He knows we're after him and so is he. Whoever gets to him brings him down. That's all he cares about."

"That wasn't what I was thinking," I said. "I was just curious as to how accurate his intel has been in the past."

"He's never pointed us in a wrong direction," Angela said.

"What did he find?"

"Three nights ago Rome antiterror cops broke into a terrorist safe house, right off the Via Veneto, if you can believe it," she said. "They made three arrests and confiscated a number of laptops. Frantoni recognized one of the three as a Raza cell member, low-tier but who might have been around the group enough to have overheard something that might help."

"The police didn't find anything at the last attack site," I said.

"And what Frantoni got from the associate may not lead to anything, but it's worth a look."

"What is it?"

"A sketchbook, same in style and design as the one found at the train station," Angela said, pausing as a waiter put a large bowl filled with lemon chicken and broccoli rabe in front of her. She waited as a second waiter placed a steak pizzaiola and roasted potatoes at my end. We both declined fresh pepper on our meals and sat silently until the waiters were out of earshot. "The cell member told Frantoni the book belonged to Raza."

"Was there anything in it?"

"Charcoal drawings, just as with the first one," Angela said. "Replicas of Michelangelo, Caravaggio, and Raphael's works along with some scrawled notes."

"Raza loves art," I said. "It's the world he hates."

"It's what he loves that he may choose to destroy," Angela said. "If we take away anything from the sketchbooks, it might be just that."

We ate in silence for a few moments. I was comfortable around Angela, always had been, and felt free to let my guard down. I hoped I wasn't making an error by doing so. I don't trust easily. You don't reach the top levels of organized crime by giving your trust to anyone, let alone another mob boss. And I could not lose sight of a cold, hard truth—that behind the beauty and charm of the woman across from me was the brutal head of one of the largest criminal organizations in the world. The Camorra was involved in so many areas, legal or very much not legal, that they had long ago earned the nickname "the Octopus" from law enforcement authorities.

Then there was the issue of a potential mole at work either inside my own organization or in league with one of the other syndicates. Having a traitor in my circle is something I feared and did everything within my power to prevent. All mob bosses are concerned with betrayal and look at everyone—from within their inner circle to those on the periphery—as potential suspects. The reasons for an ally, business associate, or confidant to turn are as simple as they are numerous—profit is a reliable motive, as is the promise of more power. Sometimes it is done out of petty jealousy, other times to correct a perceived wrong. Find the Judas and the reason becomes clear.

I had considered everyone, and each would have sound reason to make the case to bring me down:

Angela's father might have allowed her to work as my partner while he was free to lurk behind the scenes undetected and close a backdoor deal.

Uncle Carlo might be less willing to put our crew through a costly war and more willing to line his pockets with Russian money.

Angela might have agreed to help in order to keep me under her gaze and, in Italy, within reach, prime for a setup.

Or it could be any one of the crime syndicate bosses at that initial meeting. All with good reason to have me put out of commission.

In other words, the knife in the back could come from anyone at any time.

"There's something else Frantoni told me," Angela said.

"What?"

"Police found something in Florence two days ago," she said. "In a car, parked outside a Raza safe house near the Ponte Vecchio."

"What?"

"Several picture postcards of the *David*," Angela said. "On its own, nothing special. Still . . ."

"Raza practically lives in museums, they're like a second home," I said. "He walks the halls planning his terror attacks. I wouldn't put it past him to bomb one of them."

"Maybe," Angela said. "Or maybe a postcard is just a postcard."

I looked around the restaurant that had been crowded when we first came in but now was down to a few couples lingering over afterdinner drinks and dessert. We were both sitting with our backs against the soft leather of the booth, able to gaze out at the street. It was a few minutes after ten and this section of Naples, bustling, loud, and congested during the heat of the day, was silent and empty. I could see the steps leading to the courthouse and, on the other side, the narrow street that led to the old but still reliable train station.

It was then I spotted the car, a late model Mercedes four-door sedan, its windows tinted, white puffs rising from the dual tailpipes.

"Right now all we're doing is guessing," Angela said. "We need to get hard information and fast."

"How far away are your two?" I asked, still looking out the window, wondering now if the parked car was a decoy and the hitters would come at us from another direction.

Angela was quick to catch my gaze. "If there's trouble, fifteen seconds, no more," she said.

"Is the back way out of here by the bathrooms?" I asked.

"Leads into an alley that takes you to the street across from the courthouse," she said.

"I don't plan on using it," I said. "I needed to know, in case they come at us from behind."

"Let's not wait for them to come to us," Angela said, easing out of the booth. She snapped open her shoulder bag and pulled out a black nine millimeter and looked at me. "I have a second one in case you're light."

I smiled, stepped out of the booth and pulled a Glock from a hip holster. I scanned the restaurant, making sure the remaining patrons were still at their tables and the wait staff at their stations. "Are three hundred euros enough to cover the meal?" I asked, reaching for my wallet.

"Leave your money where it is," Angela said, her eyes locked onto the car outside, walking in slow, measured steps toward the front door. "My city, my treat."

"When we go out, you head for your car," I told her. "I'll deal with the ones in the sedan. When they show, your guys can cover you and watch my back at the same time. If it gets too heated, you pull out of here."

"That's a good plan," Angela said. "I'm not going to follow it, but it is a very good plan."

I reached for her left arm and held her, looking at the warm eyes and tilted smile I had known since I was a boy. "Anything happens to you, your father is going to have me killed," I said.

Angela laughed. "My father's wanted to have you killed since you decided not to marry me."

She looked up at me, leaned in and kissed me gently on the lips. Then we slowly parted, neither one saying a word as we headed for the front door.

We walked out of the restaurant in casual fashion, our guns down by our sides. Angela slid one hand under the crook of my right arm and slipped in closer to me. The street was empty, the overhead lights shielded by a humid mist. We stepped off the curb, Angela's head resting now on my shoulder, her gun hand leaning against her lower back. We kept walking even as the four doors to the sedan swung open. Four men, each more physically imposing than the next, rushed out of the car as if they were responding to a fire, guns out and aimed in our direction. I gently eased in front of Angela, looking to shield her from the fuselage that was heading our way, lifting my Glock and firing two rounds in the direction of the four men, now less than twenty feet away. Bullets cascaded against the cobblestone street, sending small pieces of sand and mounds of dust into the air.

The shots fired from out of the darkness did not miss their mark.

Hidden deep in the shadows of the courthouse to our left, Brunello and Manzo hit their targets with pinpoint and deadly precision. They didn't squander their ammo, keeping their aim steady, taking only the kill shot, bullets to the head and heart. Within seconds the four men lay on the ground, dead or dying, their guns out of reach.

It had happened in less than three minutes, four armed men barely getting off a half-dozen shots and each missing his targets. I looked down at the bodies under the shielded glow of the streetlights and knew they were not the ones sent there to kill us. They were the lambs sacrificed for the slaughter, dispatched to make me think the worst was over when in truth it had not yet even begun.

"Setup," I shouted, loud enough for both Brunello and Manzo to hear.

"The alley next to the courthouse," Angela said. "Or the door leading out of the restaurant kitchen. Those are the only two places they could come at us from."

"Would anyone left in that restaurant bother to put a call to the cops?" I asked.

"Not here, no," Angela said.

The street was as quiet as any I've ever been on. No one walked by, no car drove past. It was as if we were in an abandoned part of the city. I glanced over at Angela standing still as stone, listening for the slightest noise, her body poised to spring to action. Brunello and Manzo remained hidden under a blanket of darkness somewhere behind me.

Then came the footsteps, hard soles scraping against stone and sand and heading toward us from both the alley and the rear door of the restaurant. There could be as many as eight gunmen rushing our way, maybe even more. This was not Raza's move; this had the smell of the Russian mob all over it. Leave it to Vladimir to sacrifice four men simply to dupe us into thinking we had lived through an attempt on our lives.

While I admired the audacity and brutality of the move, it was one I never would have made. I would never openly recruit someone to my organization to be nothing but a decoy. It was clear from their movements, the cut of their clothes, and their inability to hit two still targets within close range, that the four young men lying dead on the street beside me were amateurs who bought into the promise of a fast rise through the criminal ranks. They probably weren't even paid for the job, and the sedan left idling nearby was a fresh lift from the streets of an upscale neighborhood.

"Take the car," I said to Angela, pointing with my gun hand to the sedan nearby, the four doors still open. "The three of us will give you cover."

"They're my men and you're my partner," Angela said. "I don't leave either one. But I'm charmed by your concern."

"Wasn't asking you to run," I said. "Take the car and turn it toward the direction of the shooters. Throw your high beams on and fire into the alley. Keep the driver door open."

Angela began to move toward the parked car. "Why?" she asked over her shoulder.

"Because you're going to step out of the car right before it makes it into the alley," I said.

"What about the ones coming out of the restaurant?"

"Your guys are positioned better to handle them," I said. "Soon as they see the car move, they'll know what to do."

"Where will you be?"

"I'll be on the passenger end of the car," I said, "giving you as much cover as you'll need."

Moving faster, Angela jumped behind the wheel of the sedan and turned it toward the alley, kicking on the high beams as she swerved the car slowly toward the entrance. She had one leg out, high heel skimming the cobblestones, right hand on the wheel, left hand and gun resting on the open window, firing rounds into the alley in the direction of the approaching gunmen. Bullets from the gunmen hit the front end of the sedan and smashed one side of the windshield.

Over by the narrow street leading to the courthouse, I heard rapid gunfire coming from both ends, Brunello and Manzo now in a heated battle.

I was on the other side of the car, firing my Glock into the alley, the lights from the high beams giving the gunmen a poor line of vision. I counted seven through the smoke and saw that three were already down and one was about to fall.

The sedan was inches from the entrance to the alley when I saw Angela lurch from the driver's side and stumble onto the pavement, gun still in her hand. I walked behind the car, jammed a fresh clip into the Glock and reached for her.

"I'm out of bullets," she said as I helped her to her feet.

I held my left arm around her waist and fired at the shooters now trying to ease their way past the sedan blocking the alley, their figures visible in the heavy light. "Start moving toward your car," I said to her. "But stay behind me."

"How many more?"

"Two," I said. "Maybe three, but one of them is wounded."

"Brunello and Manzo," Angela said. "I won't leave without them."

"We're not going anywhere until every one of these shooters goes down."

"You're running low," Angela said. "We're going to need more guns."

Angela left my side and started to run toward the bodies of the four gunmen who had initially approached us, their weapons strewn on the cobblestone street. As she left, I caught sight of one of the gunmen, bleeding from a gash on the side of his neck, squeeze past the sedan and aim his weapon toward her. There wasn't enough time for me to warn her and I could see she was still several steps away from picking up one of the scattered guns. I ran toward her, firing at the gunman as I moved, the two of us spraying bullets into the humid night air.

I was right in front of Angela when I felt the sting in my left shoulder. An instant later the force of it brought me to my knees. Angela, now with a weapon in hand, stepped in front of me and fired three rounds at the gunman standing less than fifteen feet across from us. Two of the bullets found their mark, the fatal one making a small hole on the left side of the man's cheek. He fell facedown onto the hard pavement.

Angela turned back to me, pushed aside a flap of my black leather jacket and tore open my blue shirt, drenched now in blood. "It's deep," she said of the wound, "but clear. You'll lose blood, but you'll be fine when we have a chance to patch you up."

"It's my favorite Armani, the shirt you just tore open," I managed through gritted teeth. "I've had it for years."

She laughed, then helped me to my feet. We both peered into the lit alley and saw nothing but crumpled bodies and heard nothing more than the groans of the wounded. All was quiet on the other end of the street, the narrow one by the courthouse. Then we heard the shuffling of feet against stones and saw Brunello and Manzo turn past the courthouse steps heading toward us. Manzo was dragging his left leg, blood flowing freely from a gunshot wound, his right arm draped around Brunello's shoulders.

They both held semiautomatic weapons at the ready and smiled when they spotted us standing between the sedan and the four bodies. In the distance we could hear the sounds of police sirens heading our way. "Let's go," Angela said, turning toward her car, one arm gripped around my waist. "There's a clinic nearby that will patch up you and Manzo. Once you're both cleared to go, you'll rest up at my place until you can get around on your own."

As the four of us walked slowly toward Angela's car, I gave a quick look back at the bodies we were leaving behind and wondered how many hundreds more would die before this war I declared would be brought to an end. "We were lucky tonight," I said to Angela, ignoring the shooting pain in my shoulder.

"We need to stay that way," she said.

37.

37.

Florence, Italy

There was at least one dead terrorist in every room.

The thirteenth-century palazzo was once the home of a duke re-nowned for his collection of wines from around the world. Through the centuries, there had been royal galas, lavish dinner parties, and dozens of weddings attended by the city's cultured and deep-pocketed.

On this day the stately rooms of the palazzo were witness to their first bloodbath.

The Silent Six had made their first major move on Raza's net-work.

They attacked in the dead of the morning, the city still asleep, the rushing waters of the Arno the only noise. They moved through the house with efficiency, under the cover of smoke bombs. The palazzo was one of six safe houses being used by Raza's cell. There were four-teen rooms spread across three floors, and sixteen terrorists living and working inside. The rooms had been stripped of most of their illustrious furnishings, replaced by foldout tables topped with computer monitors, printers, and cell phone tracking devices. There were also enough weapons stashed in the rooms to help set off several dozen terrorist attacks.

Each member of the Silent Six used their skills to take out the sleeping terrorists—Malasson utilized knives and ropes, leaving behind four dead; Kinder took out an equal number with close range kill hits to the head and heart; Pierce put his martial arts to the test, snapping necks with abandon; team leader Burke, a muzzled gun in each hand, shot and killed every target guarding the halls and entryway.

While the slaughter was under way, Weaver and Anderson worked as a team to position timers in corners of the house and set them to go off within fifteen minutes of their expected departure time.

The entire operation, from entry to the team meeting in the main hall, had taken less than twenty minutes.

"Strip the hard drives," Burke said. "Go through the printed material and take anything that catches your eye."

"What about the phones?" Anderson asked. "In this room and the others, I counted at least thirty."

"Match them with our list of existing cells," Burke said. "Take the ones not on the list."

Pierce pulled six folded-up duffel bags from his pack and slapped them open on the marble floor. "Fill these with the weapons you find," he said. "We leave nothing behind but bodies."

"And do it fast," Burke said. "Timers are set to go off in less than ten minutes, and it would suck for us to be here when that happened."

Malasson sat on a foldout chair scrolling through a computer screen when she stopped and reached for a cell phone resting close to the monitor. She scrolled through the phone numbers listed under contacts until she settled on one. She stared at the number for a few seconds and then said, "Burke, I need you to come look at this."

Burke stepped over a dead terrorist and handed an armful of

weapons to Kinder. He stood over Malasson's shoulder and peered down at the cell phone.

"What am I looking at?" he asked.

"You tell me," Malasson said.

Burke surveyed the list of phone numbers and stopped at the one he recognized, the one he had burned into his memory and called only four times since he was given access to it. "Take this with you," he said, handing the cell phone back to Malasson. "When we get back, we need to find out all the calls that number generated and all the ones it received. Get the Greek to help you."

"Do I tell him why?"

"You won't need to tell him," Burke said.

Burke turned from Malasson and shouted to the rest of the group, "Load up and let's get out of here. We have less than four minutes to get to the truck."

The Silent Six zipped the heavy duffel bags stuffed with weapons, ammo, scrawled notes, and ledger folders, tossed them across their shoulders and walked quietly and quickly out of a palazzo built to withstand the test of time but not the blast of a dozen high-end explosives.

They were in the van, Kinder behind the wheel switching gears, careening down a narrow side street, when the explosion lit up the night sky, shattering windows a mile in each direction, setting off car alarms and smoke detectors. The blast was so intense it forced the van to tilt to one side. Kinder held tight to the wheel and veered the car north, toward the highway that would lead them out of the center of Florence.

They left behind sixteen dead followers of Raza and a ruined palazzo. Sitting in the front seat across from Kinder, Burke was lost in thought, content with the success of the mission, conflicted over the troubling information found at the scene. He gazed at the scenery whizzing past and a morning sun that still lay hidden, not yet ready to greet a new day. He pulled a cell phone from the front flap of his flak jacket, held it for a moment and then pressed down on a number.

....

I PICKED UP on the second ring.

"Package gift-wrapped and paid for," Burke said.

"Good," I said. "Everyone get out before the store closed?"

"With time to spare," Burke said.

"All good then," I said, and was about to end the call.

"Not all," Burke said.

I paused and sat back in my chair. "I'm still here," I said.

"There is one problem."

"What kind of problem?" I asked.

"It's an internal," Burke said.

"How close?"

"Not sure yet," Burke said. "But close is bad enough."

I put the phone down and rested it on a coffee table to my left. I leaned my head against a thick pillow, my left arm bandaged and sore from the bullet wound. I stared out into the garden of Angela's villa, alone in her guest room, and knew I had more to deal with than Raza and his cell or Vladimir and his Russian crew.

I knew now the traitor was in my camp.

38.

Rome, Italy

Raza watched as two of his men duct-taped Santos to a steam pipe against the far wall of the cramped basement.

"My people get wind of this shit, you are going to get a taste of serious trouble," Santos said to Raza. "There's no need for this. You want something from me, you ask. You don't tape me to no damn pipe."

"You have no people," Raza said. "You're just a gunrunner and I can find one on any corner, in any city."

"Maybe, maybe not," Santos said, still not certain what Raza wanted and what information he had on him.

"I trusted you," Raza said.

"I never burned you, Raza," Santos said. "The deliveries were always on time and merchandise was top of the line as promised. If this is about your team getting wiped out the other night, that's not on me. That's bad luck on your part."

"You weren't there," Raza said. "But that doesn't mean you didn't have anything to do with what happened."

"I don't know what you're talking about."

"Let me refresh you, then," Raza said, "and see if I can help you remember."

Raza walked over to a small wooden table, picked up a shearing knife and held it in his right hand, blade first, running his fingers along the serrated edges. "You know the man who killed my men and stole the weapons I bought from you," he said to Santos, speaking without looking at him, his eyes focused on the knife in his hand. "You might even know some of the people who work for him."

"I know who he is," Santos said. "I wouldn't be any good in my line of work if I didn't. But I know who all the bosses of the syndicates are. It's a part of my business to know my business."

"You would do anything for money," Raza said. "I knew that when I started to work with you. I didn't think you would betray someone for a payoff. But then that mistake is on me."

Santos didn't respond. He stared at Raza, still with the shearing knife in his hand, and knew he had been outed as a snitch. He also knew there was nothing he could offer Raza—no weapons, no information, no amount of money—that would allow him to walk free and clear from that stifling hot basement.

Santos knew he was going to die today.

"I took a gamble," Santos said. "The Wolf had me in a corner, like you do now. When you're stuck in the middle, you got no choice but play both ends, and that's what I did. I fed you guns and I fed them info about the guns and I got money in both hands. It was the best deal I could make for myself and I took it. So would you."

"I doubt it," Raza said.

"You say that because you never been there," Santos said. "If you got any luck at all, you won't ever be. Now, I may have told them when your shipments were due and what was in your buy, but I never told them about any safe house and there's a good reason for that."

"Which is?"

"I don't know about your safe houses," Santos said. "You never told me and I never asked. It was never a part of our deal. So you can find fault for me tipping off the Wolf about our deals. But that wipeout the other night? That's not on me. That's on one of your people."

Raza stepped up closer to Santos and slapped him across the face with the back of his free hand. "There are no traitors in my group," he said.

Santos smiled, a tear running down the side of his face, his cheek red from the blow. "Baby, everybody's a traitor."

Raza glared at Santos. "A traitor dies a horrible death," he said. "It's deserved and it sends a signal. I might even send whatever's left of your body to the Wolf. Show what happens when he sends a turncoat into my camp."

Santos let out a loud laugh. "You think he gives a shit what happens to me?" he asked. "And what do you think he's going to do when they show him chunks of my body? Run and hide? Men like him? Like me? We come into this life knowing what the end of the road looks like and that don't scare us. And guys like you scare us even less. The Wolf's a gangster. You're a punk. A whole world of difference."

Raza held the wooden end of the shearing knife and plunged the blade deep into the center of Santos's stomach. He held it there, looking into the older man's eyes, waiting for the first signs of the death tremble, feeling the warm blood flowing over his hand and wrist. Raza moved the knife up, cutting through tissue and veins, seeing Santos's eyes roll back and blood form at the corners of his mouth. He released his grip on the knife, stepped away from the pool of blood forming around his feet and nodded toward the two young men hovering in a corner of the basement. "Have him bleed out," Raza said, "and then torch the body. It will be as if he never even existed."

**39.**

New York City

"How long have you known?" I asked.

"About a week, give or take," Big Mike said.

We were sitting at the bar of a restaurant in downtown Manhattan. We had the place to ourselves, the lunch staff not due in for work for at least another hour.

"But you waited until now to tell me," I said.

"I needed to be certain, Vincent," Big Mike said. "I needed to be one hundred percent nailed down sure on this before I brought it in."

"How did you track the calls to him?"

"It wasn't easy," Big Mike said. "He's good; always has been. Almost as good as I am. Bad for him that almost doesn't cut it. His biggest mistake was thinking no one would be looking in his direction."

"There any way this could be a setup?" I asked. "Have us look inside our house while it's someone else doing the dirty work?"

"I was hoping it would fall that way as well," Big Mike said. "Had it double- and triple-checked. There is no one else. Jimmy is Vladimir's inside man."

The news had devastated me. I had difficulty coming to terms with it on so many levels, from the personal to the professional. At first glance it was a senseless and foolish move, even a cruel one, knowing what had recently happened to my family. Acts of betrayal are common in my line of work and expected. I was never so naive as to think it could not happen to me and was always on the lookout for any sign someone had his eye on more than just my back.

But I never thought it would come from Jimmy.

He was my closest confidant, the one I went to with my doubts, concerns, fears, and he was always ready to give me sage, sound, and comforting advice. If there was anyone who knew my secrets, who could discern my motives and anticipate my actions, it was the brilliant young man confined to life in a wheelchair.

And then there was Jack, who Jimmy had been watching. Jimmy's betrayal endangered my son's life.

"What are you going to do?" Big Mike asked.

"I don't know," I said. "For the first time since I've been doing this, I don't know."

"You can't let this sit," Big Mike said. "And you can't let the fact the traitor is family stand in the way."

"There's more to it than that," I said.

"Only if you let there be," Big Mike said. "Tell me something. If it were me instead of Jimmy that had betrayed you, would you be this unsure of what to do?"

I shook my head. "No," I said. "You would be taken care of, no doubt. I wouldn't like it, but that wouldn't stop me from doing it."

"And Jimmy's different why?" Big Mike asked. "Because of his condition? Because you like to think the two of you are brothers? All that's out the window now, Vincent. You got a traitor, and that traitor is on the inside as close as close is. He is a risk to the entire operation. And to you, to the Strega, to me, and most important of all, to Jack."

"You think Jimmy would let harm come to Jack?" I said.

"To my way of thinking, he already has," Big Mike said. "Your enemies have access now, the kind they could never get without an inside connection."

"What about what happened on the plane?" I asked, barely able to get the words out. "Was he part of that plan?"

"Very unlikely," Big Mike said. "It was the first thing I had checked, and so far he comes up clean in that regard. In all likelihood, Jimmy made the flip sometime this summer, a week, maybe two after we had the council meeting."

"Is there any way we can make use of Jimmy?" I asked. "At least until I get a handle on how to deal with the situation."

"Give me a for instance."

"What if we tell Jimmy we know where Raza is planning to hit, that he may even be thinking of a double attack?" I said. "That we're on to him and we're going to make a move."

"And he relays that info to Vladimir's crew, who then pass it on to Raza," Big Mike said. "That happens, what does it do for us?"

"One of two things, if it works," I said. "We may pick up chatter about their actual plans, which will point us in the right direction."

"Or?"

"Or they rush the plan," I said. "Move up the date and put their pieces in motion at a faster clip. And from their movements we can pinpoint the attack sites."

"Could work," Big Mike said. "I'll rig it so Jimmy will never get wise he's being tapped incoming and out. But like I said, he's good at this and a lot smarter than any of the guys on the other end of his relay. We've been on him for about a week, light touches mostly, not enough for him to pick up a trace. But with a full 24/7 it won't be long before a guy like Jimmy figures he's being monitored."

"Will he be able to tell who's doing it?"

"He won't need to," Big Mike said. "We'll be his only suspects."

I sat quietly for a few minutes and then walked from the front of the bar toward a large coffee machine. I looked over at Big Mike, who seemed as crushed as I was by the news. He caught the look and shook his head. "I'll buy as much time as I can," he said. "But I don't think I can run it for more than another week before he catches on."

"That's enough time," I said.

"This is really going to shake your uncle," Big Mike said. "Old school mob like him do not take this kind of news well. My father was cut the same way. They don't care who it is or why they did it or how sorry they are. You betray the family, you're no longer part of the family. You're gone."

"Have you been monitoring the old man's phones?"

"Never had reason to," Big Mike said. He seemed taken aback by the hard shift in my tone. "We weren't looking Jimmy's way, either. He just fell into our laps."

"Who initiated contact with the Russians?" I asked.

"I have to go deeper into Jimmy's phone logs to answer that and it might not even be there," Big Mike said. "There's really no way to tell. I had to guess, I would put it on Vladimir. I doubt very much Jimmy, no matter his intent, would reach out to the Russian mob."

"How does he communicate with them?" I asked. "They can talk to him, but how does he respond?"

"The calls are always from the Russian end," Big Mike said. "Jimmy answers either by coded text or through an audio relay patched in through his laptop. Perfect inside man if you think about it—guy who can't speak. Who would ever suspect?"

"I should have," I said.

"You want to give a heads-up to the Strega?" Big Mike asked. "She's been on the money with us. And not only is she close to Jimmy, she trusts him. Up to today we all did."

"Let's leave everything the way it is," I said. "I'll deal with Jimmy when I have to. Maybe there's more to this than a clear betrayal. Or maybe I just would like to think there is."

"You mean he's working Vladimir?"

"Something like that," I said. "You said it yourself—Jimmy is very smart and I don't give him much to do, other than look after my son and run the computer end of the business. Maybe this is his way of showing us he can be a bigger help. He sees us focused on Raza and his cell. He also knows that other than the Strega, none of the syndicates are stepping into this in a big way. They're letting it play out, see who's still standing once the smoke clears."

"So he pretends to do a flip?" Big Mike said.

"I'm not saying that's what it is," I said. "All I'm saying is that is what it could be."

"Which is why we wait," Big Mike said.

"Exactly," I said. "If I'm going to have to dust Jimmy, I have to be sure that he's a traitor instead of somebody who's looking out for me and the family."

"Which of those two you really think it is?" Big Mike asked.

"I wish to hell I knew," I said.

40.

Vatican City, Italy

"This is the room where the cardinals gather when they need to choose a new Pope," Raza said, gazing up at Michelangelo's massive and stunning work, *The Last Judgment*. "The smoke they show on television? It goes through a tube in the rear of the room. If it's brown, they have yet to decide. If it's white, there's a new man in charge."

"The guidebook says they sit in these wooden chairs along the walls and discuss the possible choices," Avrim said. "Hard for me to believe it's all done in such a civil way."

"That's because it isn't," Raza said. "It's all corruption and deal-making and back door agreements. Religion plays no role in the selection of a Pope. It's a business like any other."

"It is an impressive room," Avrim said, staring now at the massive ceiling filled with the beauty of Michelangelo's *Creation*. "I've been here on five, maybe six occasions and it never fails to move me."

"The artist has little to do with the religion," Raza said. "In his own way, Michelangelo was a rebel. They all were—Raphael, Da Vinci, Caravaggio."

"Yet, look at the work," Avrim said. "It's as spiritual as any I've seen. They must have had some degree of faith to agree to such undertakings."

"They had faith in their talents," Raza said. "Their true beliefs rested in their skills. They ignored all who dared question the work and had contempt for the mildest of criticism. They wanted nothing from their patrons other than the funds needed to complete their work. In many ways, they were no different than the two of us in league with the Russian. I don't value his opinion. I don't seek his counsel. All that concerns me is that the money keeps flowing in and he helps keep as many of our men safe as possible until our mission is complete."

The enormous Sistine Chapel was packed wall-to-wall with tourists, as it is most days of the year. Vatican guards walked among the crowd asking for silence and looking to prevent photos being taken with flash lighting. The art in the chapel, originally commissioned by Pope Julius II, took up every inch of the third level in the room.

Avrim stared at each of the frescoes that lined the walls along the second tier, overcome by the sheer majesty of the work. "I know you don't want to hear this, but I feel I must say it," he said to Raza.

Raza looked away from *The Last Judgment* and gazed over at him. "I'm listening," he said.

"I wish you had chosen other targets," Avrim said, hesitant even to speak the words. "A government building, perhaps, or a bridge, a tunnel, a harbor. It seems wrong to destroy something that comes this close to perfection."

"I know," Raza said, "and that's why they are perfect choices. Their destruction will be an emotional blow of epic proportions. Look at these people, lost in wonder and useless prayer, gazing at the work as if the figures on the walls were real and could walk among them. To have such an effect on so many speaks to the power of a great artist. And that's exactly what I will be doing, only in reverse. I will strip them of this perfection, tear away their dream, rip apart their beliefs. After this mission is completed and the sites are brought to ruin, people will be left with nothing but memories. And when they think of Michelangelo or even mention his name, they will have to think of me and mention mine. For I will be forever linked with the Divine One."

"You once thought yourself an artist," Avrim said, uncertain if he should push the conversation further. "You had the talent to be one."

"I *am* an artist, Avrim," Raza said.

"We are on a path of destruction," Avrim said, speaking freely now, no longer concerned with the consequences that could result from such an act of defiance. "We do not create anything other than bombs fools like me strap on because of their belief in people like you. We go out and destroy and are hated for it."

"You do not yet understand the importance of our task," Raza said. "And perhaps you will die never knowing. That would be a shame, since what we do is not for glory or gold. We ask only to be allowed to live our lives on our own soil and worship in our own fashion. We have never declared war on anyone. But war is always declared on us. And you are correct when you say we are hated because of the destruction we caused. But we are also feared, and I would much rather people tremble in my presence than find comfort in it."

"If these missions prove successful, we will be more than hated," Avrim said. "We will be despised until the end of days."

"All the more reason to pray for their success," Raza said, smiling. "For if I am to be judged, let it be by my enemies."

Avrim lowered his head. Then he looked up and stared at the work, relishing each second of pleasure.

41.

New York City

Big Mike Paleokrassas, the fisherman's grandson who grew up to be one of the brightest stars in the criminal universe, got behind the wheel of a remodeled and refurbished 1967 black Mustang, eight cylinders of pure power, built for speed and comfort, and laid his head back against the plush headrest. He had wanted such a car since he first saw the movie *Bullitt* with Steve McQueen on his tenth birthday, a VHS gift from his father who handed down his love of fast cars to his son. He had to wait eleven years until he found the one he wanted. It was beaten down, engine run to the ground, body ruined by weather and age, but Big Mike knew it was the one, and he took the time and the money needed to restore it to its full glory. As he rose through the ranks of the Greek syndicate, he collected a number of other cars, all copies of those he had seen on a movie screen. These were Big Mike's real loves—cars and movies.

"If I had a chance to do it over again," he once told me over the course of a long dinner at his summer home outside Athens, "I would get on a plane and head straight for Los Angeles. Work in the movie business, and not from our end of it—shakedowns, budget shuffles, blackmail, protection—I mean just make movies."

"Why didn't you?" I asked. "I doubt your father would have stopped you. I never got the sense from him he was that keen on you going into the family business. You could have made the move."

"I was thinking about it," Big Mike said. "Then he got sick and it seemed like every Greek I ever met wanted a piece of his action, and he wasn't even dead yet. He had built it all from nothing, Vincent. I couldn't walk away and let it fall into the hands of people who had no business running his business."

"Any regrets?"

"Everybody has regrets," Big Mike said. "Part of life, I suppose. I may not have lived out my dream but I kept my father's dream alive. We're not a big outfit, can't even compare us to your crew, the Yakuza, the Triads, and forget about the Russians. But we've earned our seat at the table and nobody makes any moves on our turf. We're never under anybody's scope and that's a good thing, a very good thing for a criminal organization. I don't have the pressure on me that you do on a day-to-day. I can't imagine this is how you pictured your life turning out."

"If my parents had lived, the results would have been different," I said. "My father, especially. Now, he loved my Uncle Carlo, looked up to him and respected him, but truth is he hated what he did for a living. My dad was a hard worker who put in long hours every day for not a lot of money. Guys like that don't care much for gangsters."

"I figured you for law school," Big Mike said. "You got the head for it and the mind-set. I would have hired you."

I smiled and shook my head. "I don't think so," I said, "though I wouldn't mind the billing hours. And they call us thieves. No, medicine would have been the way for me. I was always interested in it, even more so after my mom got sick."

"Dr. Wolf," Big Mike said, laughing. "Has a nice ring to it."

"Who the hell are we kidding?" I said. "We were born to be gang-sters. I would have sucked as a doctor and you would have made those movies that go right to DVD without sniffing the inside of a movie theater, and we would both have been miserable."

BIG MIKE WAS on the top floor of a midtown park and lock garage. He looked out at the opening between two thick concrete beams and could see a hard rain begin to fall. He also noticed a second car parked in the large space, big enough to fit eighty to a floor. He didn't need to look long to catch the make and model of the sedan and see it for what it was, a car on his tail. The windows were up and tinted, so he couldn't tell how many were in the car, though he fig-ured it to be a driver and three shooters.

The car hadn't been there when he had parked his Mustang two hours earlier, prior to his meeting with John Loo and members of his surveillance team, who were getting an update on Raza's where-abouts and the killing of Santos. He rubbed his eyes, reached for a pack of gum in the glove compartment and rolled three slices of pep-permint Wrigley's into his mouth. He then slipped on a pair of thin black leather gloves and checked his rear- and sideview mirrors. He turned the ignition key and smiled when he heard the eight-cylinder 427 cubics of power he had installed kick over, the inside of the car doing a slow tremble. He turned and saw the driver of the sedan start the late model Mercedes and let it idle, thin puffs of white smoke coming out of the rear dual exhaust. Big Mike figured he could out-drive the shooters, the swerving incline out of the seven-story struc-ture working more to his favor. He knew, however, he couldn't outgun them. "Well, Bessie," Big Mike said, addressing the car by the nick-name his father had given it when he first saw the then-damaged wreck his son craved, "I always knew you were better than any Benz. Time to prove it."

Big Mike released the brake and shifted the car into reverse, its front end now facing the Mercedes. He shifted into first and drove toward the winding incline leading out of the seventh floor, the sedan following him out. As he neared the incline, he switched into second, hit the gas heavy and gripped the steering wheel tighter, moving fast down the thin concrete passageway, careful to avoid the double iron railings on one side and the solid cement wall on the other. The sedan was fast behind him, tinted windows now rolled down, three of the passengers tucking their arms out of the car, semiautomatic guns in hand.

The left rear bumper of Big Mike's Mustang bounced against an iron rail as he swerved onto the sixth-floor curve heading down to the next flight. One of the gunmen's bullets shattered a taillight and a second knocked loose the passenger side mirror. Big Mike shifted from second to first as his front end scraped against the cement wall, leaving a stream of sparks in its wake. The sedan was closing in, its tires squealing against the pull of the curves, the driver choosing to lurch closer to the wall and avoid contact with the railings.

Big Mike's Mustang jumped off the landing onto the fifth floor and he swerved it away from the next incline and maneuvered around forty cars parked throughout the space. He checked his mirror and saw the sedan was on his trail, the gunmen hailing bullets his way at a faster, steadier clip. One bullet shattered his back window while another volley tore through the leather upholstery, shredding the seats open as if sliced by a knife.

One bullet found its intended target.

Big Mike looked down and saw blood oozing out of a small smoking hole on the left side of his stomach and dripping onto the black mat by his feet. His left leg was turning numb and the burn from the wound caused his eyes to sting. He swung the car around the back end of a white van with out-of-state plates and then slammed on the brakes and carefully guided the Mustang as it did a 180-degree turn to face the oncoming Mercedes, a fuselage of bullets slamming in his direction. Four of the shots cracked the front end, causing a stream of dark smoke to snake its way through the hood.

Big Mike shifted easily into third gear, feeling the power of the engine come to life, less than twenty feet from the advancing sedan. He knew that if he lost the chicken game and crashed into the Mercedes, he would not survive the hit. He had no driver air bags and had not even bothered to put on his seat belt. His only chance would be if the driver of the sedan blinked and backed off.

Through the pain in his side and the smoke limiting his vision, he caught the eye of the driver behind the wheel of the Mercedes and smiled. "He's scared of you, Bessie," Big Mike said, "as fucking well he should be."

The Mercedes hit the brakes and swung away from the Mustang inches before a crash could occur. The sedan skidded to a stop against the open side of the fifth floor, a two-foot concrete embankment the only separation. One of the gunmen jumped out of the car, a gun in each hand, and poured bullets into the Mustang. One of the slugs clipped Big Mike in the left shoulder and a second nicked his right elbow. He ignored the blood and the pain, jammed the gear shaft into fourth and slammed his foot down on the gas pedal, heading straight for the center of the sedan.

The crash was sudden and loud, killing the crouching gunman instantly, his body wedged between squealing tires and crushed steel. The blow from the Mustang toppled the Mercedes over the concrete barrier, floating it out into the heavy rain as it crashed into the alley below, landing hood first, tires popping, gas tank exploding, smoke engulfing the front and rear, flames emerging out of the engine.

The three men inside dead.

Big Mike's Mustang was left dangling, the front half hanging over the edge of the barrier, the rear still on solid ground. The car was smashed and riddled with bullet holes, the rubber on its tires down to bare thread, smoke pouring out of the engine, the top of the Mustang torn off and resting against the far side of a wall.

Big Mike's head and chest rested on a bed of glass on the front hood of the tottering car. His body was soaked in blood and only one eye was open. He took in slow, shallow breaths, each one as painful as a hard punch. A heavy rain fell on his head and back.

He took a deep breath, patted the hood of the car as if in congratulations, and then he was gone.

42.

East Hampton, New York

"What was the promise?" I asked Jimmy. "What could they have offered that would make you turn your back on your family and on me?"

Jimmy stared at me, his body still as stone. We were in the library of the big house by the beach, surrounded by floor-to-ceiling bookcases filled with everything from the classics to the newest thrillers. In the center of the large room were two large oak tables, surrounded by several handcrafted wooden chairs. On top of each table was a chessboard—one filled with pieces carved from characters taken from Sherlock Holmes stories, the other made up of Italian medieval knights prepped for battle. Jimmy and I had spent many hours in this room with the large picture window looking out at the ocean waves a half mile away. We read, we played endless games of chess, and we talked for hours on end as I learned to communicate with a disabled boy I had come to think of as a brother.

"You want me to answer for you?" I asked. "Because I think I know what drove you to do what you did. It had nothing to do with Vladimir or Raza. It wasn't about any concerns you might have had about the war or anything to do with your family. It was none of that. It was about me. It's always been about me."

I stepped away from the thick wooden chair I had been standing behind and moved closer toward the open double doors leading out of the room and into the lush garden. I stood next to Jimmy's wheelchair, my hands in my pockets, and stared out at the beach, crowded at this early morning hour with dogs running in and out of the water, chasing tennis balls and Frisbees tossed to them by their owners.

"I get it," I said. "I took the one thing you wanted but could never ask for—control of the family. It was your birthright. It belonged to you, not me. You went along with it, pretended all these years it didn't matter to you which of us was in charge, that all you wanted to do was be heard, your advice given weight, your counsel sought. But all along you wanted to be seated at the head of the table, and I was the one who stood in the way."

Jimmy looked up at me and there were tears welling in his eyes mixed with a harsh glare of anger. His upper body trembled slightly and his hands gripped the leather folds of his wheelchair. "It wasn't my decision," I said, as much to myself as to him. "Your father is the one who made the choice. Right or wrong, it's his call. If I had turned him down, he would have gone to someone else, from here or from Italy, didn't matter. It would never have been you, as much as he wished it could have been. I think we both knew how it was going to play out from the first day I came to live with you. And now I wonder if you planned to betray me from the start, sitting back, waiting for the right opportunity to come along. And then Vladimir comes through with the offer you always wanted—me out of the way."

Jimmy shook his head from side to side, shifting the wheelchair with his sudden movements. I moved away from the window, leaned down and pressed my hands against his chest, my face mere inches from his. "You were willing to let me die to get what you wanted," I said in a low voice. "That part I can understand. In your place, I might have done the same. But my family, Jimmy. Lisa, Paula, Sandy were murdered, and I need to know and I need to know now and believe it when I hear it—did you have anything to do with what happened on that plane?"

Jimmy's eyes widened in horror and he nearly bolted free of his wheelchair, his hands clutching my arms tight enough to cause a bruise, his head shaking violently, his eyes filled with a sadness that gave weight to the pain he felt at their death.

I released his firm grip and stepped back. "I always felt you loved them as much as I did," I said. "Glad to see that part still holds."

I know the penalty for betrayal. Under any other circumstance it would have been an easy call to make, and one that would not have bothered me in the least. I've made such decisions many times in the past, and never have I regretted the actions taken. But now, for the first time since I was anointed the head of our syndicate, I was weighed down with indecision. I loved Jimmy and knew that despite his act of treason he loved me, and I had so few left in my life to love that to lose one more could prove an unbearable weight.

But to let what Jimmy had done pass without recourse or penalty would be a risk as well as a potentially devastating mistake. Once word got out, it would weaken my position in the eyes of the other crime bosses at a time when I needed a tight hold on their respect.

I was not the first to be betrayed by someone within his inner circle, and I would not be the last. In my position, you always brace for such an action, anticipate it, look to prevent it before it happens, often predict who it will be and monitor that suspect until he does indeed make the move. I did that with everyone in my group but never thought to look Jimmy's way. I didn't doubt there was a level of resentment on his part toward me, not only in superseding him as crime boss but winning over the affections of his father. But I was dissuaded by Jimmy's kindness to my own family and by the brave and noble way he handled the harsh reality he faced each day, refusing to be confined by illness and disease, never becoming a slave to his condition, and building a life when the easy option would have been to be dependent and bitter.

Jimmy reached for his notepad and scrawled a note, tore the sheet off the binder and handed it to me. I took it, read what he had written, and handed it back to him.

"It's not that easy," I said. "You know that as well as I do. There's only two ways this can go. I give you a pass on what you did, ask for your word that it won't happen again, and leave here believing you will stick to your promise. The other option and the safer one is to have you taken away and killed. Just as I would any other traitor."

Jimmy scrawled another note, this time choosing his words with care, taking his time. He held the pen in one hand and gave me the notepad with the other. I read his words and looked at him and nodded.

"Is that really what you want?" I asked.

Jimmy's look answered my question.

"Is it because you want me to do it or because you don't think I can?" I asked.

Jimmy smiled for the first time that day and made a gesture with his hands.

"It's going to be hard to live with no matter who it is kills you, me or someone in the crew," I said. "You're the one that gets off easy on this, not me."

"Nobody gets off easy." Uncle Carlo's still strong voice, shielding a weakening body, came at us from the rear of the room, near the double-oak door that led into it. "Not on something like this. In here, the three of us are victims."

I had yet to tell Uncle Carlo the harsh truth about his son.

I had wanted to talk to Jimmy first and then sort the entire affair out in my mind before I went to deliver the news. But I should have know an old school crime boss like Uncle Carlo has eyes and ears in all the places they're needed.

Uncle Carlo walked across the room, his pace slowed by a troublesome right hip. He stopped when he reached Jimmy's wheelchair and hovered over his son, his eyes filled with an anger I had not seen in all the years I lived under his roof. He lifted a still powerful right hand, leaned over and slapped his son across the face, the blow so hard and so unexpected it caused the wheelchair to lurch. Jimmy, his right cheek now beet red, stared up at his father and shook his head, tears streaming down his face.

"Yeah, I'm sorry, too," Uncle Carlo said. "But guess what? In our business, in our life, sorry doesn't count for shit. It's what you do, it's what you say, it's how you act that matters. The rest is all for show."

"He didn't tip them off to anything major," I said, feeling I had to say something in Jimmy's defense. Despite his actions, I hated seeing him cowering and defenseless in front of his father. "Just general information that the Russian probably already knew."

"I don't give a shit if all he gave them was a weather update," Uncle Carlo said. "It doesn't change what he did. A betrayal is that, no matter what one side tells the other."

Uncle Carlo looked down at his son, glaring into his eyes. "You might understand how to work computers and the rest of the technological crap that's used today, but you never took the time to understand who the hell we really are and how we do the things we do. That's why I passed you over and chose Vincent to run the organization. Not because you were in a wheelchair. You're smart enough and tough enough to figure out ways to overcome that, and you might have been able to take our syndicate in the same direction Vincent has. But your feel for our history would have made you a weak boss, and I don't need further proof of that other than your act of betrayal."

Jimmy could only stare back and nod in agreement.

"Here's what I'm guessing is the line of shit they sold and you bought with your eyes wide open," Uncle Carlo said. "That the Russians would steer clear of the terror business if we cut them in on some of our action. And they would let you broker that arrangement. Which would make you a player. You, a kid in a wheelchair, helps broker a peace and bring an end to a war without speaking a single word. After that happens, how could I not make you a boss? Did I land close to the truth?"

Jimmy lowered his head and nodded.

"Now," Uncle Carlo said, "someone needs to die for what you did, and it is the boss of the family who is the only one who can order someone to be killed. Am I right, Vincent?"

"That's right," I said.

"I handed the reins over to Vincent, let him run things for the organization while I moved back a few feet," Uncle Carlo said. "But no mistake, I'm still the official boss of this outfit and will be until the day they toss dirt on me. Either one of you feel different on that score?"

I had a gut feeling as to where all this was going and was tempted to step in and see if I could bring it to a stop, but I knew Uncle Carlo, and no words were going to bring about a shift in his thinking. He had made up his mind long before he walked into the library and was set on seeing it through.

"The betrayal happened under my watch," Uncle Carlo said. "Hell, it happened with me in the same damn house and I didn't come close to smelling it out. That tells me I'm losing my touch. There was a time I could smell a flip across the ocean, now I can't even sniff it when it happens down the hall from my bedroom. You look at it that way, then I'm as guilty as Jimmy. I may not have connected with the Russians or whoever the hell he slid information to but I didn't do anything to stop it, either. Now since somebody's going to go down for this, then that somebody had better be me."

Jimmy shook his head and nearly bolted out of his chair, straining to reach his father, hands shaking, veins in his neck bulging.

"I'm the boss and I decide who lives and who dies," Uncle Carlo said. "But there's something I want in return from you for my death, and you better damn well give it to me."

Jimmy jabbed his right hand into his chest, his eyes stained with tears, willing his father to change his mind.

"Yes it was you," Uncle Carlo said. He was calm now, no need for him to display any show of anger, his words all the force he needed to make his position known. "And you're going to make it right. My death will settle the score with Vincent. But in return, I want your word, Jimmy, that you will never do anything to bring shame to this organization again. It's something I helped to build, and I will never

allow anyone, blood or otherwise, to do anything to cause it harm. So
I want your word. Your word as my son, as a man, and as a member of
this syndicate, that you will always treat what I made strong with the
respect and honor it deserves. You think you have guts enough to
give me that?"

Jimmy struggled to gain his composure, taking slow and deep
breaths, ignoring the cold sweat forming across his brow, his dark
hair wet and matted to his forehead. He cast a glance in my direction
and I looked away. I felt like an intruder on an intense father and son
conversation. Though I played a key role in the outcome of the dis-
pute, for the first time since I came to live with them I was an ob-
server and had little say about how the situation would be resolved.

After a time, Jimmy nodded.

Jimmy and I both realized that when Uncle Carlo made a decision, there was nothing that could be done or said to change his
mind. He had lived by gut and instincts all this time, surviving in a
business where only the toughest and hardest of the bunch are left
standing, and he was not about to alter his ways, especially not now,
in the face of a betrayal.

"It's settled, then," Uncle Carlo said. "Now the both of you can set
aside your differences and keep them buried. You have each other,
and you have a war to fight, one you need to win, and you'll need
each other to do it. It won't work any other way."

He looked at Jimmy and then at me. "I love you both," he said.

"There anything you want me to do?" I asked.

"You know that spot on the hill, the one just past the house?" he
asked. "The place we used to go when you were kids, sneak some
wine past Jimmy's nurses and sit and look at the ocean?"

"It's where you used to tell us stories about the start of the Camorra
and the Mafia," I said, my mind flashing back on those simpler days
that now seemed so deep in the past. "And taught us the difference
between Fernet Branca and Averna."

"That's the spot where I want you to bury me," Uncle Carlo said.
"Facing the smell and sound of the ocean. That's the best place to
end up for an old hood like me."

He reached over and grabbed each of our hands and held them tight, his grip still coal miner strong. "Those were happy times, just the three of us, talking, laughing, our own special place," he said. "But here now, today, seeing the two of you together, is the way I meant for it to be. And that's the memory I'll take with me."

Uncle Carlo looked at each of us one final time and then let go of our hands and turned to walk out of the room. Jimmy and I stayed silent as he crossed the oak wood floor in bare feet. He opened the library door and closed it softly behind him, never turning to look back.

Carlo Marelli, an organized crime boss for more than half a century, was gone, off to die the death of a warrior.

43.

I sat on the empty beach and stared at the angry waves pounding the surf. There was a full moon overhead, and behind me the lights of a dozen houses reflected across the vastness of a dark ocean. I took a drink from a bottle of Bordeaux and wedged the bottle in the sand next to me. The last few days had been long and tragic ones, and the weight of them felt heavy on my shoulders.

The death of Big Mike hit me hard.

He was a true friend and there are few of those in my line of work. He was also a trusted ally and good at what he did. I was proud of the way he died, going down gangster hard, taking every shooter with him, behind the wheel of that car he loved so much. I would miss his comforting presence, his no-nonsense approach to business, and his dedication to be the best at what he did. We shared a lot across a short span of years, good and bad, but as with most things in the crime world, it all ended sooner than either one of us would have liked.

And that end is always bloodstained.

There's a part of me that wonders how much Jimmy had to do with helping the Russians orchestrate the setup that killed Big Mike. I have not asked him to spell out the information he fed to the Russians, nor will I. That's for him to either tell me or keep to himself. I gave Uncle Carlo my word I would work together with Jimmy and fight this war I started with him by my side. But how can I ever trust him again, trust him the way I did Big Mike or my Silent Six or even Angela, as deadly and as treacherous as she can be? And how can I know Jack will be safe under his care, believe he would not do anything that would put my son's life in jeopardy? I know what Jimmy did was out of anger and jealousy, but it was a move made against me and it led to Uncle Carlo's death, and that's a truth that is difficult to bury. It will always be there between us.

I will always love Jimmy. But there will be a barrier that will keep us apart, and one I need to ensure is never breached. Jimmy proved to be weak, and it had nothing to do with his disability but with his character. I don't know how long the bitterness he felt toward me lingered before he acted on it, and I have no way of knowing if Uncle Carlo's death washed away all remnants of it or further fortified it.

But I would take no chances. Jimmy's every move would be monitored. He would be given no access to computer or phone. He would be left isolated and alone. And his future would rest now in my hands.

Uncle Carlo's decision to sacrifice his life so his son could live was much more than an act of courage by a tough, brave old man in the homestretch of his days. It was also a direct link to our criminal history. For centuries the heads of families have made the critical decision of whose life would be taken and whose spared. But no indiscretion can be left unpunished, especially one so egregious as a betrayal by a member of the family. Under those circumstances, a crime boss can offer a life sacrificed in return for a life saved. I had heard stories of crime bosses taking their own lives in place of that of a brother, a daughter, and even a wife. In return, the survivor swears fealty to the organization for the rest of his days, working closely with the new head of the crew.

I respected such traditions and was in awe of the men who had the courage to give up their own lives as payment for the treachery or indiscretions of either blood relatives or trusted criminal partners. I'm not certain I would have the bravery to make such a move. I doubt very much I would have spared Jimmy's life as the price for mine. But then again, I would not hesitate to do for Jack what Uncle Carlo did for his only son, but that's a price any father, regardless of occupation, would readily agree on. Part of my reluctance may rest in the fact that I was not born into the criminal life like Uncle Carlo. I fell into it through circumstances beyond my control. Maybe, in some respects, that allows me to look at it from a different perspective and also makes me a more effective crime boss.

But right now, gazing out at loud, aggressive waves slamming against a white sandy beach, I knew I had been weakened in my battle against Valdimir and Raza. The deaths of Big Mike and Uncle Carlo stripped me of a powerful partner and a valued advisor, and those are deeper losses to sustain than any on-the-field casualties. I would miss their skill and counsel. My position had been weakened just as I was about to venture into unknown zones where the difference between success and defeat came down to who had the more precise information and was better prepared for any eventuality. "Go in with your best and be prepared to do your worst," Uncle Carlo had told me in the days leading up to the last skirmish we fought together, against a rogue faction of our organization. "And leave behind no prisoners. They have memories, and that will only lead to more battles down the road."

I still had Angela and David Lee Burke and his team working with me, and I controlled the most powerful branch of organized crime this side of the Atlantic. But even with all that, what loomed ahead would be my toughest test since I took over the reins of the syndicate. I was concerned about the outcome, but not afraid to confront it.

There was one factor fueling my desire, made even stronger now by what had happened to Big Mike and Uncle Carlo.

My hunger for revenge was at its zenith.

The next days would mark the first steps in my quest to destroy those who had killed my family and now had left my friend's body ruined and bloodied on the front end of a car. My uncle Carlo needed retribution as well, his own life put on the line because of his son's treachery.

The time had come for them to pay. It was the moment to show them the side of the Wolf they had heard about but never seen. I looked away from the waves, up toward the sky, and stared at the full moon above. What the Gypsics call a "wolf's moon."

It was a call to battle.

It was a call for revenge.

44.

Florence, Italy

The room was dark and quiet. Ruslan Holt sat in the middle of a peach-colored couch, head resting against his chin, sound asleep. On the oak coffee table was an empty bottle of Jack Daniel's, a crystal ashtray filled to the brim with cigarette butts, and a semiautomatic handgun. To his left was a room service cart filled with the remains of a late evening meal.

I sat on the bed and watched as Holt slept. The intel that had been gathered by my New York crew pointed to him as the man who planned the operation against Big Mike. John Loo picked up enough chatter from cloned cell phones to further back up that fact. Now, it would have been easier and probably safer to send David Lee Burke and the Silent Six to deal with Holt or even one of the crew's top-line hitters. All that mattered was that he would die for what was done to Big Mike. But I didn't see it that way.

Big Mike was my friend and that made it personal. If Holt were going to die, it would be by my hand.

I stood and pressed a switch to turn on the overhead light, an old chandelier that sparkled when lit. I walked toward the couch, on the other side of the coffee table, waiting for Holt to feel my presence and slowly open his eyes. He wiped a hand across his face and gazed up at me. "This is a five-star hotel," he said. "You would think they would have adequate security and not let just anyone into your suite."

"I'm not just anyone," I said.

Holt nodded. "The minibar is near the television," he said. "Why don't you get us both a drink?"

"I'm not here to drink," I said. "And you've had enough."

"You had your chance to kill me when I was asleep," Holt said. "You should have taken it."

"That would have let you off easy," I said. "The Greek deserves better than that."

"So that leaves you against me," Holt said, smiling. "Old-world way."

"I don't know what they call it in Russia," I said, "and I don't care. We call it a Brooklyn beat-down. It's just you and me, and only one of us is going to walk out that front door."

Holt jumped and reached for the gun laying on the coffee table. I grabbed the empty Jack Daniel's bottle and slammed it against the side of his head, sending the gun to the carpeted floor. I held the back of Holt's head, fingers gripping strands of hair, and pounded his face onto the glass coffee table. I kept at it until the glass shattered, sending shards into the air and cutting the front and sides of Holt's face. He reached for a thick chunk of glass and swung it against my arm, slicing through my leather jacket. I reared back and landed three fast, solid punches to his face, the force of the blows tossing him back onto the couch. I grabbed a fork off the dining cart and jammed it into Holt's right leg, pushing down as hard as I could, watching the blood flow from the open wound and onto the couch.

Holt jumped to his feet and swung a series of wide hooks against my rib cage. I head-butted him and then tossed him over the coffee table. I started kicking him with my right boot, landing hard shots against his chest, stomach, groin, going at him with full fury.

I had an advantage from the start. He was still groggy from the sleep and the drink and had been caught off guard by my appearance. It was all the edge I needed.

Holt rolled to his side, blood flowing out of his mouth and nose, trying to regain his footing, gasping for breath. I rained blows against the side of his head and neck and then dropped to my knees and replaced the kicks with closed fists. I hit him again and again and again, losing all track of time, wanting nothing more than to inflict punishment on the man who had ordered the death of my friend.

I finally stopped, my upper body drenched in sweat, my hands and boots thick with blood and bits of bone. I looked down at Holt, beaten beyond recognition. I turned him on his stomach and lifted his head. I jammed one knee against the center of his back. I then pushed his head toward me with both hands, leaned down and whispered into his left ear. "For Big Mike," I said.

I then pulled Holt's head back until I heard his neck bone snap.

45.

East Hampton, New York

I walked into the library, coming in through the garden door, and saw Jimmy in a corner, a large pile of his father's art books strewn around a nearby table. It was the first time I was alone with him since Uncle Carlo's funeral, and I hesitated before I moved deeper into the room. We had kept a distance in the days since the incident, and I was unsure how involved he should be in my plans.

I stood next to him and gazed down at the open art book resting across his legs. "You got something?" I asked.

Jimmy pointed to a large photo in the art book. It was a fresco of *The Last Supper* by Raphael, a full-length rendering of Jesus Christ sharing his last meal with the twelve apostles. I picked up the book and studied the drawing.

"What am I looking for?" I asked.

Jimmy closed the book and pointed to its cover.

"The Vatican," I said.

Jimmy nodded. Then he moved his wheelchair over to the big table in the center of the room. He reached for an open book and handed that one to me as well. I picked up the thick paperback and looked at the cover. It was a biography of Michelangelo.

I rested both books on the big table. "We're on it," I said. "We're checking every museum in Italy that has the works of either artist. But until we pinpoint a location, we're doing nothing more than guessing."

I walked over toward the large window and looked through the glass at the dark ocean outside. "I'm taking you off the phone monitoring operations," I said to Jimmy. "John Loo has been put in charge of that."

I turned and looked at Jimmy, who gazed back at me. "Don't worry about Jack," I said. "I moved him out last night. So you'll be left here on your own, free to do what you please. Now, am I taking a risk by doing that?"

Jimmy moved his wheelchair to a small coffee table next to a large lamp. He picked up a framed photo of Uncle Carlo that was on top of the table. The photo was in black and white, my uncle as a younger man in the early years of his reign as a crime boss. Jimmy pressed the photo against his chest.

He looked at me, tears in his eyes.

I walked over to Jimmy and put my hand on top of his, both our fingers resting on Uncle Carlo's photo.

"Let's get this done," I said.

46.

Vatican City, Italy

I stood next to Angela and stared at Raphael's fresco.

"I've looked at this fresco dozens of times," I told her. "Of all his works, it's the one that stands out. It stays with you."

"Imagine, then, what impact the work has on an art student," Angela said. "A young man wishing to emulate the master."

"And if you can't emulate him, then destroy him. What could be more memorable for an art student turned terrorist than to ruin what he most loves?" I asked.

"This room?" Angela said.

I shook my head. "Not this one, but close to it. Raza admires Caravaggio, likes the streak of rebellion as much as he does the paintings. But in his world, he's more like Raphael, a talent who looked up to a greater talent."

"Michelangelo," Angela said.

"Put it in terrorist terms," I said. "Raphael would be Raza, and Michelangelo would be Bin Laden. And that's Raza's goal—to topple Bin Laden. To wear the crown. What was it they called Michelangelo?"

"The Divine One," Angela said.

"You break it down and brush talent aside, Caravaggio's nothing more than a street thug," I said. "Raza sees himself under a bigger spotlight than that."

"And Raphael was a womanizer who died of an STD," Angela said. "That won't play well with the followers, regardless of how many wives these guys bring into the family."

"But the Divine One," I said. "All these centuries later, he's still the biggest player in the room. If you don't know square one about art, you still know his name. And that's what matters most to a guy like Raza. To be remembered."

"There's that," Angela said. "And we can't lose sight that back when Raza was an art student he may have loved Caravaggio, but guess which artist whose work he did his best to imitate?"

"But he sucked at it, blown off as nothing more than a color-by-numbers pretender," I said. "So if you can't match the works, then all you're left with is one option—destroy them."

"He has the money and might even have the ability to plan it, but would he dare make such a move?" Angela said. "If he did, and was successful, he would be the most wanted terrorist in the world. That would mean the rest of his days on the run, hiding, moving from one location to the next, always under the scope."

"And you don't think he would pay that price?"

"I'm not sure," Angela said. "From what I've read about him, from the reports I've seen, he's a terrorist who enjoys the limelight. And he's found himself a heavyweight banker in Vladimir. He pulls this off, the Russian drops him and cuts off funding. He would avoid any link between himself and Raza."

"You would string Vladimir for a while?" I asked.

"Why not?" Angela said. "Pull down a few jobs that keep his attention on me and the money flowing my way and continue to build both my reputation and organization. So long as Vladimir sees results, he'll continue to feed Raza."

"It's too big a risk for us to ignore," I said, still staring at the Raphael. "It's a big-time move for a kid who sees himself a big-time player. If it were me calling the shots, the Vatican would be one of my targets. And if I really wanted to make a score, I would go for the double hit."

Angela nodded. "Which puts us where?" she asked.

"Raphael is the pace horse in the race," I said. "It's Michelangelo Raza will want. That puts us in the Vatican and at the Galleria in Florence."

"You're swayed by a couple of sketchbooks found in a few safe houses?" Angela said.

"And by knowing who it is I'm chasing," I said.

"How soon?"

"It's height of season," I said. "There's no better time. He can do maximum damage to the property and take out hundreds if not thousands at the same time in two different cities."

"Let's walk," Angela said, resting her left hand on my right arm.

We passed through several of the rooms of the Vatican, lost in thought, only occasionally glancing up at the art on display. The rooms were crowded as always, eager tourists pushing and prodding to get a closer look at works they had until this day seen only in books.

"So much money comes through the Vatican doors each day," Angela said, "and not one single euro goes into the pocket of an Italian. If that weren't enough greed for you, they also collect a tax from the citizens of Rome."

"You're just jealous," I said, "because none of their theft will land any of the red hats a jail sentence. If we tried to pull something like that, we'd be serving life in some gulag."

Angela shrugged. "We make more money than they do," she said. "And we've even managed to make a few deals together."

"You have someone in there?" I asked.

"I make it a point to have someone everywhere," Angela said. "If there's something brewing within the Vatican, we'll know about it. Whether we'll know in time to stop it is another matter."

"You trust him?" I asked.

Angela stopped and turned to look at me. "Do you trust Jimmy?" she asked. "Because if he's a risk, it's not just to you."

"His father gave up his life for him," I said.

"What Carlo did was noble," Angela said. "I don't know if I would have the courage. I also don't know if I would have let it come to that."

"You would have killed Jimmy?"

"A traitor is a traitor," she said.

"It was taken out of my hands," I said. "Uncle Carlo decided and I abided by it."

"I won't work with Jimmy," Angela said.

"You won't have to," I said. "John Loo will slot into Big Mike's place. He'll be in charge of cloned phone information and whatever he and the team pick up through surveillance and computer monitoring."

"I was pleased to see Holt take the hit for Big Mike's death," Angela said. "A friend's death should never be left unpunished. Nor should a traitor be allowed to walk among us, regardless of whose life was given up."

Angela, I knew, would not have handled the Jimmy situation as I had. She would not have respected the wishes of her boss, and instead would have taken it upon herself to rid the organization of a traitor.

"I worked up a plan to deal with the Vatican and the Galleria attacks," I said. "I'd like to run it by you and see what you think."

"Let's do it over a long lunch," she said, leading me out of the Vatican. "I've had enough religion for one day."

47.

Florence, Italy

Raza and Avrim stood across from the Galleria watching a long line of students, tourists, and locals make their way to the entrance and a viewing of the *David*. The line snaked around the corner, but there were few if any complaints about the wait, most of the visitors engaged in either animated conversations or reading up on the work that was only a short distance away.

"It's like this every day," Raza said with a smile.

"The guards in front let in a certain number of people at a time," Avrim said. "They wait for word from the ones watching the exit to tell them when to let more in."

"Don't be too concerned about body count," Raza said. "I assure you a blast strong enough to destroy *David* will be sufficient to cause damage outside the Galleria. Many will die. Ease your mind on that concern."

Avrim glanced at the armed guards stationed near the Galleria entrance. "The men with the guns make visual contact with practically everyone on the line," he said. "They are trained to pull someone like me out of a crowd. Maybe the security only seems lax, but it really isn't. There's never been an attack here and there must be a reason why."

"There have been attempted attacks everywhere," Raza said, his back against a thick old wooden door leading to a five-story apartment building. "We only hear about the successful ones. The failures are done by amateurs, men lacking the skill to pull off such difficult jobs. They go in with explosives meant to damage but not destroy, and as the moment of truth draws near, they panic. Even the most inexperienced guard in the unit can spot such would-be bombers. But rest easy, my friend. You are not destined to fail. I would not have chosen you for such an important mission if I did not believe that."

"I am not a coward, Raza," Avrim said, wiping his brow with the sleeve of a white cotton shirt. "But I would be less than truthful if I did not admit to fears about the mission."

"You are the bravest man I know," Raza said to him. "In fact, your bravery is such that it has inspired me."

"In what way?"

"While you will be here in Florence, doing work blessed by all who have come before you," Raza said, "I will be at the Vatican doing the same. We will be giving up our lives together for the greater good. And in doing so, we shall be remembered forever."

"Do the others know?"

"You are the only one I have trusted with this information," Raza said. "I can't risk anyone in our group knowing, at least not until it is too late for them to prevent it from occurring. Not even the Russian knows."

Avrim looked at Raza with renewed admiration. He was having serious doubts about the sacrifice he had been asked to make, unsure if it was the right thing to do or whether he had the courage to go through with it. But now, hearing that Raza would be giving up his own life in the name of their cause, Avrim felt empowered, that he too would be remembered along with his leader, each a martyr to a great and noble battle. That thought alone helped strengthen the resolve needed to strap on an explosive device and pull the pin.

Raza gazed past Avrim and stared at two men standing half a street away, pretending to look at the goods in the bins of a souvenir shop. "Those two have been following us for three days," he said, tilting his head in their direction.

"How much do you think they know?" Avrim asked, his confidence once again sliding into concern.

"It doesn't matter what they know or what they think," Raza said. "They cannot prevent the inevitable from taking place."

"They could warn the authorities," Avrim said.

"And we would be charged with what?" Raza asked. "All we are guilty of to this point is expressing our interest in art. They need to catch us in the act and that will never happen."

"Why do any of them care?" Avrim asked. "These places—the Galleria, the Vatican—mean nothing to them, not to the American nor to the Russian. What we do here will have little impact on what they do."

"It's about the money stream, Avrim," Raza said. "If our goals are met, then the Russians will take in even more than they do now and eventually the American will bring in less. Their world is ruled by money. Our world is ruled by faith. That is why they can never defeat us. Each one of us who gives himself to the cause will be replaced by hundreds of others walking in our shadows."

"They could kill us so easily," Avrim said, staring at the two men, now standing by a fountain. "Foil the attack even before it is attempted."

"They're too smart for that," Raza said. "They know how replaceable we are. Within a matter of weeks if not days there will be another cell, also funded by the Russian or someone who senses profits in our actions, primed to do what we are planning to do. They will not make any attempt on our lives until they know for certain when and where the attacks are to take place. And despite their best attempts at audio and video surveillance and tracking our movements, they have yet to figure that out."

"There's still time for them to put it together, and then they can move in and eliminate us," Avrim said.

"I'm not concerned," Raza said.

"Have you settled on a day yet?"

"Thursday," Raza said. "August fifteenth."

"Why then?" Avrim asked.

"It's a day before a national holiday," Raza said. "Both places will be filled to capacity. We bring ruin to what they hold sacred and kill as many of them as possible."

Avrim took a deep breath and felt a cold line of sweat run down the center of his back. He stared across at the two men still standing by the fountain, both reading newspapers and occasionally glancing their way. "What about our friends?" he asked. "What do we do with them when it's time for the attack?"

"We give them the honor of dying with us," Raza said.

Raza stepped onto the street and walked toward the long line waiting to enter the Galleria. "Where are you off to?" Avrim asked.

"To see the *David*," he said over his shoulder. "It's my favorite work of Michelangelo and I'd like to see it one final time."

48.

Paris, France

Vladimir sat in a center seat on a tour boat making its way down the river, a silk scarf around his neck to protect against the late afternoon breeze. Klaus Marni sat to his left and pointed toward the huge spires of the Cathedral de Notre Dame.

"Impressive," Marni said. "One of the guidebooks says it was built by hand and designed with little idea whether it could even be completed."

"This boat runs every hour on the hour until eleven tonight," Vladimir said with a tinge of impatience. "Do your sightseeing then. *This* is a business trip."

Marni leaned his back against the slants of the wooden bench. "Raza requested one more payment and it was made this morning," he said. "That puts this week's total at close to $1.5 million. I have no idea what we're getting in return for all that money."

"Have we managed to pinpoint his target?" Vladimir asked.

"Targets," Marni said. "They are going to hit two sites at once. That is as much information as we were able to get from their end."

Vladimir glanced over at Marni, his eyes as cold as winter. "I am sick of playing second fiddle to a common street punk. He has cost me time, millions, and a trusted hand in Holt. None of that would have occurred had we not aligned ourselves with bottom-feeders."

"On top of which, he stripped us of our contact on the inside," Marni said. "All communication with the young man in the wheelchair have gone dark."

"He's occasionally foolish, but not a fool," Vladimir said. "He had to watch his father surrender his life in return for saving his. That will harden him in ways you cannot imagine. Never again expect him to act as a pawn in anyone's game. Unless he's eliminated, he will prove, over time, to be more of a danger to the Wolf than he was when supplying us with what proved to be meaningless information."

"Our people managed to pinpoint two potential Raza targets," Marni said. "Not nailed down but solid enough to be followed up."

"Do I need to guess?"

Marni pulled a slip of paper from the front flap of his light blue windbreaker, passed it to Vladimir and waited as he looked down and read the two lines typed across the front. Vladimir handed the paper back and stayed silent for several minutes. "Do you think he can pull it off?" he asked.

"If he hits one, it will be all we will need to set in motion our plan," Marni said.

"That wasn't what I asked," Vladimir said.

"He'll need what we all need to succeed," Marni said, "luck and skill. He's had both in the past but he's never attempted anything on this grand a scale."

Vladimir nodded. "Raza seems to thrive when the pressure is greatest. That might well be the edge he needs."

"He has the makings of a piss-poor gangster," Marni said.

"But the potential to be a master terrorist."

"We've kept our distance," Marni said. "Our focus has been to keep the Italians from disrupting his activities."

"The time has come for us to ramp it up," Vladimir said. "I want a dozen of our best hitters sent to each city. They should be put in place near the Galleria in Florence and the Vatican. I want you to monitor the teams, bring in Alexi to help."

"Raza's been bounding from one city to the other at a rapid pace the last ten days," Marni said. "He practically lives at the train stations."

"The attacks can't be more than a few days away," Vladimir said. "I would wager he selected his targets long before he and I ever met. It's been his plan all along, to go out in a religious blaze of glory."

"What's our plan?" Marni asked.

"Raza is to do what he does best," Vladimir said. "The same holds true for us. Once the mission is completed, successful or not, he is to be eliminated along with anyone else that comprises what can be referred to as his inner circle. I don't want anything that links him back to us. It is to be as if the first time we heard Raza's name or saw his photo would be on the evening newscast."

"We'll still be suspected of funding his cause," Marni said. "Especially if he succeeds."

"Being suspected won't do us harm," Vladimir said, "and may even prove useful. But no one in law enforcement circles is to know for certain we were the central bank for this operation. I want our fingerprints nowhere near Raza."

"We've kept the transactions between us as clean as possible," Marni said. "I've secured every location whenever the two of you have met and had them swept again afterward. And the cell number he was given to initiate contact is registered in the name of a Belgian woman who passed away three months ago."

Vladimir stood and walked toward a railing, gazing down at the swirling river below. "Give the phone to the first vagrant you find on the street," he said, "and keep it active. The more dead ends the police have to run down, the better."

"And what about the Wolf and the Strega?" Marni asked, stepping in alongside him. "They pose a larger threat to us than anyone with a badge."

"They will need to keep their focus on Raza," Vladimir said. "They are probably closing in on the two target sites by now. They have access to the same information we have, perhaps better."

"We can monitor their activity as we keep track of Raza," Marni said. "Sooner than later, they will all be in the same location."

"Raza is the one we must be rid of," Vladimir said. "But if in the exchange of fire, one or both mob bosses goes down? It would not be a tragedy."

"They have so many men at their disposal, yet the Italians seem to be heading into this battle practically solo," Marni said. "Doesn't make sense."

"It's for the other crime bosses to take note of," Vladimir said. "They still need to be convinced the war the Wolf wishes to wage is one they need to fight. By taking Raza head-on, he and the Strega are leading by example, and nothing impresses the other syndicates more than a show of leadership. It's what the old school gangsters would have done. We may be in a new century, but the codes of conduct are firmly planted in the past."

"They're good enough to foil Raza's plan," Marni said. "We could help prevent that."

"We remain invisible, until the last possible moment."

"I'm not certain how it will play out," Marni said, "but I believe it will be bloody and messy before a conclusion is reached."

"No different than any other skirmish," Vladimir said. "Granted, this is being fought on a larger scale with deadlier ramifications. The risks are higher, as are the rewards. But a battle is still a battle regardless of where it is waged. All that matters is that we are the ones left standing once the bodies and debris have been cleared. It is the only truth that has ever mattered."

49.

Rome, Italy

I walked with Angela past the crowds gathered on the Spanish steps, Brunello and Manzo close behind us.

"Did you know these steps are not owned by Italy?" Angela asked.

"No, Professa, I didn't."

"The steps are property of the French government," Angela said. "In fact, the Romans pay a small tax each year that is sent back to France."

"I'm sure there's a logical answer as to why they're not called the French steps," I said.

"Logical? In Italy?" Angela said. She pointed to her left, toward a long line of high-end clothing stores and a two-story house turned museum that had centuries earlier been the summer residence of Lord Byron. "One of the two Spanish embassies is located in the square."

"And there are two Spanish embassies because . . . ?"

"There are two embassies from every country in Rome," Angela said. "One for the Italian government and the other for the Vatican."

"You make a terrific tour guide," I said after we moved from the steps, then passed Bernini's Fountain and crossed the plaza.

"Speaking of tours, what is this you're taking me on?" she asked.

"It's an electric golf cart tour," I told her. "Best way to see the city. The driver can take us down those narrow side streets that are hard to walk on and most cars can't fit through. I asked for two carts. They're going to meet us over by the bookstore."

"What about the main streets?" Angela asked. "Are they allowed to drive on those?"

"Piece of cake," I said. "They can go as fast as twenty-five kilometers an hour and they're good for about ninety miles. It'll give us a chance to talk."

"Is there a problem?" Angela asked.

"There's always a problem," I said.

ANGELA AND I sat in the backseat of a white electric golf cart, the driver steering his way through the throng surrounding the Trevi Fountain. We were in the lead cart, Brunello and Manzo in the second, somewhere behind us.

Our driver turned toward us. "You want the full tour or you want some time to yourselves?" he asked.

"Little bit of both," I said. "For now, just focus on the drive."

"You want scenic or you want to, you know, cuddle?" he asked.

"Your English is pretty good," I said to him.

"You mean for a guy from Brooklyn?" the driver said, turning to look at us.

"You chased here or come on your own?" I asked.

"I married Italian," the driver said. "Real Italian, like your lady. You fall in love with a Made in Italy woman, be prepared to live in Italy."

I smiled. "Looks like you've made it work."

"No complaints, *amico mio*," he said. "She's a good woman, the kids are great, and this business has been solid enough to get me a house and a full table every night."

"Low overhead," I said. "Smart. The only thing cuts into your profits are the batteries on these things. They can run a credit card."

"You know the Pope mobile?" he asked. "The one they scoot the Pope around in two or three times a year?"

"What about it?"

"The battery in the Pope mobile has to be changed every three months whether he puts one mile on it or a thousand," he said.

"Why?" Angela asked.

"Who the hell knows?" The driver shrugged. "But it works out great for me. I got a friend on the inside and he puts the batteries aside and sells them to me for a hundred euros each. Simple, no?"

I exchanged a look with Angela. "The Vatican has more scams going than we do," she said.

The crowds parted to let us through, many people waving or pointing. The golf cart tours were still a novelty, in business less than a year, but the Italians seemed to have warmed to them.

"What do you think?" I asked Angela.

"It's a fun idea," she said. "Of course if we need to make a speedy getaway, we're doomed."

"We could always jump out and run," I said.

"Good to see you have a backup plan," she said, gazing at the passing shops.

"I know you came into this reluctantly," I said, "and I can't blame you. But I am glad you're on my side."

"It was a business decision," Angela said. She turned to look at me. "And a personal one as well."

"I can take it from here," I said. "Burke and his team are on their way to Florence. They'll deal with the target there. I'll work the Vatican."

"And I go back to Naples?" Angela asked.

"I've lost one friend already," I said. "And a large chunk of my family, even before it began. I'm not quite ready to lose someone else I care about."

"I appreciate your concern, Enzo *mio,*" Angela said. "But when I decided to join you in this fight, it wasn't to be your backup. I have my organization to consider as well, and these bastards are as much a threat to me as to you."

The backseat was tight and we were snuggled against one another. I hadn't been this close to her since we were teenagers, and I closed my eyes and allowed the warm memories of many years ago to wash over me. Her left thigh was resting casually against my right, tanned skin exposed, and in those brief moments I forgot the mob boss by my side and instead looked at her as someone whom I had always loved and with whom I had always felt safe.

"This is the beginning of a long war," I said. "And we can't afford to lose our best people out of the gate. I think you should go back to Naples."

"I have never left a fight," Angela said, "and I won't start—"

"If something *happens* to me," I said, "it will fall on you to lead the fight from there. That's a *business* decision."

"We walked into this together, Enzo," Angela said. "We'll walk out of it together or we'll fall together."

"No one calls me Enzo," I said.

"No one but me," Angela said, smiling.

"I don't want to lose you," I said, not meaning to blurt it out, taking a quick look at the driver as he navigated the golf cart down the Via Veneto.

"Then *don't,*" Angela said. "Because, you know, you'll have my father chasing you from one country to the next."

"I can only imagine," I said.

Angela turned away and looked out at the Piazza Navona. "You were right not to marry me," she said. "It was the wrong time. It would have been done for the wrong reasons. I was angry at first. Who wouldn't be? But you made the choice that needed to be made. You got lucky. You met someone you loved. I'm very sorry you lost that."

"And now?"

"Now?" she said. "Now we have a war to fight."

I said something then that I had felt for a long time but had never consciously thought. "You and me, Angie. We're a story of bad timing."

"We've known each other a long time," Angela said, her voice lower. "We're comfortable with each other. Perhaps we shouldn't mistake that comfort for anything other than that."

Something inside me spun the wrong way.

"Fair enough," I said.

Angela leaned forward and rested a hand on the driver's shoulder, getting his attention. "How long do these cart tours last?" she asked him.

"As long as you want," the driver said cheerfully, veering the cart toward the Pantheon. "Forty-five minutes, seven hours—whatever you like!"

"Then stop the cart at the next corner," she said.

"Where are you going?" I asked.

"For a walk," Angela said. "And don't worry. I won't be completely alone. Brunello and Manzo won't let me stray from sight."

The cart eased to a stop. Angela leaned over, kissed me on the cheek and let go of my hand. She stepped out and started a slow walk toward the Pantheon. Brunello and Manzo followed, keeping a respectful distance.

I sat there in that stupid golf cart and watched her until she disappeared into the crowd.

50.

Florence, Italy

David Lee Burke had his back to the statue of *David,* looking at the crowd mingling around the work.

Jennifer Malasson was in one corner of the room, her back against a cool wall, a sketchbook cradled in her arms.

Robert Kinder was having a quiet chat with an elderly couple visiting for the first time from England, celebrating their thirty-fifth wedding anniversary in the company of a Michelangelo masterpiece.

Franklin J. Pierce was at the entrance to the Galleria, a guidebook in his right hand, checking the faces of the visitors as they entered the large, well-lit room.

Carl Anderson was squeezed in between two art history students, a short distance away from the entrance to the Galleria, and had already spotted the two Russian shooters snaking on the same line, about a dozen feet from his back.

Beverly Weaver was inside an idling black van parked around the corner. She had six computer monitors running, three giving her visuals inside the Galleria and three outside. She also had audio transmission relays switched to green mode and could hear and see everyone on the team and alert them to any hot spots.

The Silent Six were in place.

AVRIM HAD HIS head bowed in prayer, standing in the middle of the long line. It seemed to take a lifetime to move even one step. He was wearing a black T-shirt and an oversized New York Yankees jacket, a bit too heavy for the humid weather but a perfect buffer to shield the thin but burdensome device attached by leather straps to his chest.

The device had been delivered to him earlier that morning by an unknown courier, a young, fragile looking teenager he had never seen before who knocked on his apartment door and handed him a sealed Amazon box. He nodded his thanks when Avrim took it from him, jumped back on a rusty red bicycle and peddled up Via Pietro Maroncelli under the imposing shadows of the soccer stadium.

It took Avrim slightly less than an hour to cut open the package with a dull kitchen knife and stare at the device inside. It took him even longer to bathe and choose the proper clothing, since he was unable to ease the fear that was raging inside and calm his trembling body. He sat and prayed and drank a cup of lukewarm tea. He then stood, walked over to the Amazon box, lifted the device and held it in his hands. He was surprised at how light it felt and how crudely it was put together. But he was also aware of the damage such a device was meant to cause and the number of people it could leave dead in its wake.

Avrim had placed the device on his chest, his head barely fitting through the small opening, and snapped the leather straps in place, making it as tight as he could manage. He wiped his face and hands with a damp towel and then reached for the Yankees jacket, a final gift from his mentor and friend, Raza.

Now, he glanced at the two guards stationed near the Galleria entrance, their attention focused on faces farther down the line. He handed his entry ticket to a young woman in a blue jacket and matching skirt and waited as she tore off the top and handed the rest back to him, already reaching out a hand for the next visitor on the line. Avrim walked past her into a small vestibule, turned right and entered the Galleria.

He was in place.

51.

Vatican City, Italy

I spotted the Russian shooters long before I caught sight of Raza. They were spread out, a dozen if I made them right, two to a team, mingling among various tour groups, moving from one room to the next. I was wearing a small hearing device in my left ear and had audio contact with Angela, Brunello, and Manzo, the four of us spread throughout the Vatican exhibits. I also had a miniature video camera clipped to the collar of my black leather jacket, linking me back to New York and John Loo, who was working in a room that enabled him to see and hear what I did across the faces of six large computer screens.

"Anything?" I asked.

Angela's voice popped into my ear. *"No sign of him,"* she said.

"He'll show," I said.

"Two of the Russians made me," Brunello said. *"So I won't be there alone."*

"Don't worry," I said. *"None of us are going to be alone for long."*

We made our way toward the Sistine Chapel, walking through the small entrance nearest *The Last Judgment.* I was the first one in and caught a glimpse of Angela with a cluster of teenage girls, chatting casually with one of them. She was wearing a black jacket, Nike running shoes, form-fitting J.Crew jeans, and was walking toward the center of the large room.

Brunello and Manzo took their positions, one against the wall closest to the exit, the other standing directly across, blocked from view by the guards stationed around the milling crowd.

I was facing the rear of the room, *The Last Judgment* at my back, Michelangelo's ceiling above me.

I was in my place.

RAZA STOOD IN the center of a children's tour group, eighteen boys and girls in the requisite camp outfit—matching T-shirts hanging loose over the tops of jeans or shirts, three female guides watching them. He smiled at the children, seemingly at ease in their company, chewing a thick wad of gum, an expensive camera hanging on a leather leash over his neck, a black cap on the lens. Then he paused, taking in the room. He gazed at all of it—the paintings, the centuries-old furniture, the sheer majestic power of it—and a smile came to his face. It was as if he were looking at it for the first time.

And for the last.

He was in place.

52.

Florence, Italy

"He's in," Burke said. *"He's slow walking from the main entrance, not stopping to look at anything, coming straight toward the target."*

"There are Russian guns in every direction," Malasson said into her body mike. *"They wanted to, they could spray this place and give him all the cover he needs."*

"He's the suicide bomber," Burke said, *"the one who came in here to die. The Russians won't want to join him. They must have an exit strategy."*

"Once that bomb goes, there's no way out of here for anybody," Pierce said. *"Them or us."*

"Then let's make sure it doesn't go off," Burke said.

"I got four here with me," Anderson said. *"And they keep letting others get in front of them, which means they don't plan on going in."*

"They'll give cover fire from outside," Weaver said from the van, *"aiming at either us or any guards blocking the others making a break."*

"You get a visual on where they stashed their transport?" Burke asked.

"*Two streets past the Galleria,*" Weaver said. "*Two four-door sedans, no drivers waiting.*"

Burke was twenty feet from Avrim and started to move in his direction. "*I'm going to go make contact,*" he said. "*If I'm not getting anywhere with him, I'll give the signal and you take him down.*"

"*I'll be ready,*" Kinder said. "*It's going to be tighter than I'd like with all these folks around. If you could work him toward a quieter spot, be a big help.*"

"*If you can't take the shot, don't,*" Burke told him. "*Turn your attention to the Russians. Jennifer will take him with a blade.*"

"*I'm moving now,*" Malasson said. "*I'll have him through the neck. Device will be covering his chest and back.*"

"*The rest of you, remember, drop the Russians,*" Burke said. "*But if you have to hit one of the guards, try for flesh wounds.*"

Burke walked down the center of the hall and stopped in front of Avrim, startling the young man. "Hi," Burke said with a smile and in a pleasant voice. "I was wondering if you could help me out?"

53.

Vatican City, Italy

I made eye contact with Raza, wanting him to see me, to know I was there, throw him off—if only for a moment. He looked back and I saw that he recognized me, probably from a photo somebody gave him. He looked younger than I thought he would, moved with deliberate motions, like a dancer rehearsing something he needed to learn. He was wearing a jeans jacket with a faded T-shirt underneath. He raised his right hand to waist level, waved the fingers at me and smiled. He moved away from the kids around him and began to walk in my direction, casual and relaxed, in total control of the moment.

A terrorist about to step through the door to paradise.

It was then I knew.

Raza wasn't the bomber.

He was the decoy.

"The bomber's in the room," I said into my mike. *"Find out who and where."*

"How will we be able to tell?" Brunello asked.

"You won't," I told him. *"Let the bomber tell you. Eyes, body language, nervous looks. The closer he gets to pressing the timer, the faster the adrenaline moves, the more exaggerated the gestures. They all say they want to die, but it's no easy thing."*

"Once you spot him," Angela said, *"make your move. Target needs to go down without the device going off."*

I watched as Raza moved into a crowd of Japanese tourists, pushing his way toward the exit at the rear of the room. *"Looks like Raza's not going to stay for the fireworks,"* I said. *"John, track him and make sure he doesn't get too far from range."*

"He's on my radar," John said.

"Manzo, the Russians belong to you until we get our sights on the target," Angela said. *"Don't waste bullets. Drop to kill. There's a badge in the room to help you take them down."*

"Does he have a name?" I asked.

"Frantoni," Angela said.

54.

Florence, Italy

"I look at you and don't see the eyes of a young man who wants to die here today," Burke said to Avrim.

Avrim had been startled by Burke's approach, especially given Burke's size. Burke had the casual manner of a man who was good with both his hands and with a weapon, and Avrim did his best not to show either panic or bravado, to remain as calm as possible.

"I am here same as you," Avrim managed to say, "to see the *David.*"

"You got two Russians drawing closer to your left," Pierce said.

Burke took note but kept his eyes on Avrim. "It would be so easy to prove me wrong," he said to Avrim. "Wouldn't take more than a few seconds."

"What do you want me to do?" Avrim asked. He felt the crowd closing in tighter around them and was feeling light-headed and drained.

"Pop open that Yankees jacket," Burke said, moving closer to Avrim, sensing the Russians coming at him from behind.

"Three more hitters coming straight at you," Pierce said.

"I have a clear shot on one," Kinder said. *"Once he's hit, people might scurry for cover and give me a look at a second. Still leaves a bit of a crowd."*

"There are three more on my side of the statue," Malasson said. *"It's starting to get tight."*

"I'm not going to open my jacket," Avrim said.

Burke reached over and grabbed both of Avrim's hands. The move startled the terrorist and made him flinch. "What are you doing?" he asked.

"You don't need to open the jacket, the set button is in one of your pockets," Burke said, gripping down tighter on Avrim's hands. "I'm not going to let that happen."

"You cannot hold onto me for the rest of the day," Avrim said, regaining a fraction of his composure. "Some in the crowd have started to look our way. Soon the guards will sense something is wrong and come toward us. I only need a second."

Burke looked over Avrim's left shoulder and spotted two of the Russian hitters closing in. Each held a Glock, guns low, letting them ride against their legs. *"When I start to move with my new friend here, begin to clear out some of our company,"* Burke said into his mike. *"But stay silent. Take down as many as you can before we have to make some noise."*

"Who are you talking to?" Avrim said, confused, looking around and catching a glimpse of the two Russians coming for them.

"And if it looks like the target is giving me trouble," Burke said, looking right at Avrim, *"take him out fast, center of the head. And if I'm in the way, put me down, then take him."*

Burke turned Avrim around, bending his arms behind him and began to walk him toward the Galleria exit.

He estimated he had a fifteen-second jump before the Galleria became a fire zone.

55.

Vatican City, Italy

I stood in the middle of the Sistine Chapel and looked for the face of the one person in the room eager to bring it crashing down. Raza would not select an innocent for such a monumental job; he couldn't risk any last-minute indecision or error. He would want someone to whom the destruction of the chapel would have a deeper meaning; someone who could override emotion with strength.

And someone who could squash his fears and zero in on the task.

I scanned through the crowd looking for the face of that person, the one face I needed to find. A face as marked by damage as by determination.

A face like mine.

John's voice came through my earpiece. *"I'm not picking up Raza."*

"There are two cameras in every room," I said, *"keep looking. He's not going to stray far. He'll want to see this through."*

I turned to my left and spotted a man in a dark brown sports jacket and matching slacks. He wore thick glasses and a designer scarf hanging around his neck and kept both hands inside the flaps of his jacket. He was doing his best to act calm but could do little to disguise his nerves. He was in his mid-forties, with a well-groomed beard and a visible scar that ran from the corner of one eye down the length of his cheek, partially hidden by his facial hair.

"*I have to go, John,*" I said. "*I think I found our target.*"

I took a few steps closer to the man, waiting for him to look away from the panels on the far walls and turn to me.

"*Keep your distance,*" I said to Angela and her team. "*And keep looking in case I'm circling the wrong guy.*"

"*There isn't time for you to be wrong,*" Angela said.

I walked up to the man, blocking his view of the panels over my shoulder, catching him off guard. "A son?" I asked him. "Or a daughter?"

The man stared at me for several seconds, glanced at the crowd milling around us, and then turned back to me. "One of each," he said. "Two years ago this day."

"How old?" I asked.

"My son was twelve, my daughter not yet ten," the man said. "They were walking home from school along with some other friends when the bomb . . . A bomb sent by people who look like you."

"You want your revenge," I told him. "And you've been led to believe what you are about to do will get that for you. You're wrong."

"It is the only way," the man said.

"No," I said, "it's not. All it will do is kill these innocents who wished no harm for your children. It won't bring justice. It won't give you the revenge you seek. If that's all it took, then I'd be setting off bombs in as many crowded places as I could find."

"Who?" the man asked.

"My wife," I said. "Two daughters. A terrorist attack."

"And did that not make you want to kill all terrorists?"

"Yes," I said, "as long as they lead me to the one I need."

"Is Raza the one you seek?" the man asked.

"I don't know," I said.

"I still have two children," the man said. "Raza will send them money. For education. To buy a home. To live a better life than I can give them."

"That's what he told you," I said, feeling the man's conviction starting to fade. "It's what he tells anyone. Any up-front cash?"

The man shook his head.

I grasped his shoulder. "Your children will be without a father and there will be no money."

"Who are you?" the man asked.

"I'm the one who's going to stop you," I said. "You're different from them, and from me. But that changes if you push down on that button in your pocket. That will make you a hated man, despised even by your own country. Your own children. What you do here is how they will remember you."

The man looked at me and shook his head. "Raza gave me his word," he said. "And I left him with mine. What was meant to happen will happen. And it will happen now."

I pressed my right hand against the one he had hidden in his jacket pocket, the one whose fingers were near the trigger point that would set off the bomb.

I fired three bullets into him at close range. The sounds of the gunshots were partially drowned out by the crowd noise and the ringing of the bells outside. I wrapped my arm around the man and held him up as blood poured down on our feet. I heard a woman behind me scream and saw one hold her fingers to her mouth, her eyes frozen in fear. To my right a male voice shouted for help.

"*Get out of there now,*" Angela said, her voice coming through clearly in my earpiece.

I reached into the man's jacket pocket and felt for the timing mechanism, pushed his limp hand aside, and pulled it out. I looked into his eyes and saw he was close to gone. I let him slowly slip from my grasp. He fell to the floor like a deflated balloon as I moved toward the Sistine Chapel exit, the frightened and stunned crowd parting to give me space.

I walked until I made it past the small entryway leading out of the chapel and then began to run. *"I'm going for Raza,"* I said into my body mike.

Behind me I could hear gunfire, people shouting and screaming, police whistles echoing, alarms going off in every corner of the chapel. I knew Brunello and Manzo were in a firefight with the Russians, giving Angela as much cover as they could as she made her way toward the exit to join up with me.

"John?" I said into the mike. *"You have a location on Raza?"*

I was racing through the halls, not certain which direction to go, losing time. John's response came across garbled and then silent.

"He's heading for the bridge leading to Castel Sant'Angelo." It was a male voice coming in through my earpiece, speaking English with an Italian accent. *"The ancient route the Popes used to escape any Vatican attacks."*

"Frantoni?"

"Yes," he said.

"You on our frequency or a police intercept?"

"He's on ours," Angela said. *"He'll get you to where you need to go."*

I leaned against a wall to catch my breath, timing device still in my hand, and closed my eyes for a brief moment. *"Okay,"* I said into my body mike. *"How do I get to the bridge?"*

56.

Florence, Italy

Two of the Russian hitters were down, left for dead on separate benches in the Galleria, their backs against a wall. Malasson had killed the first, burying the blade in his stomach. The second had been taken down by Kinder, firing at close range.

Burke was leading Avrim toward the Galleria exit. Pierce walked in front of them, providing a shield against anyone looking their way. *"You got heavy company coming at you from both directions,"* Weaver said from inside the van. *"Russians on your back and waiting for you to come out."*

"Anderson, meet us by the exit," Burke said. *"I'm going to hand the target off to you."*

"Taking him where?" Anderson asked.

"To where the Russians parked their cars," Burke said. *"Weaver will lead you there."*

"Then what?"

"I'll tell you when you get there," Burke said. *"Everyone else, full loads out and secure your vests. Do your best to minimize collateral, civilian and police. Make your way to where the Russians left their cars. We'll catch up with Weaver and Anderson there."*

"There's six hitters left inside the Galleria and they're moving fast to come out," Malasson said.

"Four, maybe five more on the street heading toward you," Anderson said.

"How many guards out there, Weaver?" Burke asked.

"Four that I see on the screen," Weaver said. *"There's a blue car parked farther up, three at least sitting in there."*

Avrim, his upper body coated in sweat, his hands numb from the grip Burke had on them, was dragging his feet as he walked, trying to hold his ground. "You cannot make it out of here," he said to Burke. "You might as well have been the one to plan a suicide mission, not me."

"What do you care?" Burke said. "You were planning to die today anyway."

They were less than twenty feet from the Galleria exit.

Burke nodded at Anderson. "He's yours now. He tries to free himself from your grip, snap his neck and use him as a shield when the Russians start firing. That bomb can only go off if the button is pushed down."

"How much time before set-off and explosion?" Anderson asked, grabbing hold of Avrim's hands.

"It's a crude device, hard to give an accurate read," Burke said. "But I would guess fifteen, maybe twenty seconds tops before it blows."

They stepped into the afternoon sunlight, Anderson and Avrim out ahead, Burke trailing, Russian hitters rushing down the corridor behind them, Malasson and Kinder somewhere nearby.

"Here we go," Burke said into his mike. *"Treat every bullet as if it's your last and I'll see all of you on the other end."*

57.

Vatican City, Italy

I was running down the Passetto di Borgo, a narrow and exposed red-brick corridor that led out of the Vatican and toward Castel Sant'Angelo.

The structure had once functioned as a jail and a refuge, but was now a tourist attraction approached by crossing the Bridge of Angels that led to its front gates.

I was halfway across the corridor when I heard what had to be Raza's footsteps ahead of me. Luca Frantoni had navigated me out of the Vatican and onto the corridor, moving me from one corner to the next, one stairwell to another, before I finally broke through and caught some daylight.

Inside the halls of the Vatican behind me, I could still hear heavy fire and knew the battle between Angela and her men against the Russians raged on.

"Anyone have eyes in there?" I asked.

I heard Frantoni's voice. *"Don't worry,"* he said. *"Angela's got plenty of backup. I have a dozen men inside and another twenty making sure the crowd gets out in one piece."*

I picked up my pace and made my move to close in on Raza. I heard footsteps coming up behind me and turned and saw Angela heading toward me. Just seeing her, jacket open, a gun in each hand, sneakers kicking up dust on the stone and sand pavement, brought a smile to my face. I continued my run toward the Castel and did not notice the three Russian shooters bearing down on her. Not until I heard the shots and her painful moan as she took a hard fall, her face scraping against the side of the redbrick wall.

I turned toward her, catching a glimpse of the three Russian shooters. Angela was on the ground, on her side, her back to the wall, her guns out of reach. I jammed the bomb device into my pocket and pulled out a second gun, another Glock from my left hip holster, aimed them and fired off rounds in the Russians' direction. They returned fire, bullets whizzing past me, chipping at the wall and kicking up dust from shattered stones.

"Angela's down," I said into my body mike. *"Three Russians are coming my way, and they'll get her. Raza is on the run and should have reached the Castel by now."*

I could barely make out Brunello's voice amid all the shooting going on across both ends. *"The three coming your way and the two we've got cornered down here are the last of the Russians. The cops have either rounded up or killed the rest."*

"You're on your own up there," Manzo said. *"We won't be able to get to you in time."*

I was twenty feet from Angela when I stopped running. I dropped out my empty clips, jammed in two new ones and took aim at the Russians. I was working off adrenaline and anger, afraid to look straight. Afraid to know.

I felt a burning sensation in my right leg and knew a bullet had found its mark. I kept my ground and held my aim steady. I hit one of the Russians just below his jawline, sending him sprawling on his back.

I heard him before I saw him, his words coming across my earpiece. *"Make your way to Angela,"* Frantoni said. *"Leave the last two to me."*

Frantoni was a dozen feet behind the Russians and taking aim at his two targets, one falling quickly to his knees before a final bullet to the head laid him down.

I limped over toward Angela and cradled her head in my arms. Her right arm was drenched in blood, thin red lines flowing past her fingers and onto the pavement. I stared down at her, holding her close to me, the blood from the wound in my leg dripping onto her jacket. She opened her eyes. There was a long gash on her forehead and some of the blood had streaked down onto her shirt and neck.

"You think you can stand?" I asked.

"I know I can," she said, "but I'm not too sure about you."

We both struggled to our feet and then stopped when we heard the footsteps coming at us from behind. I kept my arms around Angela and whirled with the two guns still in my hands.

The man coming toward us was in his mid-thirties, dark hair, muscular build, two guns in his hands, blood staining the white T-shirt he wore under his jacket.

"Relax," Angela told me. "It's Luca Frantoni."

I looked at him and gave him an appreciative nod. "We've met," I said to her. "Sort of."

I scanned the terrain behind Frantoni, glancing at the bodies of the three fallen Russian shooters.

I gripped his shoulder. "I owe you," I said.

"It will even out soon," Frantoni said.

Angela pointed to the Castel over my shoulder. "Raza's holed up in there," she said.

"He could have made it out by now," I said.

"We would have heard," Angela said. "I have half a dozen of my crew by the exits and Frantoni has his team in place as well, both eager to take him down. No, he's in there, waiting."

I took the bombing device out of my pocket and handed it to

Frantoni. "You probably could make better use of this than I can," I said.

Frantoni took it from me and jammed it in the rear pocket of his jeans. "Bomb's already been dismantled," he said. "My guys stripped it off the body while the fireworks were still going on."

Frantoni then reached down, picked up Angela's guns and handed them to her. She took each one, holding them in her bloody hands.

"Let's finish this," I said.

I turned and limped toward the Castel, walking between the boss of the Neapolitan mob and the head of the Rome Antiterror Squad, each of us bloodied but ready for one more fight.

58.

Florence, Italy

Anderson slammed Avrim against the trunk of one of the two Russian sedans parked on a side street, two up from the Galleria. Behind them, the area had turned into a hot zone. Smoke from gunfire and tear gas canisters filled the street. Bodies were strewn on the road, the sidewalk, hoods of parked cars. Store windows and apartment doors were riddled with bullet holes. Three uniform officers were down, two wounded and one dead. Four of the Russian gunmen lay sprawled on the pavement, two with guns still in hand.

Burke's Silent Six had not gone untouched. Pierce was sitting against a wall, around the corner from the parked sedans, his right arm lacerated. Malasson lay facedown on the street across from him and wasn't moving. Burke had taken a bullet to the shoulder and one that grazed the side of his head. Even Avrim had been shot in the leg and was losing blood at a rapid rate.

Anderson had taken the device from Avrim's jacket during the skirmish and waited as Burke turned the corner and approached them.

"There are still seven, maybe eight Russians heading our way," Burke said to Anderson. "Check on Pierce and Malasson and get ready to help load them on the van. Weaver should be here soon."

"I'm coming toward you," Weaver said into their earpieces. *"Less than a minute away."*

"Are we taking him, too?" Anderson asked, tilting his head toward Avrim.

Burke shook his head. "He rides with the Russians," he said, taking Avrim from Anderson. "And give the set-off device to Weaver soon as you get in the van."

Anderson walked toward the corner to retrieve his two fallen comrades.

Avrim turned to Burke, bleeding, frightened, and tired. "You can't leave me with the Russians," he pleaded. "They'll kill me as soon as they make eye contact."

"You're going to surprise them," Burke said. "You're going to kill them before they have a chance to kill you."

Burke pulled a Swiss Army knife from the front pocket of his jeans and slid the small blade into the trunk's key slot. "They didn't lock their car," Burke said with a smile. "Russians never lock their cars."

He had the trunk popped in less than thirty seconds and then turned to Avrim. "This is where we part company," he said to the terrorist. "Get in."

"Why?"

Burke stared at him for a moment and then slammed the butt end of his gun against the side of Avrim's head. The first blow stunned, the next two made him wobbly, the fourth put him out. Burke caught Avrim's limp body just as it was curling toward the street, held him in both arms and slid him into the trunk, resting his head against a brown duffel bag. He unbuttoned Avrim's Yankees jacket and checked on the bomb strapped to his chest, then slammed the lid down on the trunk.

He waited as the van with Weaver at the wheel turned the corner at a sharp angle and came to a stop right next to the two sedans. A side door slid open, and as Burke jumped in, the van pulled away. "How bad?" he asked, looking over at Pierce and Malasson.

"They both lost a lot of blood," Kinder said. "Pierce has a clean wound, just needs the bullet removed, the sooner the better."

"And Jennifer?"

"Stomach wound," Kinder said. "Her vest took one of the bullets, other snaked in just below. She needs a hospital and a doctor who knows what he's doing."

Burke turned to Weaver. "How close do we need to be to set off the device?" he asked.

They were three streets away from the Russian sedans and could see the remaining shooters making their way to their cars. Weaver slid the van toward a curb and brought it to a fast stop. "Right about here ought to get it done," she said, holding the set-off device in her right hand.

Burke slid open the panel door and stepped out of the van. He looked down the narrow streets and waited until the Russians had all piled in and started the cars and put them in gear, the lead sedan moving at a much faster speed. "Can we get them both?" he asked Weaver.

"How raw was the bomb?" she asked.

"Pretty basic," Burke said. "Half a dozen sticks of low-grade dynamite, coiled wires, and a weak timer. It would have been enough to knock *David* off its pedestal. Raza figured the walls and the marble floors would do the rest of the damage."

"You'll get the one car for certain," Weaver said. "Might smash out some windows and pop a couple of the tires on the second if it's close enough."

Burke stepped away from the van and walked into the middle of the street, the sedans less than two blocks away. He lifted his right hand, bunched it into a fist and raised his thumb. Inside the van, Weaver looked at the set-off device and pressed down on the red button in the center.

The explosion brought the first sedan to a halt. Its four doors, the hood, and the trunk flew off in different directions, shattering glass and landing hard against parked cars and doorways. A fireball hurtled toward the sky, and dozens of wooden shutters from the apartments above were blown off their hinges. The four passengers in the car were incinerated instantly.

In the trunk, Avrim's body all but disappeared, a few scattered and charred remains amid the smoke and debris.

The second sedan also sustained damage. Rear tires were blown to shreds and the back window had shattered. Flames engulfed the front end, and the driver no longer had control of the wheel as it slowly weaved to a stop half a block from where Burke was standing.

Three Russian shooters stepped out of the car, guns in hand, their clothes covered in soot and dust. Burke pulled two guns from his waist and started to walk toward them. Kinder jumped out of the van and followed, Anderson right behind.

"Let's see if there's any fight left in them," Burke said as they came up next to him. "Weaver, turn the van around and follow behind us. Keep it nice and slow."

The Russian shooters, wiping the burn from their eyes, watched Burke and his team approach and held their ground, guns at the ready. "Seems like they're giving it some thought," Kinder said.

"Let's give them something else to think about," Burke said. "Soon as we reach the corner, start pouring bullets in their direction. If they shoot back, then we'll know they're in this until the last."

The three Russians stepped away from the smoking sedan and moved into the center of the street, still dazed by the force of the explosion, not yet able to focus. Behind them, they could hear the approaching sirens and knew the police couldn't be more than a few minutes away. The heavy smoke from the burning car covered the narrow street like a blanket, making it hard to see clearly, forcing them to aim more toward footsteps than actual targets.

Anderson and Kinder stopped at the corner and spread out, using stone walls as a shield, Burke holding steady in the center of the street, peering through the haze at the Russian shooters, his guns raised. Weaver eased the van forward, only a few feet behind.

"Say when," Anderson said.

"When," Burke said.

The three each fired off heavy rounds into the smoke that was starting to flow their way. The return fire was minimal and sporadic, shots hitting stone or bouncing off chipped pavement, and then it stopped.

Burke and his men held their fire and waited.

"They could all be down," Kinder said. "We tossed a lot of ammo their way."

"They might have had enough and cleared out," Anderson said. "There are cops all over the place. Should be swooping down this street any second."

"Turn on your headlights," Burke said to Weaver. "The smoke's too thick, might help us get a better look."

Weaver was the first to spot them, the three Russians rising out of the smoke.

A bullet hit Kinder in the shoulder, forcing his weapon to the curb. Anderson turned and exchanged close fire with a second Russian, the two a foot apart, each bullet finding its target.

Burke was empty and reaching for fresh clips when he was hit on his left side, the blow forcing him down on one knee.

Weaver opened the door to the van and emptied a Glock in the direction of the gunman who had hit Burke. Four of the slugs found their mark and left the shooter flat on his back, dead.

Burke jammed in the two ammo clips, his movements slowed by the wound, and turned his guns toward the Russian looking to finish off Kinder.

"Stay down!" Burke shouted.

Kinder tossed himself onto the sidewalk, his face inches from an open sewer. The Russian standing above him, his body sideways, turned his aim toward Burke.

Burke sent a flurry of bullets at the Russian. The force of the slugs caused the man's arms to flail, his gun falling from his hand, his legs pushing him back into the dark smoke. He landed on the street with a hard thud.

Burke turned toward Anderson and the last Russian. Both men were down and neither was moving. Kinder eased up off the pavement, picked up his weapon and walked toward Anderson. He gazed down at the Russian, kicked the weapon next to his hand farther up the street, and bent down to check on his friend.

"Still breathing," he yelled out. "He's got two holes in him, one serious."

Burke came over and helped Kinder lift Anderson to his feet. Weaver moved the van to the corner, jumped out and slid the panel door open. One by one she put each of the wounded men into the van and slammed the panel door shut. She ran to the front, got back in behind the wheel and put it in gear.

"We're all in," Weaver said. "Snug as bugs."

"Let's go," Burke said. "We're done here."

59.

Parco Adriano, Italy

I was on the second floor of the Castel, its walls as thick and fortified as any I'd seen. Angela was next to me, walking on the other end of the stairwell, Frantoni slightly ahead of both of us.

Raza was somewhere inside these ancient walls and needed to be found.

"How are you both on ammo?" Frantoni asked.

"I've got two full loads," Angela said.

"I'm low," I said.

"There's a medieval weapons room one floor above," Frantoni said. "If you don't mind breaking the law, you can help yourself to a few pieces. Some of the things they have there could do a lot more damage than a gun."

"If Raza is anywhere, he'll be on the top floor," Angela said. "It gives a vantage point, limits the ways we can come at him, and allows for plenty of open space to fight."

"He might think I came in alone," I said. "And that's what I want him to believe."

"You can't take him alone," Angela said. "Not in your current condition."

"He could have eluded both the cops and your crew," Frantoni said. "He's been on the run for a long time. He knows how to get himself out of tight spots."

"Not this time," I said.

"What makes you so sure?" Frantoni asked.

"He must know by now that whatever he thought was going to happen back there didn't," I said. "That means he's cost the Russians a lot of money, time, and manpower, with nothing to show for it."

"So if he takes one of you down," Frantoni said, "that might buy him another go-around with the Russians."

"Exactly," I said. "And if he's lucky enough to take us both, even better. Now from his vantage point he must have seen me and Angela get hit, so he knows we're bloody and figures that gives him some kind of edge."

Frantoni glanced at me and at Angela as we struggled to navigate the stairs, our wounds leaving a blood trail. "He might be right," he said.

"A wounded wolf is the most dangerous animal to take on," I said.

"Maybe," Frantoni said. "But he won't be expecting to have a cop show up. So, I bring the element of surprise."

"Just so we're clear," I said, "I don't want to see Raza arrested."

"I'm not looking to arrest him," Frantoni said.

We had reached the weapons room on the third floor of the Castel. The large circular room was crammed with an assortment of guns, swords, shields, muskets, and torture devices displayed behind glass cases, place cards under each item detailing the gruesome ways the weapons could be utilized.

"Help yourself," Frantoni said to us, scanning the deadly instruments just beyond the glass.

Angela stared down at three torture devices designed to rid a man of his most private possession and smiled. "These would come in very handy," she said. "I don't know of any man who wouldn't talk with one of these strapped on."

I used the butt ends of my Glocks to shatter a pane of glass and shoved the guns back into my waist. I reached inside, avoiding the shards, and picked up a sword and a knife.

Angela, using her guns the same way I had, chose a thick silver mallet with iron spikes spread across its head. "I always wanted one of these," she said.

"How about you?" I asked Frantoni.

He held up a nine millimeter and a shuttered switchblade. "I have what I need," he said.

"Roof is two flights up," I said. "He's expecting me, so I'll take the lead. You cover Angela and come in behind me. But don't move too quickly. Let it play out. I don't want Raza down until I get some information out of him."

"If he has any to give," Frantoni said.

"I'll know soon enough," I said. "But if he's on that roof, there's no way he leaves here alive."

"That's what I'm counting on," Frantoni said.

I looked at him for a moment and then at Angela, then turned and walked out of the room, heading for the roof. It was painful for me to move. Reaching each stone step sent a jolting pain into my leg, now bleeding heavier than before. I felt light-headed and weak. I figured Angela was in even worse shape than I was, leaving Frantoni as my one backup, putting me in a position to trust a cop I barely knew.

Angela seemed at ease around him, a sign the two of them had a solid history. Frantoni had mentioned he wanted something in return for his help, and I wondered what that could be. It wasn't financial. He didn't seem the type, and if he was being greased, Angela would be doling out enough to keep him content. There are few things a mob boss hates more than not knowing everyone's angle, what someone wants in return. But for now I needed to leave it alone and stay focused on my target.

I knew with certainty Raza would be on the roof waiting for me, eager to confront the one he could blame for foiling his master plan. He was a terrorist and I was a gangster, but we both worked off our desires for money and revenge. I had cost him on the financial end, and he would be looking to cash out on the emotional.

We also shared a degree of arrogance. Raza would never entertain the notion he couldn't take me down any more than I could fathom losing a battle to him. We were programmed to win, regardless of the cost, the idea of defeat of any kind never allowed to penetrate our thinking. We would rather die than surrender.

On this day, as the sun began its slow fade to dusk, one of us would get his wish.

Raza was standing with his back against a stone embankment, the city of Rome spread out below him, watching as I stepped through the narrow opening and onto the rooftop. The view from Castel Sant'Angelo is one of the most beautiful in Rome. At any other time I would have been taking in the spectacle around me, from the dome of St. Peter's to the rushing river, the cascading hills, and the church steeples that pointed toward the sky, a vast and breathtaking eternal city that lives as much in the past as it does in the present.

But that needed to be left for another day.

I gazed up at the statue of the Angel Michael above me and walked over toward Raza. I held the knife in my left hand and the sword in my right, the guns still tucked in my waistband.

Raza had his hands spread out across the embankment, the right one holding an open switchblade.

"Tell me," he asked as I drew closer, "how did you know I would be using a decoy? That I would not be the one setting off the device?"

"You're not the one who shows up," I said. "You're a recruiter, not the trigger man. Guys like you never get their hands dirty."

"But I'm here now," Raza said. "Standing before the big bad Wolf himself."

"Only because you need a scalp for Vladimir," I said, "before he takes yours."

"I have no fear of the Russian," Raza said. "Just as I have no fear of you."

"You should," I said.

Raza moved from the wall and lowered his hands. I gripped the knife in my hand tighter and walked closer to him.

Raza looked at my leg, dripping blood onto the stones. "I could just stand here for an hour or so, relax and watch you bleed to death," he said.

I turned the knife in my hand, switching casually from handle to blade and moved several steps closer to him. "You might be right," I said. "And it would be a whole new experience for you. Usually you put in an order and wait to hear the outcome and the body count."

Raza shook his head. "I know you think I had something to do with the attack that killed your wife and daughters," he said. "And while it would have pleased me no end to have ordered that mission, I can't take credit for it."

"But you know who did," I said.

"Perhaps," Raza said. "But you never will find out. At least not from my lips."

I eased my hand back a few inches, prepared to fling the blade toward Raza, my eyes on his, when the shot rang out behind me. Raza rocked back on his heels, looking down at his stomach and the gaping wound. He leaned against the embankment and pressed both his hands against his stomach, trying to staunch the flow of blood.

Frantoni walked past me and toward Raza and jammed an open hand against the terrorist's throat. Angela stepped in next to me and put an arm under mine, helping to keep me on my feet.

Frantoni bore down on Raza with hard eyes and there was a harsh, angry tone to his voice. "Maybe you had nothing to do with the attack on the plane that killed his family," he said. "But I know you had everything to do with the bombing that happened at the

Rome airport. That killed a lot of people, too. One of them was my brother, Remi. He was a cop, just like me, only better."

I looked at Angela and she gripped my arm tighter. "We should go," she said to me. "Let Frantoni take it from here."

"You said he wouldn't be arrested," I said to Frantoni.

Frantoni spoke to me but his eyes and grip stayed on Raza. "I'm an antiterror cop based in Rome," he said. "But I was born and raised in Naples. He will be arrested. But he will be arrested Neapolitan style. You have my word."

60.

The Bridge of Angels, Italy

I walked with Angela arm in arm across the bridge, statues of angels on each side of us, lights casting the early evening in a warm glow, a platoon of police and Camorristas milling behind us in front of the Castel entrance, the river flowing past us on both sides.

We were about three angels deep into our walk when we heard the implosion of body against stone, Raza landing with a thud on the ground in front of the Castel, his ruined body silent and still.

Frantoni had avenged his brother's death.

"Do you have a favorite angel?" Angela asked me, ignoring the commotion behind us.

"Michael," I said. "A fighter from start to finish. You?"

"I always had a soft spot for Lucifer," Angela said. "He was the Lord's favorite, as you know."

"Why am I not surprised?" I said, spotting her car waiting on the other end of the bridge.

I turned and looked back at the Castel, lit up and glowing in the night, police lights twirling in all directions.

We crossed the bridge and headed for her waiting sedan. Three of her men rushed over, doors open, helping us both to the car. "When my father hears about this, he's going to want to kill you," Angela said with a smile. "All over again."

I shrugged. "I would be disappointed with anything less."

We both got in the backseat, the driver pulling out at fast speed, heading for the hospital. Angela leaned her head back and closed her eyes.

I looked out at the passing scenery and then at her. Her face and hair were matted with dried blood and her wound was deep and still bleeding. The cut on her face had darkened and was smudged with dirt.

I reached for her hand and held it in mine.

I saw her smile and felt her grip tighten. She turned her head and looked at me. "That's all I have to give you," she said. "At least for tonight."

"It's all I need," I said, and closed my eyes.

The first battle, waged across a long and brutally hot summer, was now at an end.

61.

East Hampton, New York

I walked into the library, my leg bandaged, a crutch under my left arm helping me move about. Jimmy had his back to me, staring out into the garden and the ocean below. He turned his wheelchair when he heard me come in. He knew why I was there, sensed it. He was, despite his disability, the son of a Don, and understood better than anyone why I could not allow him to live.

It was the most difficult decision I've ever made.

Uncle Carlo had only balanced out a portion of the betrayal—Jimmy feeding information to the Russian. But there was another part of it, one that only I could avenge. His actions endangered my son's life, and I could never let that stand.

I moved closer to Jimmy, his eyes never leaving mine, neither of us speaking. I was now inches from his chair, and placed my left hand on his shoulder. He made a slow gesture with his hands and I nodded.

"It will be fast," I said. "I promise."

I pulled the ventilator tube from his mouth and let it drop to the floor. I reached for the oxygen machine attached to the back of his wheelchair and turned it off. Jimmy, now straining and gasping for air, looked up at me and made a final hand gesture.

"I love you, too," I said, reached for his right hand, and held it tight in mine.

Jimmy lurched back, chest muscles straining to breathe, his face flushed, his upper body trembling, legs twitching.

I stared out at the ocean, my face smudged with tears, feeling Jimmy's body slowly lose its grip on life, his hand still clutching mine.

62.

East Hampton, New York

FALL 2013

I was on an empty beach, ocean waves to my left, my son Jack chasing Hugo across wet sand, both getting wetter than they should.

Angela walked next to me.

It had been eight weeks since the skirmishes in Rome and Florence, and while our wounds were slow to heal, we were getting stronger by the day. The once tiny puppy Angela had given Jack was closing in on sixty pounds and followed my son everywhere.

"How big did you say they get?" I asked her.

"Anywhere from 125 pounds to 160," she said. "Hugo is going to be a bruiser."

"It's been a long time since I've seen Jack this happy," I said.

"Hugo will help him heal," Angela said. "And be a friend he can count on."

I looked at Angela. "It's good to have one of those," I said.

"How are Burke and his crew doing?" Angela asked.

"They took some hits," I said, "but should all be back in action in another month or so. They're resting up in Capri, getting tanned and drunk."

"You made some points with a few of the crews," Angela said. "The potential for what could have been in Florence and Rome helped convince the Triads and the Yakuza to go all-in on the fight."

"And the Greeks are in the game now, eager to avenge Big Mike's death," I said.

"And all the Sicilians need is a nudge," Angela said. "They would hate to see the Camorra get the credit for taking down the terrorists and the Russians."

"What about you?" I asked.

Angela walked on, her bare feet kicking up sand with each step. "I will be there if you need me," she finally said. "But . . . it's complicated."

"I need time," I said to her.

"There's no rush," she said. I put my left arm around her and held her close to me, her head resting on my shoulder.

We walked the rest of the beach in silence. The only sounds around us were waves splashing against sand, the laughter of a boy, and the barking of a dog.

We were each of us, for these few moments, at peace.

Epilogue

Central Park, New York

FALL 2013

I sat on an old wooden bench across from the Great Lawn, watching the last inning of a softball game played by middle-age men. It was closing in on evening and a cold wind was starting to whip through the park, kicking up leaves and loose debris.

I kept my eyes on the game, ignoring Vladimir as he sat on the bench, a few feet to my left.

"You did well," he said. "You and the Strega. And I chose poorly. Raza was not equipped to take on the two of you."

"You asked for a meeting and you got one."

"I need a favor," Vladimir said. "And in return I'll do one for you."

"What is it?"

"Our fight this summer cost me a great deal of money," he said. "And Raza wasn't the only terrorist I'm funding."

"If you're looking for a loan, you can forget about it," I said.

"I paid them out of my own funds and I'm running low," Vladimir said. "All that can be rectified, but I need your help to make it happen."

"How so?"

"I need to launder $50 million in Russian currency and turn it into American dollars," Vladimir said. "The only one who can do that is your friend Kodoma and his Yakuza bankers. It can all be done in twenty-four hours, maybe less. Sadly, he refuses to do business with any of the Russian crews, mine especially."

"And you think if I ask him he'll change his mind?" I said.

"That's correct," Vladimir said. "You've always been close to him and now appear to be even closer, with his nephew attached to your team."

"Kodoma's a respected boss and a friend," I said. "He would never do anything that goes against Yakuza tradition regardless of who's doing the asking."

"You can convince him," Vladimir said.

"Why are you so sure?"

"You started this war to find out who it was that ordered the attack on the plane that killed your wife and daughters," Vladimir said. "You can rule me out since you know that if I want to hurt someone, I hurt *him* and not his family. And you know Raza was not the one."

I turned and looked at him. "But you know who it was," I said.

Vladimir nodded. "With these terrorists, attaining full accuracy can prove to be difficult. So many of them lay claim to attacks they had no play in. It takes a lot of time and, once again, large sums of money to even get close to the truth. But yes, I know."

"So, I get a name if I agree to reach out to Kodoma and get him to launder your money?" I said. "That's the deal you're putting out?"

Vladimir nodded. "A onetime offer. Once we part company, the name stays with me."

"I'll talk to him," I said. "But there is no guarantee he will agree to it. I'll give it my best shot. On that you have my word."

"That makes it valid," he said.

Vladimir reached into a side pocket of his suit jacket, pulled out a thin white envelope and rested it on the bench between us. He then stood and walked toward the east side of the park, his hands in his pockets, his head down against the growing strength of the wind.

I reached for the envelope and held it firmly in my hands.

I ripped it open and pulled out a folded sheet of white paper, then read the two words typed in the middle of the sheet.

Vittorio Jannetti.

The head of the Camorra.

Angela's father.

I folded the paper, put it back in the envelope and jammed it into my jacket pocket.

I sat on that bench until late into the night, gazing past the Great Lawn at the majestic Manhattan skyline.

I knew on that night there were many more battles to be fought.

I knew there would be more opponents to be defeated.

I knew there was a good chance I would not win them all.

I knew that my son, my organization, could be lost if I failed.

But what I knew more than anything else was a truth I had always feared.

I knew now I would need to confront and destroy someone I trusted and perhaps even someone I loved.

I knew now the name of my enemy.

I knew now that my war had only just begun.

Acknowledgments

Acknowledgments

This book was written during a difficult and emotional time and took much longer than expected. Its completion is owed in great part to the many hands that guided me along the way. It would be impossible for me to thank them all or to do justice to what they each mean to me. Suffice it to say that every one of them has a very special place in my heart.

To Mark Tavani, this book is as much his as it is mine. He pushed, prodded, and edited with a surgeon's skill and didn't stop until the story we wanted to tell was told. In the process he also became a valued friend. Gina Centrello has always had my back and my respect. In my darkest days, she went a step further and showed why she is more than my publisher—she is part of my family.

They all are, everyone mentioned in these few pages—Libby Mc-Guire, who has made Ballantine my home and was always at the ready with a kind word; Kim Hovey, whom I have known forever;

and Betsy Wilson and all the wonderful, hardworking, caring, and thoughtful folks who give their all for me at the only publishing house I have always called home.

To my team—Suzanne Gluck, who (along with her dynamic duo) was always there to guide, who always found the words to help me get through one more day; Erin Junkin, a terrific agent with a golden heart; Rob Carlson, with whom I've grown up (and shared many a laugh in the process); and to all the others at WME, for all that you do.

To Lou and Berta Pitt—you loved us both and care for me daily. If that's not the definition of family, I don't know what is. To the great Jake and Ruth Bloom. I owe you so much and can never repay what you've done for me. But most of all, I will never forget the two of you coming over to visit us toward the end and bringing a smile to the face of a woman who loved you both as much as I do.

To the rest of my family—Andy K.; Dr. George and Joyce; Christopher and Constantino; Maurice and Mamma; Vincenzo, Ida, and Anthony; the magical Irene; the amazing Tina J.; Steve Allie; Liz "Wine Lady" Wagner; Hutch; Hank G.; Eddie F.; Mikey; Peter G.; Rocco; Captain Joe; Sonny G. and Chris; Lorenzo Di; Deb; Alan Carter; Keith Bellows; Dan Bova; Dr. Lori; Dr. Ingerman; Dr. C.; Dr. Schlegel; Dr. Loo; Otto P.; Zoglin; the entire Murino clan of Milan; the gym rats—Sid, Steve, and Kevin; Tracy; Gethers and the Rotis gang; Lisa S.; Angela and the Ischia crew; Mr. G.; PJ Barry; Frank Selvaggi; the team at West Chelsea Vets, for keeping my Gus healthy for another go-around; Fred "Full House" Bass; Ida and Geri; the Book Club posse; Richard and Augusta T.; Kate White; Jeremy Conrady; Leah Rozen; Danny Watts; Danny Aiello; Judy P.; Gilbert from the Visiting Nurses Service; Grace from The Haven; Rebecca; Sarah and James—it is truly an honor to know and love each one of you.

To Dr. Gregory Reily and the beloved Michele of Sloan Kettering— you are indeed miracle workers and the best at what you do. I could never thank you and your great team enough.

To my children—Kate and Nick. You did all you could to help get your Mom through the most difficult battle of her life. And you did it the right way—without complaint, with dedication, with care, and with the bolt of humor that was always needed. We are judged by what we leave behind and you are your mother's greatest gift and proudest achievement. I love you both.

Finally, to Susan Jill Toepfer, who left us all way too soon. Everything I am, anything I might have accomplished, none of it, not one thing, would have ever happened without you. It was an amazing thirty-three-year ride, and one I will always treasure.

I miss you, my dearest friend, and I always will.

—Lorenzo Carcaterra
January 28, 2014

About the Author

LORENZO CARCATERRA is the #1 *New York Times* bestselling author of *Sleepers, A Safe Place, Apaches, Gangster, Street Boys, Paradise City, Chasers,* and *Midnight Angels.* He is a former writer/producer for *Law & Order* and has written for *National Geographic Traveler, The New York Times Magazine, Details,* and *Maxim.* He lives in New York City with Gus, his Olde English Bulldogge, and is at work on his next novel.

www.lorenzocarcaterra.com

About the Type

This book was set in Baskerville, a typeface designed by John Baskerville (1706–75), an amateur printer and typefounder, and cut for him by John Handy in 1750. The type became popular again when the Lanston Monotype Corporation of London revived the classic roman face in 1923. The Mergenthaler Linotype Company in England and the United States cut a version of Baskerville in 1931, making it one of the most widely used typefaces today.